THE BLUE MOON

A Novel

David Neth

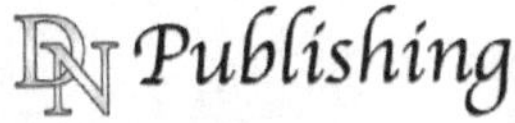 Publishing

The Blue Moon
Copyright © 2017 by David Neth
Batavia, NY

www.davidnethbooks.com

Publisher: David Neth
Copyediting: Tammy Salyer of Inspired Ink Editing
Proofreading: John Ognibene
Cover Design: kpgs.designs@gmail.com

ISBN: 978-1-945336-81-2

First Edition

Subscribe to the author's newsletter for updates and exclusive content:
davidnethbooks.com/newsletter

or

Follow the author at
www.facebook.com/davidnethbooks
www.twitter.com/davidnethbooks
www.instagram.com/dneth13

MORE BY THE AUTHOR

To find the rest of the books in the Under the Moon Series as well as
more books by the author, visit
davidnethbooks.com/books

* * *

Subscribe to his newsletter to be the first to know of new releases and
special deals!
davidnethbooks.com/newsletter

For Liam

THE BLUE MOON
PART I: CHAOS

CHAPTER ONE

Being back in Erie was strange. Everything was different; yet at the same time it seemed like nothing had changed at all.

The former magic room was now Holly's bedroom, but the floorboards still creaked in the familiar way they used to. Herbs, spices, and other potion ingredients still filled the cupboards in the kitchen, but she could tell that the stove hadn't been used for a vanquishing potion in a while. Certainly not as often as they used to cook them up.

Prior to Holly's arrival, Kathy and Josh had been the only two living in the house. They both had very busy lives. Hunting down evil no longer fit in with their schedules.

Unpacking didn't take as long as Kathy thought it would. She seemed to think that Holly would need all day to settle in. As if she needed to reacquaint herself with the house she used to spend most of her time at. Holly wasn't so sure. For a long time, this house had been a second home.

Whether she was currently a guest or a roommate was still to be determined. She hadn't decided yet if her stay was permanent. Only time would tell. All she wanted to do was find a new hiding place like the one she had had in Lily Dale. But part of her knew that that wasn't a perfect solution.

Right now she needed to focus on what she'd returned for: the Chaos. Kathy had said she thought she'd seen it in New York City, which meant that it was out and it was active. It also meant that somebody had released it, which begged the question: Who let it out? A better question was: What the hell was it?

From the warnings she, Kathy, and Josh had received, the Chaos was some big magical force. Based on the fear in each warner's eyes, the witches assumed it wasn't good. It needed to be stopped, that much was certain. With a name like Chaos, Holly could already imagine what it would bring.

She consulted the magic book, but apparently none of the Harpers' ancestors had ever come into contact with anything like it. There was absolutely nothing in the book, so her research was short-lived.

The Harper house made Holly think about Drew. He'd died shortly after she had first met Josh and Chris. She had also lost her daughter in Erie. The city was only filled with bad memories. Holly wondered why she'd ever agreed to come back.

She let her mind wander as she thought of Drew. What he would be doing now, whether they would've ended up together instead of her and Chris, or whether another demonic force would've killed him because of his connections with so many magical people.

Back in Salem, Drew used to tell her about his parents' library filled with books on magic. Tomes specializing in potions, creatures, fighting tactics, magic history, powers, herbs. She wondered if he or his parents had ever heard of the Chaos. Maybe he would've been of help if he were still alive.

No.

He'd been gone for ten years. She needed to stop thinking that he would ever come back. There had once been a point in her life that she didn't think of Drew daily. Back when she and Chris had been together. And her daughter had been alive. When things had made sense.

When she had been happy.

Holly splashed cold water on her face in the bathroom. She needed to focus. Hypothesizing about life with Drew was not helping her now.

But Drew could still be useful. If she summoned his spirit, he may have some leads that she'd be able to track down. The sooner she and the Harpers solved the Chaos problem—which Zamball was likely involved with in some way—the sooner Holly could move someplace else and put her past behind her.

When the magic room had been turned into a guest room, its contents had been spread throughout the house in various hiding places. The spare candles were now mostly stored in the attic, the various trinkets, knives, and other magical objects had been moved to the basement. The few books—including field notes in journals and other magical history books—were hidden among books on the various bookshelves throughout the house.

Holly tracked down the necessary instruments and set up her makeshift altar in the living room. She hesitated before lighting the candles.

The Harpers hadn't been actively seeking out evil since the accident. Kathy and Josh both had their own lives and were busy being normal people. What would they think about her suddenly bringing magic back into their world without their consent?

Even though Drew's spirit wouldn't be an immediate threat, she knew that sudden spikes in magical activity would alert anyone who was watching them. Her quest to find a solution to the Chaos could result in attracting other magical folk to the house. She had made that mistake before. She couldn't risk it. That would only put Kathy and Josh in danger. And, if she was being honest, that sudden danger would force Holly to stay longer than she wanted.

She needed to get out of Erie as soon as she could. There were too many memories here.

* * *

"So, are you all settled in?" Kathy passed a bowl of mashed potatoes over to Holly. The three of them were sitting at the small kitchen table for dinner.

Holly nodded and scooped out a spoonful onto her plate. "I guess so, yeah."

"It's gotta be weird to be sleeping in the room we used to fight evil in," Josh said.

"It's weird being back in Erie. In this house. The last time I was here I think I was picking up—"

Kathy offered a sad smile. "I know. We miss her too. But we're so glad you're back."

Holly's memories were still haunted by her daughter. In Lily Dale, she had found a place where she could move on. The loss still numbed her, but she had been able to get up each morning and act like she was okay. Now that she was back in Erie, she wasn't sure if she'd be able to do that anymore.

Kathy and Josh were quiet, unsure of what to say. Besides that, they hadn't sat down to a meal together in almost a year. They had become more like roommates than family. Their lives were heading in opposite directions, and they really only saw each other in passing nowadays.

"When was the last time you talked to Chris?" Holly asked.

"Are you sure you wanna talk about him?" Josh poured some gravy on his plate.

"Why not? Don't talk about him as my ex-husband, talk about him as your brother." Holly didn't want to think about Chris, but nobody was talking and something needed to be said. Otherwise, she knew Sophia's memory would get the best of her. Besides, she was curious to hear what Chris was up to.

Josh and Kathy exchanged glances, but finally he spoke up. "It's been about a year. He was always changing his number. Different burner phones. We gave up trying to contact him because he would always contact us." He shrugged. "But then he didn't. For a long time. Aunt Kathy and I were talking about just summoning him, but then he called. Said he wouldn't be able to talk to us anymore and—"

"That's enough," Kathy cut in. "Chris made his decision."

"You guys didn't investigate it more? Where he was? Who he was talking to? What he was up to?" Holly couldn't believe that Josh and Kathy would just let Chris go like that.

Kathy stood and walked to the other side of the kitchen counter.

Watching as his aunt busied herself with the dishes, Josh said, "Chris made it clear that he didn't want us involved—"

"And you listened to him? What happened to the witches I knew?"

"You don't understand, Holly!" Kathy whirled around and leaned on the counter with her wet, soapy hands. "*You* were the first one to leave this family. *You* were the one who abandoned Chris—abandoned us. Chris just followed suit because *you* blamed him—and he blamed himself—because Sophia died. *You* lost faith in him, so he lost faith in himself. There wasn't anything left after that."

"Oh." Holly stared at her plate. She wasn't hungry anymore.

Emotions had bubbled over a lot sooner than she'd expected. But it was good to lay it on the table so they all knew what each other was thinking. Still, Holly felt guilty for tearing their family apart. She suddenly felt like an intruder.

Her hatred for Chris had grown so out of control that she had lost sight of everything. She realized that Josh and Kathy had lost a niece too, but she'd never put herself in their shoes. They didn't only lose a niece. They lost Holly and Chris too.

Holly could blame Chris for Sophia's death, but *she* had been the one who'd destroyed the Harper family. Chris wasn't to blame for that.

"Whatever happened in the past, you're back now. We can start to fix things from here."

"I'm sorry." Holly looked up at Kathy. "I've only been thinking about myself since the accident."

Kathy sighed. "It's okay. You're angry, which is understandable. But don't let your anger blind you from what's happening around you. You came back because of a very real threat."

Holly nodded. "I guess that's what happens when you isolate yourself."

"You're not alone anymore," Josh said.

"Yeah, but we're all still feeling the repercussions of my actions. Chris is gone without a trace. Even if he took Sophia from all of us, I took him from you guys."

"Don't." Kathy walked over and retook her seat at the table. "Playing the blame game is not helping any. From now on we need to be united. Otherwise, the Chaos, and whoever released it, has already won. As much as we miss him, Chris isn't our priority right now."

Holly nodded. "Do you guys have any idea where he is?"

Josh shrugged. "Out west. That's all we know. But in a year's time, he could be anywhere. It's hard to say."

"Maybe he's joined some magical group like the Fire Wizards." Holly dug back into her food. Her appetite had returned, but only slightly. She just wanted to keep her hands busy, and the plate of food in front of her was a welcome distraction.

"What makes you think that?" Kathy asked.

"His specialty had grown. He was able to wield flame the last time I saw him. If he felt like he couldn't come back to you, maybe he went looking for another group to share his magic with."

"But the Fire Wizards aren't good people," Josh said.

"Well, that's debatable," Holly said.

"How?"

"Yes, Drew said that they'd turned," she responded. "They used to be good and then they were evil. But I've been keeping my eye on them. Their actions don't seem to align with good *or* evil. Out in Middletown, California, they did burn down half the town. But a small, orphaned witch was spared. Why?"

"That could just be a coincidence," Kathy said.

"Nothing is a coincidence. Besides, that witch's specialty turned out to be related to nature—causing the grass to grow higher, making flowers bloom, sprouting up trees. That sort of thing. Why would the Fire Wizards want to save her?"

"Maybe they have some sort of demonic plan for her?" Josh asked. "Evil doesn't always make sense, either."

"You're right. I could be reading too much into this. But if they got to Chris when he was desperate—and Chris likely believes he's a killer—they might've been able to sway him into joining." Holly decided to sugarcoat her belief that Chris was her daughter's murderer. She wanted to prevent another argument.

Kathy shook her head. "No. Chris wouldn't ever do that. If the Fire Wizards were evil once, they will always be evil."

"Kathy, don't let your feelings toward *your* ex-husband cloud what's going on with mine." Holly felt the sting and added, "Sorry."

Kathy crossed her arms. "Chris and Will are two different people. Will was a killer by nature. Chris is only a killer by accident."

That cleared up that debate.

"You and I both know that we've all killed." Holly sat back in her chair. "Look, I'm not saying it's definite. What I am saying is that anything is possible."

Josh and Kathy exchanged looks.

"I still don't believe it," Josh said.

Holly shrugged. "He might even be dead."

* * *

Chris woke up with a headache. Migraine, more like it. His head was throbbing. His face was pressed against metal bars, and his wrists were shackled to the plywood floor. His shirt had been removed, but he could feel the gauze wrapped around his body, pressed tightly against his burns.

When he opened his eyes, he saw two men in blue robes standing near his cage. They were outside. A series of tents were positioned in a circle around a large fire pit in the center. Other men and women in blue robes milled about.

He figured it must be some sort of camp for the Fire Wizards. Maybe even their main camp. What he couldn't figure out was the cage. Why was he being treated like a prisoner? He should've been in a medical ward or something. Anything nicer than a cage.

Chris's mouth was dry when he tried to speak. It took a couple of tries, but he managed to call to one of the guards. "Hey!" He cleared his throat and tried again. "Hey! What's with the cage? I just joined you guys. Shouldn't I be with a medic or something before I begin my training?"

Both men ignored him, facing forward toward the center of camp. Chris tried to get to his feet, but he couldn't stand up straight. His cage was only about four feet tall. About the same in width and length, too.

He sat back down and addressed his wounds: one strip of the gauze had soaked through with blood and pus, but most of them seemed to be doing okay. His back was what bothered him the most. He just wanted to stand up and stretch. And a glass of water would've been nice, too.

The men shifted and suddenly a woman towered over Chris. The light from the sun blinded him, and he couldn't make out her face. When she spoke, though, he knew exactly who she was.

"Mr. Harper, glad to see you're awake," Raven said.

"Is this how you treat all your honored guests?" Chris asked.

"Cut the sarcasm, Mr. Harper. It won't help you any."

"Well tell me what's going on then!" He broke into a short coughing fit. "You told me I'd need to train before I could lead, but you're treating me like an animal."

"I told you that you're not entitled to anything. You need to prove your worth."

"How am I supposed to do that locked in a cage?"

"Soon you'll begin your reprioritization process."

"My what?"

"It will help align you with the philosophy of the Fire Wizards. First, as promised, we will be treating your injuries. However, you have not finished obtaining them."

Chris's heart beat faster. "What do you mean?"

Raven turned to the two guards and nodded. One opened the metal door while the other entered. The guard took a position behind Chris and wrapped his arms around him, restraining him with his arms, holding his head in place. Chris tried to fight him off, but the man kept his grip.

"Don't struggle, Mr. Harper. This will be over soon enough." Raven stood over him and kicked his shoulder, pushing him down onto his back.

Weak from dehydration, Chris collapsed on his back. His restraints dug into his wrists.

"To be able to wield the magic of fire and inflict pain with it, you must feel its power firsthand," Raven said.

A moment later, Chris's chest was on fire. His skin felt like it was melting as a hot skewer pressed against him. He felt sick to his stomach, and his vision began to fade, but he didn't lose consciousness. When the skewer was finally pulled away, his skin sizzled, but he still felt the fire. He tried to reach for his chest, but two medics arrived and pushed his shackled hands away as they treated him.

Chris looked down at what they had done. An upside-down triangle was branded onto his chest.

Chapter Two

"Aunt Kathy, don't do this." Josh followed her into the living room. She had her arms full with candles of varying colors. Holly was sitting at the foot of the stairs, still in her pajamas.

Instead of sleeping, Kathy had spent half the night coming up with a ritual to summon Chris. The other half of the night was spent creating the potion. The smell of it woke the whole house up.

"Don't argue with me. I'm doing it." Kathy set candles of various sizes in a circle around a black pot on the coffee table.

In the last ten years, they had burned through most of their traditional spellcasting candles, so she had to resort to the scented candles. The colors of the candles were really the only thing that mattered. There were two of each of the three colors she was using: red, symbolizing fire and connecting to Chris on a magical level;

pink, representing love, family, and friendship; and yellow, meaning communication.

"Are you even sure this is going to work?" Holly was nervous about seeing Chris again. She hadn't spoken to him since the accident.

Kathy struck a match and lit each of the candles. "I've done plenty of spells in my lifetime. I may be rusty, but all of this is second nature to me."

"Yeah, but what are we going to say once he's here?" Josh asked.

Kathy scrunched her face. "I don't know. But getting him here is most important."

"How can we be sure that Chris hasn't turned into someone we no longer want to associate with? What if he's evil now?" Holly asked.

"Guys, this is Chris. Not a criminal."

"No, but—"

Kathy slammed her hand on the table. "We have to try! Holly, I understand if you don't want to see him, but he's my nephew. He's Josh's brother. No matter what happened, he's family. We have to try."

While Holly's words from the night before had certainly stung, they rang true. They *had* given up on Chris too easily. They had given up on magic in general, really. As much as Kathy didn't want to admit it, they were using their careers to hide from reality.

It was time to change that.

Josh sighed and took a seat on the floor across the table from his aunt. "What does the spell entail?"

Kathy smiled.

Holly crossed her arms and watched as Kathy and Josh readied the potion that would help power the incantation. Once it was finished, Josh turned to Holly.

"So…what have you decided? Are you going to help?"

She took a deep breath and sat next to Josh. "For the record, I'm doing this for you guys. Not for Chris."

Reuniting with her ex-husband had not been on her to-do list when she had come to Erie. But Josh and Kathy were different than she remembered. Less confident and more hesitant. The family bond no longer existed. The Harpers were broken. Holly knew exactly what that felt like—for many reasons—and she didn't want anyone else to feel that way. Least of all two people she cared about.

Kathy looked to Holly and mouthed, "Thank you."

"Are we ready?" Josh held the paper with the spell on it in front of him so they could all read it.

Kathy and Holly exchanged glances and nodded.

Brother, nephew, lover rise,
to the place where we reside.
Let your mind and body be free,
and return to your family.

Holly rolled her eyes once she finished the spell. Hopefully Chris's connection to Josh and Kathy was strong enough, because she and Chris hadn't been lovers in a long time.

"Did it work?" Josh asked.

Kathy tilted her head toward the center pot. "Burn the spell."

Lifting the paper to one of the candles, he dropped it into the pot.

The air began to stir and the witches stood, waiting to see what would happen.

Flames began to appear in a small cyclone. They could feel the heat licking their faces, and they each took a step back away from the magical fire.

When the wind and flame ceased, a man in blue robes stood before them, facing the opposite direction.

"Chris?" Kathy asked.

The man turned. "Chris is not here. I am Nootau, a member of the Fire Wizards."

"Where's my brother?"

Nootau looked to Josh. "I'm afraid that I don't have good news."

Kathy suddenly became breathless, but she tried not to show it. She narrowed her eyes and tried to determine if the wizard was lying.

"Christopher Harper was found dead along the Snake River in Idaho a few weeks ago. The rest of the Fire Wizards and I tried to revive him, but unfortunately the witch you knew is dead."

Holly was surprised at the sadness that washed over her. Now the last fragment that was left of her family and the few years of bliss she'd experienced were gone forever. Wiped away. She felt Josh's hand on her back, and she leaned in to him. She hated Chris, so why was she so upset?

"You're lying!" Kathy's voice was thick with emotion.

"I'm not. I could show you pictures, but I don't think you want to see them."

"You took *pictures*?" Josh was disgusted.

"My coven has had experience with yours. We are aware of your distrust, despite us doing the honorable thing and informing you of his passing in person."

"Please. You're only here because we summoned you," Josh said.

Nootau shifted his attention to Kathy. "It appears it was severe dehydration. He wasn't properly equipped to be out in the sun. He was barefoot, half-starved, completely unkempt."

"Tell us where Chris is." Anger was the only thing Kathy had to hold on to. The thought of Chris dying of thirst alone in some remote part of the country made her sick. She had promised his mother she'd take care of him. Protect him. Watch over him. Meanwhile, she never went to bed hungry and enjoyed her nice warm bed every night. As a parent, she had failed.

"We performed a proper ritual."

Kathy had had enough. She couldn't believe that Chris was dead. She would've felt a shift, even with being a little less connected to her magic than usual.

She leaped at Nootau and tackled him to the floor, sitting on his chest and slamming her fists into his face over and over again.

"Aunt Kathy!" Josh pulled on her arm and got her to her feet. Her fists were bleeding.

Nootau stood, his face dripping with only her blood, and pulled his wand from his robes. He waved it in the air before pointing it at Josh and Kathy. Josh pushed her to the floor, but took the brunt of the attack, flipping over the back of the couch.

"Josh, are you okay?" Kathy called. She kept her eyes on the wizard.

"Yeah." He patted out the fire from his clothes. They were charred and his skin was tender, but he was fine otherwise.

"That was a warning. I'll ignore your outburst because of your grief, but do not use your nephew's death as an excuse to attack my coven," Nootau warned.

"I don't need an alleged death for reason to go after your coven!" Kathy charged at him again. He didn't have time to point his wand before they were on the floor again.

Holly stood and watched. The use of fire magic and the news of Chris's death brought back so many bad memories. She couldn't bring herself to do anything. It had been a mistake to come back to Erie. Her hands shook and goosebumps prickled her skin.

"Freeze him!" Josh called.

Nootau had pinned Kathy to the floor and was delivering his own punches. Her legs kicked from beneath him, and her arms flailed through the air, but she couldn't push him off.

"Holly, do something!" Josh tried pulling the Fire Wizard off his aunt, but Nootau elbowed him in the face and knocked him to the floor.

Taking a deep breath, Holly had no choice but to help. Closing her eyes, she put her magic to work. Flames rose up throughout the house. At first, Nootau didn't pay attention them. Then they began to strike him.

He shouted in pain and rolled off Kathy and focused on Holly. "How are you doing this?"

"You delivered your message. Now get out." Her voice was soft. Nervous.

He stepped closer and another burst of flame hit him.

"I told you to leave!" Stronger this time, yet her hands still shook.

Nootau took a deep breath. "Very well. I would offer my condolences, but it seems they're not welcome here."

A moment later, he disappeared in a swirl of flames.

* * *

Kathy gritted her teeth as her nephew treated her battered face. She was sitting on the barstool in the kitchen. The first aid kit was open on the counter next to them.

"You were the one who attacked him first." Holly was the only one without a scratch on her. She was leaning against the counter with a cup of coffee.

"Yeah, because I thought he'd attack with magic, not his fists."

Josh pointed to his shirt. "He *did* attack with magic." He had some mild burns on his chest, but it wasn't anything a few applications of aloe couldn't fix.

"At least you guys are all right." Holly set her mug down. "It's a shame about Chris." She tried to act casual, but inside, her world had crumbled. Any daydream she might've had of piecing her family back together was shattered. Not that any of that had ever been possible anyway. Sophia was dead too. Mostly, Holly felt lonely.

"You mean, it's a shame they're lying?" Kathy winced as Josh applied more magical ointment. That had been the extent of his magic in the last few years: crafting supernatural remedies.

"Aunt Kathy, don't—"

"No. Chris is not dead. They're hiding something."

Josh picked up the first aid kit and took the seat next to her. He sighed. "Like what?"

She shrugged.

"Well, if we're entertaining the idea that he's still alive, my theory is the same as last night. He's working with them." Holly picked up her mug and took a sip. Kathy's refusal to believe the claim of his death sparked a smidgen of hope in Holly. Frankly, she missed him. She had forbade herself from even thinking about him in the last two years. Now that he was likely dead, she needed to begin to forgive him.

"That still doesn't make any sense," Kathy said.

"Why not?" she asked. "Let's think about it: Chris doesn't like them either. No matter what's happened to him in the year since you've spoken with him, that still won't change. Chris is a good—Chris wouldn't join the Fire Wizards unless he had to. Once he got in there, maybe he tried to change the way they did things, which didn't sit well with them, and they killed him."

"I really hope you're wrong." Josh stood and walked out of the kitchen.

Kathy tapped her fingers on the counter. "I won't believe he's dead until I see proof. Things just aren't adding up."

CHAPTER THREE

It was strange how quickly all the excitement from the morning could be wiped away. By the way Holly had woken up, she would've guessed the rest of the day would follow suit. From what she remembered, they always used to.

However, by midmorning, Josh had left for work and Kathy was busy upstairs getting ready. The house was quiet, save for Kathy's footsteps as she traipsed back and forth between the bathroom and her bedroom upstairs. Things were normal. Almost as if they hadn't summoned and then attacked a Fire Wizard that morning.

"Okay, I'm heading out. The promo tour for the new book continues," Kathy said as she strode down the stairs. The promotion cycle for her new book had been going on for a couple of weeks already. Ever since the launch party in New York. Up until now, she had done mostly interviews via email with some of the most popular blogs. This was her first interview locally for the new book.

She gathered her things into her purse and glanced in the mirror. "What do you think? Too much?"

Kathy had extra makeup on to try to cover the open cuts and bruises from the morning's festivities. The swelling was hard to hide, though.

Holly made a face. "You really should've put ice on it."

Looking in the mirror again, Kathy asked, "It's that bad?"

"Not horrible. Just hope they're not taking pictures."

Kathy gently touched the most swollen part of her face. "I'll just send them one of the headshots I took last week. It'll be fine."

"What are you going to tell the reporter?"

"I don't know." Kathy shrugged. "I guess I'll just try to leave it alone unless they ask."

"And what if they do?"

"Car accident?"

Holly nodded. "It could work."

Kathy took another look in the mirror and frowned. She'd done the best she could; she was already running late. She zipped up her purse and slung it over her shoulder. "What are you doing today?"

Flopping back on the couch, Holly sighed. "I don't know."

It was funny how comfortable she felt at the Harpers'. Sure, they had been family for a short while, and she was definitely no stranger to the house, but it had been two years since she'd been back. She sometimes felt more comfortable here than she did visiting her dad before he'd passed away.

"I suppose I could do some more research on the Chaos," she continued. "Although I don't know how far that's going to go. I couldn't come up with anything yesterday, and with the way our summoning spell worked this morning, I don't want to try asking spirits."

In truth, she was afraid she was going to get more bad news. Although her feelings were surprising, hearing about Chris's death hurt her. She was almost glad to have the day to mourn him. Even if Kathy wasn't completely convinced that he was dead.

"No, summoning spells are off-limits for now. Try looking online. I've found a lot of help there in the past. Oh, and isn't your uncle still researching witches? Try giving him a call."

Holly chuckled. "Sure. Just as soon as I figure out what time it is in Sydney."

"Oh. Well that might have to wait until tonight, but maybe you can email him instead?"

"Okay. Good luck today."

Kathy took a deep breath. "Thanks. I'm nervous."

"Stop! You've done this before, right? Your last two books were great."

"You read them?"

"I lived alone, Kathy. Yes, I read them."

Kathy stood over the couch and looked down at Holly. She was touched. Holly had separated herself from them, but in her own way, she had never fully distanced herself from the family.

And the fact that she continued to support Kathy after what had happened with her and Chris reassured Kathy that everything would be all right.

Especially once they found Chris. Or, at least, proof that he was still alive. Putting Holly to the task of finding him wasn't a good idea. Kathy knew how awkward things could be with exes.

Holly broke into her concentration. "You're going to be late."

Kathy looked at her watch. "Oh shoot! I might have to teleport."

"Why not? You've got it, you might as well use it."

"No, I should drive. I don't know exactly where I'm going, so I might slip up and pop in somewhere else." She looked around the messy living room. "Do you mind cleaning up a bit?"

Holly rolled her eyes. "Sure, not a problem."

"Thank you! Bye!"

After Kathy left, Holly lay where she was for longer than she intended. The quiet house reminded her of her marriage to Chris. Obviously it had ended badly, but they had been happy for a while, hadn't they? She'd enjoyed being a stay-at-home mom, but she'd also loved the time she and Chris had shared after Sophia went to bed and it was just the two of them.

She never thought she would like being a part of normal society. She thrived on the fact that she was different, that she knew things and saw things that most of the world only dreamed of. But the simplest thing had captivated her and completely changed her world: love.

Even now, as she reflected on the life she used to have, she internally rolled her eyes at how sappy she was being. When did she become *that* girl?

To her, strength had always meant independence and not letting anyone know what she was thinking. But how had that worked out for her over the last two years? She had become lonely and miserable, and at the first sign of danger, she'd gone running back to Kathy—the only real parent figure she had left.

But she couldn't be mad at herself. Not once did Kathy or Josh make her feel small for coming back. They had even admitted to needing her help too.

Their strength was in numbers, not in independence.

Holly's head perked up at the sound of water running. Ever since Kathy left, the house had been silent. There was no reason for anything to be on.

She got up and started to the kitchen, but came face-to-face with Zamball as he rounded the corner into the living room.

"I'm surprised to see you're back in Erie," he said.

She backed a safe distance away.

"Although," he continued, "it doesn't seem as though you're happy about it. I take it you've heard about Chris then." A smug expression curled across his face.

Holly wiped at her eyes. She hadn't realized she'd been crying. "What do you want?"

"Well, you still have yet to tell me about that prophecy you heard back in Lily Dale." He picked up a picture frame from one of the end tables in the foyer and glanced at it. He set it down a moment later. "I'm assuming it was something important. Otherwise, you would've never come back here."

"And what makes you think I'm going to tell you?" Holly crossed her arms, trying to look tough. Trying to make up for the tears. "It's not like I have anything left to lose."

"Don't be so sure." He opened his arms and looked up. "Seems like you've got a pretty nice house here. By the way you were able to come running back, it's clear you and the remaining Harpers are still pretty chummy." He shrugged. "That could change."

"We've been through this before. They know how to handle themselves. You don't think I've told them that you came to my house in Lily Dale?"

A swirl of flames appeared next to Holly, and she moved away from the heat, putting herself behind the couch for some added distance. A woman in blue robes appeared. She had dark skin and short-cropped hair.

"Zamball, what are you doing back in Erie? I thought you moved on to New Orleans?"

He smiled and nodded. "Raven, always a pleasure."

"Leave the Bowen girl alone. I need to speak with her."

He motioned to Holly. "She and I were in the middle of a conversation."

"A conversation that started in Lily Dale. Based on the fact that she moved to get away from you and that you're still standing here, I think it's safe to say she's not going to give you the information you want. Now leave us."

They studied each other a moment. Holly thought she was going to have to run for cover. By the way Raven and Zamball stared at one another, it was as if they had forgotten she was even in the room.

"Fine." He faced Holly. "I'll see you again."

After he returned to the kitchen, Holly could hear another splash of water.

* * *

"Why have you been so mopey today?" Josh's girlfriend, Natalie, tipped back what was left of her fruit cup and sipped the juice. She and Josh were sitting in the hospital cafeteria for their midshift break.

"I haven't been mopey." Josh folded his napkin in half and tucked it under the edge of his tray.

"Uh, yeah you have." Natalie waved her hand between them. "This whole conversation has been completely one-sided."

"Whatever, just leave me alone."

"Moody, too."

"Natalie!" Josh barked. He looked around and lowered his voice, his face burning with embarrassment. "Sorry. Just drop it."

"No." She reached for his hand. "Josh, something is bothering you. Let me help."

"It's a long story."

She looked up at the clock. "So talk fast."

He sighed. "Well, you know how I said my brother was out west?" When she nodded, he went on. "It's because he got carried away with his magic here and…some bad things happened."

"He got divorced."

"I told you that?"

"You tell me everything." She brought her feet up to the chair and tucked her knees up against her chest, leaning them against the edge of the table.

"Anyway, so he's been out of touch for a long time. Then this morning—it's a long story."

"Josh…"

"I think my brother might be dead." He covered his mouth with his hand and looked down at his empty tray.

Natalie got up and moved to his side of the table. She rubbed his back and asked, "What do you mean? Why would you think that?"

"I haven't heard from him in a year." His voice cracked. "Holly thinks he got involved with some bad people."

"Holly's his ex-wife?"

Josh nodded.

"Well, of course she's going to say that."

"No, she thinks that because he is—*was*—a good person, he wanted to straighten them out and they killed him for it." He sniffled.

"What do you think?"

He shrugged. "I don't know! My aunt doesn't believe it, but she might just be in denial. She's pretty mad."

"At the person who killed him?"

"And herself for not trying harder to save him."

Natalie shook her head. "But you guys didn't even know he was in danger."

"But he wasn't with us!" Josh finally met her eyes. "He's my little brother. I'm supposed to protect him. We didn't even see a body." He ran his hands across his face, wiping away the moisture.

"Who told you he was dead?"

"One of the guys from the group Holly thinks he joined."

Natalie sat back. "Let me get this straight: you *think* he joined some bad group and someone from that group told you he was dead without offering proof? This theory being provided by your brother's ex? I don't know. Seems like a lot of speculation to me."

"It's not like that, exactly. We had cast a spell to call my brother, and the wizard came instead. Why else would someone from that group come from a spell focused on Chris if he wasn't a part of that group? At this point, his involvement with the Fire Wizards isn't in question. His death is."

She studied him a moment with her fist propped against her mouth. "I guess I just don't know how magic works, then. All I know is that you shouldn't rule him out until you've had some closure. It seems like you need it."

"And when am I going to have time to find that?"

"Why don't you take some time off? Be with your family."

He shook his head. "No, that'll just make it worse. Getting messed up with all the people that he did would only result in me getting killed too. I'm better off here."

"I meant grieve with them."

"No. My aunt's not grieving, and Holly…" He missed how united his family used to be. Sure, the rift between Chris and Holly had started the disintegration of his family, but he wasn't exactly doing his part to keep them close, either.

"Well, next time you start thinking about the possibility of your brother's death—which I wouldn't count as certain until you have proof—come talk to me. I don't want you to be sad and bottling this all up. It's not good."

"No, Natalie, I can't do that. If they knew you and I were… you're better off not knowing anything."

She smiled. "But you tell me everything. Look, if I'm going to date a witch, retired or otherwise, I'm going to need to be able to understand the world you come from. Don't put me in a bubble. Look at Lois Lane."

"Lois Lane?"

"Yeah. If Clark Kent had told her from day one that he was Superman, maybe she would've been smarter about which hard news stories she chased. Maybe she wouldn't have kept getting kidnapped all the time."

"This isn't a comic book. I'm not Superman and you're not Lois Lane. This is serious, Natalie." He kissed her hand. "I'll come to you next time. But don't expect details."

Chapter Four

The tattered sleeping bag wasn't enough to keep Chris comfortable. It was better than the hard plywood floor, but it wasn't exactly memory foam. Not that he was used to memory foam anyway, but usually his worst nighttime shelters were bookended with a night in a motel or squatting at someone's house. That had been his extent of luxury.

There wouldn't be any more squatting or wandering or any of that. He was a member of the Fire Wizards now, for better or worse. Right now, things were looking worse.

The medics had given him some sort of magical ointment, but he still needed time to heal. The burns on his side had subsided, but the intense itching of his chest was almost too much to bear. He clenched his fists and gritted his teeth as he fought the urge to run his nails over his skin.

Chris was about to roll onto his side to try to get more comfortable when the door to his cage opened. He tried to remain still. Tried to act like he was sleeping. The two women were talking about him—in very thick Spanish accents.

Where *was* he?

"Do you think once he's reprioritized he'll tell us who released the Chaos?" She sounded middle-aged, maybe even older. Her voice was a bit scratchy, like she was a smoker or had screamed a lot recently. Chris guessed she was a smoker.

"I don't know. From what I've heard, he's not going to remember anything from before. Everything will be for the Fire Wizards." This one was definitely younger, but she seemed more knowledgeable. More experienced. Maybe she had been with the Fire Wizards longer than the older woman.

Chris felt them pulling at the bandages wrapped around his torso. They weren't gentle, which made it difficult to lie still. He did his best not to react to any pain. Luckily, he had experience with that.

"Let's just get him cleaned up quick," the older one said. "The sooner we do this, the sooner we get away from him."

"Raven just wants the job done. This man is important to her. He needs to heal."

"I don't like that she's in charge. This coven is not the same as it was."

"Watch what you say aloud," the younger one snapped.

So Raven was the leader of the Fire Wizards. Then why had she asked him to lead? He figured she had a prominent role in the coven, but he'd never assumed she led it. What was with the initiation ceremony then? Raven had taken the place as the leader of the Fire Wizards, but he figured it was due to lack of proper representation. Was he actually a member or just a prisoner?

Soft hands ran over Chris's healing skin. His side felt cool and less itchy, but he could feel that something was still off about his chest. The two women spent most of their time treating the spot with the triangle. The mark that had been branded into his skin. He felt cool gels and lotions rubbing into the spot, and his skin prickled with goosebumps.

"It's a shame, though."

"What is?" the younger woman asked.

"That he doesn't know the truth."

"Stop. Raven will kill us."

"But it's his daughter. He has a right—"

"*We* have no right! It's not our place to tell him about Sophia."

Chris sat up. "What about her?"

* * *

"Who are you?" Even though Zamball had left the room, Holly still wasn't sure what to make of the other intruder.

Raven studied her for a moment before speaking. "You're an interesting girl, Ms. Bowen."

"How so?"

"Well, you've come from a long line of strong witches—mostly female, in particular. I admire that. You've overcome the odds and defeated your family's long-fought enemy at the young age of fifteen—"

35

"Get to the point." Holly could see right through the sugar-coated story Raven was feeding her. After the way she and Zamball had barged into the house, Holly was not in a good mood. She hadn't missed this part of living in Erie. "Who are you?"

"I'm a leading member of the Fire Wizards. I'm sure you've heard of them."

Holly's mind flashed to Drew's charred body resting on her dining room table when she had been a kid. All at the hands of the Fire Wizards. A coven he used to call his friends. His family.

"I know all about them. What I don't understand is why you think I would help a bunch of murderous *sorcerers*."

Raven flashed brilliantly white teeth that contrasted with her dark skin. "You may be needed to sway your ex-husband's intentions."

Holly's heart fluttered, but she tried not to show it. Still, she couldn't help but ask, "Chris is alive?"

"For now."

If Chris was alive and Raven was asking for Holly's help, that meant he was with the Fire Wizards. So she had been right. Even after all this time, she still knew Chris. That idea was scary in itself.

What was more confusing was why Raven was telling her this. A few hours earlier she had been told by another member of the Fire Wizards that Chris was dead. Something was up. She decided not to believe it one way or another until she had further proof. Any member of the Fire Wizards wasn't trustworthy.

When Holly didn't respond right away, Raven continued, "We're anticipating some...resistance from Mr. Harper. If he was persuaded by someone he trusts, maybe he would see the value in our proposal."

"And what proposal is that?"

"That isn't your concern." The wizard took a breath. "For now, we're asking for your help."

"Why come to me? Couldn't you ask Kathy or Josh? Or maybe Chris's new girlfriend or something? Isn't there a spell to cast to bend him to your will?"

How could Raven think Chris still trusted her? He had been the one to leave Erie first. Holly assumed he didn't want to see her any more than she wanted to see him.

Raven sighed. She was getting frustrated. "It needs to be his free will. But that doesn't mean he can't be misled."

Holly chuckled. This was exactly the kind of stuff that Drew had left the Fire Wizards over.

Manipulation.

Hidden agendas.

Holly didn't want a part of it. But if they had Chris, Holly knew she'd have to play along to get more information. She owed it to Josh and Kathy.

"We knew his family wouldn't agree to such an arrangement. In fact, it's better that they go on believing he's dead. But we figured his ex-wife would be more than willing to get the vengeance she was looking for. You don't care what happens to him, right?"

Reflexively, Holly shook her head. "No."

It was a lie, wasn't it? The thought of Chris being alive made her feel relieved—happy, even. It still didn't change anything.

She didn't want to see him, but it didn't mean that she didn't still care about his well-being.

"Good. Do you have any more questions?"

Holly could tell from the way Raven looked down her nose at her that she was aware of Holly's hesitation.

"What am I convincing Chris to do? What'll this do to him?"

Raven rolled her eyes. "If you must know, it'll fully empower him. His powers will unite with ours. He will *officially* become one of us. Which means, he won't be able to act out of order. The Fire Wizards have a strict conformity policy. At the moment, his membership as part of the coven is still in a probationary period."

"What happens if he doesn't fully conform?"

"You mean the very thing he's facing now? He'll be exiled, like your friend Drew. Only this time, we will employ our full persecution methods on him."

"You're going to torture him?"

"We'll make sure he won't be around to figure out what it's like to be a Fire Wizard outcast." Raven smiled. "However, if you help, he'll be free of any outside temptation. By persuading him to join the Fire Wizards, he will realize the true potential of his specialty. Isn't that what he's always wanted?"

Ambulance lights and fire engine sirens filled Holly's memory. The smell of smoke and the roar of flames that had taken everything away from her came rushing back. Yes, Chris had always been interested in magic, but he became obsessed once he was able to create fire in the palms of his hands. Convincing him to join the Fire Wizards would give him exactly what he wanted. It would also mean that Holly was casting him out of his family. Did she hate him that much to hurt Josh and Kathy in her spite? Would manipulating Chris's free will really make her feel free?

"Why should I help the man who is responsible for my daughter's death?"

Raven shook her head. "She didn't die."

"What are you talking about? She's buried in Erie Cemetery." Holly felt her temperature rising. Raven had no right to make that kind of accusation.

"She has a marker in Erie Cemetery. There is no body."

"She was *burned alive!*"

Holly didn't want to let herself believe that Sophia was alive. It was one thing for her to play with the idea of Chris's death, but it was another to play with the idea of her own daughter's. Chris had a callused spot in Holly's heart, while Sophia was still a wide-open wound that would never be healed. She couldn't allow herself to go back to that dark place. She wouldn't ever recover.

"You only believe she was burned because you gave up too easily."

Holly's eyes flashed with anger. "Don't tell me I gave up on her! I tried for *months* to find any sort of lead on her!"

After the accident, Holly had lingered in Erie, not only to divorce Chris but also to hold out hope that Sophia was alive somewhere. Holly knew just how far some people would go to get their hands on a magical child. She had nearly driven herself insane trying to find anything. There had been no signs that suggested Sophia was still alive. Eventually, she'd just had to let her go and move on. Dwelling on the loss wasn't doing any good.

"I'm not here to discuss your child, I want to know if you'll help sway Chris's intentions," Raven said.

"If Sophia wasn't killed, then what happened to her?" Holly was not about to let this go. She didn't know what to think. If Sophia had never died, then where had she been the last two years? As a mother, Holly felt guilty for not knowing—not *feeling*—that her child was still breathing somewhere.

The wizard sighed. "Kidnapped. Now, your answer?"

"How can I believe you?"

"I'm done talking about this. Are you going to help or not?"

"Where is my daughter!?" Holly stepped closer with each question until she was within arm's reach of Raven.

Flames momentarily rose up in the small space between the two women, and Holly backed up a step.

"Your compliance is no longer an option," the wizard declared.

Holly tried to put more space between them, but Raven grabbed her T-shirt and threw her to the floor.

"You and Mr. Harper are both stubborn. That's how you lost your daughter. What she was needed for was too great for her to achieve in your care. She needed to be removed. Where her parents ended up is more proof that her capture was justified."

Holly swung her feet and tried to knock Raven to the floor, but the wizard created a wall of fire that burned the witch's feet.

"She should've been with her parents," Holly shouted from the floor. "You made us the way we are."

Raven knew more about Sophia and the night of the fire than anyone Holly had ever come in contact with. Even if Raven hadn't physically been there she would've been the one dolling out orders. After all, she was a leading member of the Fire Wizards.

Raven knelt next to Holly, who was nursing her foot, and grabbed a fistful of her hair. "This conversation has taken too long. If you won't convince him, maybe you can be used as leverage instead."

In a swirl of flames, the two women disappeared.

* * *

Kathy kept checking how bad her face was in the pocket mirror she kept in her purse. By the time she met the reporter at Bicentennial Tower—where a major scene in *Spellbinding* took place, and the inspiration for the cover—the swelling had gone down a bit. However, the left side of her face was puffier than usual.

Despite how she felt, it was a beautiful day out. The sun reflected off Lake Erie, and Presque Isle could be seen in the distance. A few people gathered at the end of the pier to admire the view.

Kathy and the reporter, Jean, sat at one of the picnic tables at the end of the pier. Jean jotted down notes as Kathy talked.

"The opening scene in your book—the murder scene—really sets the tone for the rest of the story. Tell me, what was it about this pier that inspired you to write that?"

Jean beamed as she waited for Kathy to start. Everything about her was perfect. Her hair was pulled back in a tight bun, and she didn't have any flyaways that blew in the breeze. Her skin had a glow that only seemed to be enhanced by the sun's rays. And her teeth were a brilliant shade of white.

Kathy envied her. While she had certainly aged well, she *had* aged. These days, she was so busy doing one thing or another that she didn't have as much time to spend on her appearance, perfecting every little detail like she had when she'd been younger. With the early-morning attack, she was certainly far from her best self.

"Well, this pier is a great date spot, even if not all dates are great."

Jean threw her head back and laughed loudly. "Oh, let me write that down! It's so funny because it's true!"

"Anyway, so I had a date here once, and all I kept thinking was how beautiful it was with the lights and everything. And, you know, with my twisted mind, I thought about how a murder could take place right here in a public place and it could be hidden pretty well."

Kathy thought about her first date with Will when Vepar had nearly drowned her. Will had chopped him up, and they'd buried him in a farm field. The investigation that followed had been no fun to clean up, but it had made for a funny story.

"Well, it helps when your characters have magical powers. How creative." Jean buzzed with excitement. A practiced mask that she likely slipped on for her professional meetings.

Kathy nodded. "Not as crazy and you'd think."

"With the magic stuff, there are rules that need to be followed. How did you come up with your character's limitations?"

For an interview in the local newspaper, Kathy was surprised that Jean had actually read the book. Most of the interviews she had done featured general questions, or questions that could be asked based on the back of the book.

Kathy chuckled and rubbed the back of her head. "Um… again, not as crazy as you might think. I helped my sister raise her kids, so I've been around…active imaginations. But in order to have interesting characters, they need to be faced with challenges."

"Kathy?" a man's voice cut in.

She looked up and saw him approaching. He wore a fitted suit, and it took a minute for Kathy to recognize him. His perfectly combed hair gave him away, though.

"Jeremy?"

He walked over and she stood. Before she knew it, he had wrapped her in a hug. "It's so nice to see you. You look great."

Kathy touched the swollen part of her face and looked down. "Thanks."

"Who's this?" Jean asked.

"Oh, this is…uh, an old friend," Kathy said. "Jeremy, this is Jean. We're actually in the middle of an interview." She was hoping it would get him to go away. Jeremy was the last person she expected to see. It had been years since they'd spoken.

"Right! You're an author now. That's exciting."

Kathy's head perked up. "Have you read my stuff?"

Jeremy rolled his eyes. "Like I have time to read. I'm the CFO of Tyler Harris Insurance—not that I'm trying to brag. I'm just saying I'm busy."

"I know what that's like." He was *definitely* trying to brag.

"Hey, why don't I get out of your hair? We should get dinner sometime and catch up. You still out on Arlington?"

Kathy nodded. "Yeah. That, uh, sounds nice."

"Great, I'll see you later. Nice meeting you, Jean!"

The reporter waved and turned back to Kathy. "Is he the pier boyfriend?"

"No, that was a different guy."

Jean patted the bench next to her. "Sit! I have more questions."

Chapter Five

The two women stared dumbfounded at Chris. A moment later, the older one stood and started toward the entrance of the cage.

"What is it about my daughter that you're not telling me?" Chris struggled to stay sitting up. He only had a limited amount of water, and his body was tired. Not to mention the sores that had been melted into his chest that still throbbed with pain, despite the medicated ointments.

"Don't ask questions." The younger woman fussed with his bandages, but Chris grasped her arms.

"No, tell me!"

"Guards!" the older woman shouted. "Guards! The prisoner is escaping!"

Two men rushed over. One of them raised his wand, and

hot embers shot into Chris's face. He shouted and wiped them away.

By the time he opened his eyes again, the women were gone and the cage was locked. The two guards stood a few feet away from the cage with their backs to Chris.

He needed to come up with a plan. While he was stuck in the cage, he was at their mercy. He needed to get out and dig around for information himself. Maybe even try to make contact with someone outside. Maybe even his brother.

No.

Josh was a doctor now. He had the life he wanted and had finally escaped the world of magic; something that had always been a burden to him. Chris couldn't justify drawing him back into this dangerous world.

His Aunt Kathy was out of the question as well. She had a career now too. Chris had seen a review for one of her books in a newspaper when he had been in Portland. He remembered when she had just been jotting notes down on a pad of paper when the Queen put her in the hospital. That had been a mess. Kathy was better off without magic too.

Besides, as much as Josh and Kathy would also want to know what it was that the Fire Wizards knew about Sophia, they would try to put an end to the group to stop future attacks. Chris didn't care for that.

The world hadn't been kind to him, even after he'd gone out of his way as a teenager to save the nonmagical from supernatural attacks. He didn't want to live that life anymore. He was done. Once he learned what they knew about Sophia, the Fire Wizards were no longer his problem.

Chris's stomach ached, which brought him back to his current situation. While he was used to that feeling, he usually tried to alleviate his hunger a bit with extra water. He was short on that, as well. Besides, the nurses hadn't finished tending to his wounds. He would need to find a medic tent and steal some supplies before he could go anywhere.

That was if Raven hadn't cast a spell on him to track him. Chris had no idea what kinds of samples she had taken while he was unconscious. Just a strand of hair containing his DNA could offer Raven so many possibilities.

The first thing to do was to get out of the cage. If he could get the guards to just *talk* to him, he knew he could whittle them down enough to let him out. Or look the other way while he escaped.

"Hey man, do you have any water?" Chris asked. "I'm really thirsty."

Neither guard acknowledged him.

"Look, I'm sorry about grabbing that girl like that. I didn't mean to scare her. I just haven't heard any news about my daughter in so long that I got excited." He tried to swallow, but his mouth was too dry. "Do you have any kids? I'm sure any parent would—"

"Shut up," one of them said. He was shorter—rounder—than the other guard, who gave him a look.

That was good. Now that they were responding, Chris had an in.

"I really miss her. She was my world, you know? After she...

went, I lost everything. I've been on my own ever since. Just looking for anything to help give me some answers."

Chris felt a lump forming in his throat. For the last two years,
he had been so focused on his hatred of the Fire Wizards and the
person who'd killed Sophia that he'd never allowed himself to properly mourn her. He needed to be a stone-cold killer if he was going
to be taken seriously and get some answers. Or, at least, act like one.

But that had taken its toll.

The truth was, he was lonely. He hadn't been able to trust anyone—not even himself sometimes—and he was tired of it. Sometimes he wondered if his loneliness was a worse pain than losing
his daughter.

He couldn't think like that. Losing Sophia was the worst pain of
all. She hadn't deserved to die. She had been so young. She hadn't
done anything to anyone. Her life had been taken from her—from
Chris. And Holly, too.

Chris wiped at his eyes. Raven knew that he would do anything
for Sophia—or anyone else in his family—but the rest of the coven
didn't need to know that. They didn't need to know his weaknesses.

"Look, if you could just get me—"

A third man came running from the center of camp.

"We need help. One of you stay here with him, the other come
with me."

The shorter one stayed behind, which Chris was thankful for.
He had shown a chink in his armor. Chris just needed to keep
working at it.

"Hey man, if you could tell me anything about my baby girl.

Anything at all. I need some glimmer of hope."

The guard gave a quick sideways glance at Chris and then faced forward again.

"Put yourself in my shoes. Imagine what it's like not hearing *anything* about your kid for two years. Wouldn't you want some answers when someone mentions their name?"

The man cleared his throat and spoke softly. Chris needed to strain to listen.

"I don't know much. And whatever I do tell you, you have to keep to yourself. *Do not* let Raven—or anyone else—know that you know. That would end up in *my* daughter getting killed. Got it?"

Chris leaned close to the bars of the cage and nodded fervently.

"Mr. Harper!" Raven's voice cut into the exchange. "It looks like you've got a new neighbor."

She was leading two guards, the one who had just been guarding Chris's cage a few moments before and another. The guards were dragging a woman with a burlap sack over her head.

Now that we have a new inmate,
this cage we need to replicate.

Chris's cage began to shake after Raven cast the spell. He buried himself in the corner and held on to the bars as it rattled. Another set of bars began to form to Chris's right, so that the cage was a large rectangular shape with a dividing wall separating the two cells. Once the shape was complete, the shaking ceased.

"I believe you are acquainted already." Raven stepped up to the woman and pulled the sack off just before the guards tossed her in.

"Hey! What are you going to do with me! You told me you were going to train me!" Chris reached through the cage. Raven had begun to walk away, so he needed to shout to get her attention.

Instead of answering him, Raven turned and offered a smile before continuing to the center of camp.

Chris slammed the bars in frustration. She hadn't ever planned on letting him lead. He was a prisoner; he had been fooled.

"Chris?" a familiar voice called from the cage next to him. Crouched down in the cell connected to his was the last person he'd ever expected to see again.

Holly.

* * *

When Kathy pulled into the driveway, she had a list in her head of everything she needed to do: call DJ Books and tell them to send over a headshot for the paper; mark in her calendar when the rest of her interviews were; and check in with Holly to see what she had come up with about the Chaos. Finding who had released it, and stopping them before they could do any damage, needed to be their top priority.

Oh, and dinner needed to be decided as well.

As she walked to the front door, she searched for her publisher's number in her phone. It was just after five. Someone would still be in the office. They usually worked until six.

"You haven't changed a bit."

Kathy jumped. Jeremy was coming up the walk from the street.

"Same old house, still just as beautiful." He indicated her hand. "Still single."

"What makes you think I'm not seeing someone? Maybe we just haven't gotten married."

"Are you seeing someone?"

"No."

"Good."

"Good?"

He nodded. "That way it won't be awkward when I invite you to dinner tonight."

"Tonight?"

"Yeah."

"Like when?" She ran through her to-do list again.

"Now works for me."

She stuck her thumb over her shoulder toward the house. "I just—I have so much to do."

"Stuff that can't wait until after you've had a proper meal? What were you going to have for dinner? PB&J?"

"I *have* learned to cook, you know." Since her sister had died, Kathy had watched enough of the Food Network to make it look like she knew what she was doing. Nobody had gotten sick from her cooking yet. That was a win in her book.

"Prove me wrong."

"Excuse me?"

"Show me how different you are. Show me that I don't know

you as well as I think I do."

The thought was tempting, but she had been through Jeremy's games before. Their relationship had worked when they had both been young and she'd fallen for his lines, which she had once thought were charming. As adults, they just didn't work.

She sighed. "Jeremy, we've been through this before…"

He shook his head. "I have no intentions, promise. All I know is that I'd love to catch up with an old friend, and, judging by how dark your house looks, you'd be eating alone tonight anyway."

Kathy thought of Holly. She was probably in her bedroom reading or something. She wouldn't notice Kathy was gone. Besides, with the way the house was so dark, she likely wanted to be left alone.

Sighing again, Kathy asked, "Where are you taking me?"

* * *

"The diner? You drove me all the way out here for the diner?"

Kathy was surprised. The diner used to be their spot. All their friends would hang out here, too. Back when Jeremy was going to Penn State, he'd lived with a friend in Lawrence Park, and the Lawrence Park Diner was the only twenty-four-hour eatery within walking distance. That had been over thirty years ago. She hadn't been back since.

"It's got history!" Jeremy got out of the car and waited for Kathy to meet him on the other side.

The place looked like a standard American diner. It was as if a mobile home had been renovated to work as a restaurant. The resulting space was tiny, which was fine for the owners. The whole place seemed to be stuck in the 1950s. When Jeremy was in college, it was perfect for a late-night meal to help keep away a hangover. Now, as adults who had just gotten out of work, she and Jeremy both stood out by the way they were dressed.

After they got their seats and ordered, an awkward silence fell on them. The place was too quiet to have a private conversation. It was small enough that the whole room could be discussing the same thing with one another.

Once an old man at the breakfast bar began talking loudly with another man seated next to him, the quiet faded.

"I'm surprised," Kathy started.

"Why's that?"

"I thought you would've outgrown this place. Here you are, in your—what is that? Armani? Being the CFO of a huge company, I expected you to wow me with your millions."

Kathy herself was dressed nicer than she needed to be for the atmosphere. She felt out of place, afraid everyone thought she was better than them.

She tried to relax. The diner brought back memories from when she had been younger. She had been a different person then. Maybe Jeremy had been too. But she'd been burned by him plenty of times before. Especially after everything she'd gone through with Will, she was reluctant to put herself out there again.

"You think I have millions?"

Kathy shrugged.

"Okay, maybe *a* million. But this dinner isn't only to see how you've changed, Kathy. It's to help show you that I've changed too. A lot of time has passed."

She leaned on her elbow. "Don't remind me."

"So what've you been up to? I saw that your sister passed away. I'm sorry to hear that. I wish you guys would've had a memorial or some other service."

"We did."

"Oh. I must've been out of town or something."

She raised her eyebrows and straightened out the edges of the card advertising the pie selection.

"Did you ever get married?"

She turned her attention back to him. "Yeah, for a bit. It didn't work out."

"Gotcha. Anyone I know?"

"Maybe. He was an attorney. I'm sure you've had to have some scandal swept away." She immediately regretted the jab. They were adults now. She didn't need to condemn him for what he'd done in his twenties.

"What was his specialty?"

"Lying." She slapped her hand down on the table. "Is this what you want to talk to me about? My dead sister and my ex-husband?"

He looked down at his hands. Kathy loved it that a few strands of his perfectly combed hair fell out of place. But damn, he still did look good. When he swept his hand up to correct it, his hair looked perfect once more.

"No."

"What about you? Did you ever marry?"

"Yes."

"Really?" He used to be a lot of fun. Never serious. Couldn't hold down a job. His idea of a good time was usually limited to activities that involved alcohol. Definitely not marriage material. When had that changed? Now he was a Penn State graduate and one of the leading men of a huge insurance firm. But she still couldn't bring herself to see him through a different lens.

"We were married about seven years. We have a daughter. She's a senior in high school now."

"Oh wow." Kathy leaned in on her arms. "I gotta be honest, I'm surprised."

"How come?"

She shrugged. "Never thought you wanted all that."

Their food came over, but neither of them touched it. Jeremy rattled his knuckles against the edge of the table. The room quieted for a minute until the old men at the bar erupted again.

"I realized after I got divorced that the girl I had imagined marrying and starting a family with was you."

Kathy rolled her eyes.

"And I know you have no interest, and I've certainly missed my chance, but after seeing you this morning I just wanted to say that I know I took you for granted all those years ago." He shrugged. "It might not mean anything now, but I'm sorry for the way I acted back then."

Jeremy gave her a quick smile and reached for the ketchup to add to his fries. Kathy sat frozen. Did her ex-boyfriend—who she'd once envisioned being with forever—actually just admit that he wished things had gone differently? When she'd broken up with him, all he'd said was, "Okay," as if it didn't matter to him one way or another.

That had been the first time she had let her guard down for a guy. The first time she'd allowed herself to love someone without any hesitation. When he'd blown her off, it had broken her heart. It wasn't until Will had come along that she'd felt that way again—and that had obviously ended a lot worse than her relationship with Jeremy.

Things were different now, though. They had both been married, raised children, and yet the universe brought them back together again. She had given Will of all people a second chance, shouldn't she do the same with Jeremy? Kathy didn't believe in coincidences, but she no longer wanted to let herself fall in love again. She needed to remain focused. Isn't that what she'd told Greg the last time she'd gone to New York?

The rest of the dinner was quiet. Kathy listened as the two men at the bar talked about labor unions and retirement packages. Jeremy was obviously uncomfortable, too. He didn't try to strike up any further conversation.

When he walked her to the door, he kissed her cheek to say good-bye, but Kathy turned and met his lips. Her hands found the familiar resting spots: the back of his neck and his side.

She felt a mixture of disappointment and relief when he finally pulled away. Nostalgia. That's all it was. Her feelings for him were dead in the water.

But she'd be lying if she said she didn't enjoy the kiss.

The Blue Moon

* * *

Heading out now.

Josh plugged the message into his phone and sent the text to his aunt. It was two in the morning. His shift had gone two hours longer than expected. One of his patients had gone into cardiac arrest, which meant more paperwork for Josh to fill out on top of the fact that he'd saved someone's life.

He walked through the empty parking garage toward the staircase. His car was probably the last one on the top floor—the only level left with available parking when he'd arrived at noon.

When he came out from the top of the stairs, Zamball and a young woman stood side-by-side with their arms crossed. Josh recognized her as Collie, the one who'd exposed him as a witch to Natalie on their first date.

"Holly told me you were back," Josh said. He wasn't particularly surprised to see them. At the moment, he was more annoyed that there was another obstacle between him and his bed.

"I believe you've already met my friend Collie." Zamball motioned toward her.

"Yeah, I remember her."

"How's your girlfriend?" Collie asked. "You two have been getting pretty cozy here at work."

Josh gritted his teeth. The fact that they knew about his personal life was suspicious. How long had they been watching him? Why?

"I have a proposition for you," Zamball said.

Josh put up his hand and started toward his car. "I don't want it." He just wanted to get home to bed.

Zamball pointed his wand. A burst of water slammed Josh into the brick wall containing the staircase. He fell to the ground, soaking wet and freezing from the night cold.

"Hey! I haven't done anything to you!"

"Focus, Windy." Collie knelt beside Josh. "He's got a great offer for you."

From the look on her face, Josh could tell she wasn't happy about it.

Zamball stepped closer. "I'm a member of the Pentad. A group of magical beings with very specific specialties all related to the elements."

"So what?" The visit Zamball had paid to Holly flashed in Josh's head. If Zamball had a new coven *and* he was seeking out old enemies, trouble was ahead. They needed to be careful.

"So there's an opening, and lucky for you, it's the air branch." Collie tried to ruffle Josh's wet hair, but he pulled away.

"Obviously, I represent the water branch," Zamball continued. "Collie represents earth, and spirit and fire are already covered. To be at full strength, we need to have the air branch filled."

Josh studied them, unsure of whether or not this was a trap.

Zamball held out his hand. "I'm asking you to work alongside us as an ally. This is a very powerful position, and we operate based on majority vote. Will you join us, Josh Harper, and become a member of the Pentad?"

CHAPTER SIX

Josh stared, uncertain. He couldn't tell if they were serious or not. He knew Zamball was demonic, and he guessed from the attack at the Downs that Collie was too. So why would they ask a white witch—who hadn't really practiced magic in some time—to join them? Were they desperate to fill spots? What did the membership cost? What was the reason the group existed to begin with?

"Why me?"

Zamball crossed his arms. "Your wind specialty makes you—"

"No, you told me that already. I'm asking why you want me, specifically. It doesn't add up. There are plenty of other people who have a wind specialty. Plenty of *demonic* people."

"I didn't make the choice."

"Then who did?"

"Our leader."

"And who is that? I thought you guys operated by majority vote?"

Zamball sighed. "Eleanor is not in charge of us, per se, but her specialty makes her the perfect candidate to assume a leadership role when an agreement can't be made. Since there is currently an even number of voters, our decision was split. She made the final call."

Josh didn't like that. What happened if one of them left or died and he was stuck in a group without a say in how they proceeded? He wouldn't do it. Besides, for the most part, he enjoyed his life without magic. He didn't want to tangle himself in it any further.

"Why would she choose me? She doesn't even know me."

Collie held up a hand. "What do you think that attack in the parking lot was for?"

"You were testing me."

She nodded.

"And you couldn't have waited until I was alone?"

She shook her head. "You might've run. Or played dumb. I needed to find you when you were worried about the safety of someone else. Where you would have to use your magic to protect them."

"You—"

"Either way," Zamball cut in, "Eleanor saw potential in you."

"She saw potential in *me*? It still doesn't make sense."

"She admires your knowledge both magically and medically. Besides your specialty, she thinks your other assets will be of use as well."

Josh stared at them. He didn't like the fact that he was being watched. Worse, he didn't like the fact that he *didn't know* he was being watched. He had never been that naïve before. Separating himself from magic had its downsides too. But magic was going to follow him whether he liked it or not.

"What's it gonna be, Windy?" Collie asked. "We're kind of on a deadline here."

"It's a big decision, don't you think? I need some time to think about it," Josh said. He had no intention of saying yes, but Zamball's visit to Holly in Lily Dale meant that he had some connection to the Chaos. Or at least knew who was connected.

"It's a very big decision, yes, but time is something we don't have," Zamball said.

"What do you mean?"

"There's a force that has been awakened—"

"The Chaos. Yeah, I know about it. What does that have to do with me?"

"It has *everything* to do with you! You and your damn family!"

"My family hasn't done anything to you since Will died!" He left out the part where Zamball was supposed to be dead.

"It's not only me who's at risk. It's everyone who's magical— maybe even humanity in general," the wizard countered.

Josh narrowed his eyes. "What do you mean?"

"The Chaos was created by two very powerful people using a combination of white and black magic."

"That doesn't make sense. Since when do they blend?"

"They don't," Collie chimed in. "Hence, the Chaos. So much

for being the smart one."

Josh turned back to Zamball. "But you said it was created."

He nodded. "The two who created it knew what would happen if they gave up their magic and combined it: insanity."

"But *why* was it created?"

"It's funny how little people have changed over the years. Always greedy. Always seeking power. Always at the expense of someone else. Back then, the number of people who possessed magic was growing. Worse, the power they possessed was naturally growing as well. Battles involving the supernatural were harder to fight. Harder to stop."

"Sounds like it was already chaos," Josh said.

Zamball shook his head. "No. They saw what the future held—what we're living in today. They saw that insanity would happen naturally over the course of time. They created the Chaos to stop magical people. Wipe us out completely. People, regardless of whether they possess magic or not, are driven to extreme insanity once they're exposed to the force."

"Why would they create something like that?"

"To speed up the inevitable: the day we all kill each other in our quest for power."

Josh tried to process it all. He remembered Kathy's story about what she had witnessed in New York City. She had seen the effects of the Chaos firsthand. She was lucky she hadn't been infected by it herself.

Zamball broke into his thoughts.

Josh could see the fear in his face. "Then how do we stop it?"

The Blue Moon

"First off, you need to join us. Eleanor has a theory that since the Chaos was created by white and black magic working together, it can be destroyed in a similar fashion. Your joining the Pentad would be a step in the right direction."

"Why do you need me? Couldn't you find someone else?"

"Not with the time we have!" Collie shouted. "The longer we sit here and explain it all to you, the more we risk being wiped off the face of the earth."

Zamball gave her a look and turned back to Josh. "Without a complete quintet, we're not at full strength. The threat of the Chaos—and the current phase of the moon—requires us to fill the vacancy quickly."

"What do you mean 'the phase of the moon'?" Josh looked up and saw the full moon directly above them. The lights illuminating the parking ramp weren't even necessary due to the glow of the orb above.

"Ordinarily, we can only add new members to the Pentad during the harvest moon; however, we found a loophole that allows us to add new members on another occasion: the blue moon. Tonight."

"Before dawn," Collie added.

"So you're saying that if I decide to join you, it's gotta be *tonight*?"

Zamball nodded.

"Forget it." Josh gathered his things. "I'm not going to be strong-armed into some demonic group and be brainwashed into thinking I'm helping the greater good. Nope. I'm a good person, all right? I go to work, pay my taxes, all of that. But I'm not stupid. I won't be fooled into trusting someone I used to call my enemy—who I thought was dead." He set off toward his car.

"If that's your choice." Zamball watched as Josh walked by. "But joining the Pentad wouldn't only eliminate the threat of the Chaos. It could also save your brother and your niece."

Josh spun around. "What about them? What do you know!?" He would've given anything to see another part of his family restored.

Collie crossed her arms. "Well, that got his attention."

"At full strength, the Pentad is capable of anything—including resurrection."

* * *

Chris and Holly stared at each other, both too afraid to move. Chris took in the small changes: Holly's shorter hair, how thin she had gotten, the faint worry lines by her eyes. Despite it all, he still thought she was beautiful. Perfect.

He wanted to say something but didn't know how to start. What did Holly think of him after so much time had passed? She hadn't tried to contact him, maybe she had moved on. At the same time, for the last year he had been out of reach, deliberately out of contact. Maybe she had tried to make contact, but he had severed all ties.

The bigger question was: Why was she here? He decided to start with that.

No. He should ask her if she was all right first. Or maybe he should lead with what was going on…

"Are you okay?" Holly broke the silence first.

"I've been better." Chris smiled. After everything, she still made him smile without even trying. No matter the circumstances.

"I barely recognized you. You look so…different." Holly studied him. She didn't care for his long hair, but she didn't know how long he had been held captive. Maybe he didn't have a choice in the matter. His beard could use a trimming, too, but she liked it otherwise.

His torso was the worst, though. The first thing she noticed was the upside-down triangle burned into his chest. It had begun to scab over, but it was also red and puffy. Infected. He had more burns on his side. Those looked better, like they'd had longer to heal.

She could see almost every one of his ribs. His hip bones stuck out just above the waist of his dirty shorts. She remembered when he used to be so fit. He used to work out every day—his body and his magic. Now his body barely resembled the man he'd once been. But wasn't she a different woman too?

So much had happened since they'd last seen each other that Chris was practically a stranger to her. But his smile was familiar. Her chest burned and her eyes began to water. Despite everything she blamed him for, she missed him. Judging by the state of his tattered body, the last two years hadn't been easy for him.

Instead of the heartbreak and anger that she thought she'd be filled with when she saw him again, she was filled with pity. And guilt. If Sophia really was alive, he didn't deserve the punishment he had gone through. The punishment she had helped dole out.

Chris looked down and tried to see himself through Holly's eyes. "I've looked better."

She nodded and laughed nervously.

"Are you okay? What are you doing here?" he asked.

"Raven wants me to convince you to join them."

"Why?" It came out harsher than he intended. "I mean, why would they think you'd help me?" He dropped his eyes. "You hate me."

Holly shifted her eyes away from him. "I don't hate you, Chris."

His head perked up. "You don't?" He never thought he'd hear her say that—never thought he'd even speak to her again.

"I don't know what I feel. I'm…I don't know. I *am* happy to see you." She met his eyes for a moment and then looked down again. If she looked at him, she would lose her confidence. She could already feel the lump forming in her throat. "I wish you were in better health and, you know, *not* locked in a cage, but it's good to see you."

He smiled again. "It's good to see you too, Holly. I've missed you."

"I—" She stopped herself before she admitted anything. This morning she'd thought Chris was dead. Now she knew he wasn't, and neither was their daughter. Whatever she was going through, she needed to work it out in her head before she told him anything. There was still a mystery to be solved. But one thing did need to be said: "I owe you an apology."

"For what? I should be the one apologizing to you." He played with a wood chip sticking up from the plywood. "And I am sorry, Holly. Really sorry. I loved Sophia. I would never have done anything to hurt her. I just… I loved her so much. And you." He looked down again and muttered, "Still do."

Holly pulled at a loose thread on her shorts. She heard what he said but tried to act like she didn't. She didn't want to think about it. Not here. "What happened that night?"

"You really want to talk about it?"

She shrugged. "No. But I realize I never gave you a chance to explain. I just assumed the worst and left. I'm sorry for not hearing you out. Or trusting you."

He shook his head. "You weren't completely wrong. It was partially my fault."

Holly's heart sank. She closed her eyes tightly and tried to hide her sorrow behind her hair.

"The Fire Wizards showed up because of me. If you had been the one watching her, they wouldn't have…"

Her head perked up. "Wait, the Fire Wizards were there that night?"

He nodded. "Yeah. Where do you think the blue flame came from?"

"I just thought it was you."

"Holly, why would I practice my fire magic when I had Sophia? We were going to watch a movie. I went into the kitchen to make popcorn, and then I heard the smoke alarm go off. Sophia was gone by the time I got back."

Chris felt like a weight had been lifted off him. Since the accident, he had wanted to tell Holly the truth. Even if it didn't change anything, it was a burden he was carrying. She deserved to know. Now, he only wondered what she thought of it. Whether she believed him or not. His story might be too convenient for her.

"So why didn't you just tell me that the night of the fire? Or any night since then?" She felt guilty for damning him all this time when he was an innocent man. Chris was simply a parent who was just as distraught over losing their child as Holly was.

He shrugged. "You just assumed. I couldn't blame you. I *was* obsessed with the growth of my powers. It wasn't until after you filed for divorce that I realized that. The only other option I could think of who could wield flame like that were the Fire Wizards. I left Erie to hunt them down and found out it was a woman named Q who had killed her. Ordered by Raven, apparently."

"So that's what you've been doing all this time? Looking for who was responsible?" Holly felt like she hadn't done enough. She had accepted the fact that Sophia was dead and moved on. Meanwhile, Chris was trying to get justice for her. Apparently, he was on the right track. Maybe if she had been helping him all along, they wouldn't be locked in side-by-side cages.

He nodded again. "Yeah, basically. I've been across the country town-hopping, looking for answers. A lot of good that did me. Raven asked me to lead, and I thought I could use them to find Q and then take the Fire Wizards down from the inside. First thing they did was throw me in here and put their mark on me." His hand hovered over his chest. "I fell right into their trap."

Holly chewed on her thumb. Chris had been living in hell for the last two years. Unlike her, he didn't have a home or a guaranteed warm bed to come home to every night. Through all of this, she had been selfish while Chris was being selfless. He was a much better person than she was. She didn't think she could ever apologize enough.

"Chris, there's something you need to know."

"No, Holly. Let's just be done apologizing and move on. Look, we're both in here now. Let's figure out a way to get out."

"And then what?"

He shrugged. "I don't know. Go our separate ways, I guess."

Holly hesitated, her breath shuddering. "I don't want that."

"What are you saying?"

"I don't know, exactly. But I know that I'm going to need your help to find our daughter."

He studied her, not sure what she was saying.

Holly confirmed it: "Chris, Sophia's alive."

Chapter Seven

Chris's mouth hung open. Sophia was alive? That didn't make sense. After all of the spells and rituals he had performed to find any information on her, why hadn't her location revealed itself? As her father, didn't he have a strong enough connection? More importantly, who was keeping her hostage? Was it Q, or had she just been a hitman? If she—or whoever Sophia's captor was—was able to keep her hidden from his magic, what kind of power did they wield?

"How do you know? When did you find out? Why wouldn't you try to contact me to tell me?" All of his questions came rushing out at once. He tried to hold off his anger, but he couldn't control it. He pressed against the bars.

Holly put up her hand. "Hold on, Chris. I just found out. Raven told me before she threw me in here. She said Sophia didn't die, but that she was kidnapped."

He rubbed his beard. "Did she sound like she was lying?"

She shook her head. "She was kind of matter-of-fact. She didn't give me any details, though."

"Weird."

"Yeah."

"No, it's weird that she even told you."

"Why's that?"

"Well, clearly she knows something. Maybe everything." Briefly, Chris let himself fantasize that Sophia was here at this camp. But that would be impossible. They would be able to sense her. He just hoped that wherever she was, she was being cared for.

"It seemed that way. Has she mentioned anything about it to you?"

He shook his head. "That's the thing. She's been leading me to believe that Sophia's dead. She even made several accusations that I'm the one who killed her."

Holly wondered if she had forgiven Chris too easily. If Raven said he killed her, maybe Chris was just remembering wrong?

It didn't add up, though. Raven had told Chris that he'd killed Sophia while she'd told Holly that she had been kidnapped. That right there proved that Raven's word couldn't be trusted. And if they were going to get Sophia back, Holly needed to start trusting Chris again.

"If she told me one thing and you another and then put us in side-by-side cages, she had to have known that we would talk," Chris said. "But why would she want us to call her out on her contradicting stories?"

Holly shrugged. "It's not like we can do anything about it anyway."

"Something has already been done, Holly." Chris buried his face in his hands.

"What do you mean?"

He moved his hair out of his face. "I'm so stupid!"

"What?"

"I'm a member of the Fire Wizards now. Raven tricked me into joining."

"But then why would she need me? She made it sound like I was going to convince you to join."

"Convince me to join or convince me to abandon my search for Sophia?"

"How would she make you do that? Especially if she expected me to tell you that Sophia was alive?"

He shrugged. "Paranoia, maybe. Make me think that I was crazy with two sides telling me different things. I've been alone for two years. She must think that I have trust issues."

Holly let out a deep breath. She hated to hear about the pain Chris had gone through alone. "So trust *me*. I just told you that I was wrong about you." She held out her hand. "We have to be a team again."

"Are you sure that's a road you want to go down again?"

She shook her head. "I'm not sure. But first things first: getting Sophia back. Neither of us can do it alone. We'll go from there."

He smiled and took her hand. "Right. So what's our plan then?"

"I guess you should just play along for now. Maybe see if they'll let me go. Or give you a free moment to contact Kathy and Josh."

Chris raised his eyebrows. "It's been a long time since I've talked to them. I'm not even sure they want me back."

"They do."

"How do you know?"

"They told me so. This morning, actually—or maybe it was yesterday. Either way, it was recently."

"Wait, you've seen them?"

"I'm kind of living with them again."

"How did that happen?"

She smiled. "Long story."

"That must be weird for you." He studied her hand in his. He fought the urge to kiss the back of it like he used to. He never did it for any particular reason: when she was cooking dinner, when they lay down to bed, or if they were just watching TV. It was little things like that that he remembered about their marriage when he missed her most. How easy everything had been. How comfortable they had been.

She nodded. "It was weird. Until I learned that Sophia is still alive. Now I know I'm going to need all of you guys to get her back. She was a part of this family. We all lost her. I need to remember that."

Chris tightened his grip. "We'll get her back, Holly."

She looked down at their hands. Chris's used to be so rough from the steel plant he'd worked at. Whatever he'd been working with used to stain his clothes and his hands. She remembered how angry she would get with him when he ruined another pair of jeans. Their lives had been normal for a bit. It was a strange feeling to think that her best years were behind her already.

"I feel like a failure," she admitted.

"Why?"

She took a deep breath. "I turned out to be exactly like my parents."

"Holly, you had great parents."

With tears in her eyes, she looked up at him. "I had one parent. My mother left me before I was born. My father didn't even bother getting me back until I was a year old. I guess life really does go in cycles. I missed *two years*."

Chris shook his head. "That wasn't your father's fault and it's not yours, either. Okay, so you were a year old when your father got you away from Toxanna, but after that you had a normal childhood. Until you learned you were a witch."

"And then what happened? I was too inexperienced and needed to run away while my dad and Drew fought my battles for me."

"But look at you now."

"Now? Now I'm a woman who gave up searching for her kid and gave up on what was left of her family. Sometimes I wonder if everyone would've been better off if Toxanna had just raised me. Then someone would have put me down a long time ago." Her words surprised her. She hadn't consciously thought that before, but everything just seemed to get worse. Life was supposed to have been smooth sailing once Toxanna was defeated, but that couldn't be further from the truth.

Chris squeezed her hand again. "Hey, look at me." When she

met his eyes, he kissed the back of her hand. "I would not have been better off. Even if it was only for a little while, you made me so happy." He reached through the bars and wiped a tear from her cheek. "Can I tell you something?"

She shrugged, unable to find her voice.

"I've thought about you and Sophia every day since the accident. And not just the moments with the three of us, but when it was just you and I. Before we had Sophia. When we first moved in together and got married. How everything was exciting and I couldn't wait to get home from work every day—even if all we were doing was lying around the house." He smiled. "It's funny. With all of the magic we've both seen, nothing quite captivated me like you do."

"Chris, I—"

"Mr. Harper." The guards moved away from each other, making way for Raven.

Chris dropped Holly's hand and turned toward his captor.

"It's time to begin your training."

"My training?"

"Yes. I made you a promise and I intend to keep it. As a member of the Fire Wizards, you are subject to proper training." She shifted her eyes to Holly and then back to Chris. "I can only trust that you'll keep your promise." She turned to one of the guards. "Get him out. Start him with laps around the camp. He needs to stretch his muscles."

"Wait! He needs a medic!" Holly called after Raven. "He needs food and time to rest. He's not ready to train."

Raven turned her head over her shoulder but didn't look at Holly. "I'm training a soldier, Ms. Bowen. He'll toughen up."

* * *

Josh was grateful he had the day off. By the time he got to bed, it was almost four in the morning. He didn't allow himself the luxury of sleeping in. He had a list of medical journals to read on top of the paperwork he brought home from work—which now needed to be reorganized, thanks to Zamball and Collie's attack.

He was sitting at the kitchen table reading through an article and eating a bowl of cereal when Kathy came downstairs.

"Hey, I didn't hear you come in last night." She wore black leggings and a hoodie. Her brown hair was pulled back in a bun.

"I got in late." He kept his eyes on the paper.

She pulled a water out of the fridge. "Did Holly text you last night?"

"No. Why?"

"Oh."

He looked up. "What is it?"

"I just haven't heard from her since we all left yesterday morning. When I got home she still wasn't back. I think something might be wrong."

"I don't know."

"She's been back in Erie for three days and suddenly she's MIA?"

"She's used to being on her own. I'm sure she just forgot to check in."

Kathy shook her head. "Who does she know in Erie?"

"Lots of people! She lived here for eight years."

"I don't buy it. She wasn't exactly excited about coming back here, why would she reconnect with old friends?"

Josh shrugged and sipped the milk from his bowl.

Kathy sat at the table across from him. "Hey, what's going on with you?"

"Nothing. I'm fine." He set his bowl aside and tried to focus on the article. He had reread the same paragraph three times now, never once actually processing it.

"You're not fine. You're acting weird. Is it Natalie?"

He shook his head. "No, it's not."

"Then what is it?"

"It's nothing."

"You just said it wasn't Natalie, which implies that it *is* something. Josh, tell me what's wrong."

He tossed the article on the counter and let out a puff of air. She was going to find out eventually. Better she hear it from him. He had been hoping to tell her and Holly together, though.

"Last night something happened. Zamball found me when I was walking to my car."

Kathy's face dropped. "Honey, are you okay? Why didn't you say anything?"

"He didn't want to hurt me." He hesitated before he continued. "He had a proposition for me."

She narrowed her eyes. "What kind of proposition?"

"He's a part of this group called the Pentad. He said that with good and evil working together, we could stop the Chaos…and save Chris and Sophia."

Kathy's mind raced. The name Pentad sounded familiar, but she couldn't remember why. Whatever it was, she hadn't heard it in a long time and she was sure it wasn't good. Especially if Zamball was involved. "Josh…tell me you didn't…"

He nodded.

She slammed her hands on the table. "What were you *thinking* getting in bed with Zamball!?" She paced the room. "Why? Do you think he's actually *capable* of finding Chris?"

"Bringing him—and Sophia—back to life." Josh was perturbed with Kathy's denial of his brother's death. Why couldn't she accept it so they could mourn him? It didn't feel real, but he knew it was.

"Nobody has that power, Josh! The few necromancers who've tried ended up getting themselves killed. Once someone is dead, a corpse is a corpse. They're never the same again." She turned away from him and shook with frustration. "Oooh, I can't believe you did that! Do you realize what you've done?"

"I'm trying to help put our family back together! Isn't that the same reason you summoned a Fire Wizard here yesterday? You can't tell me that wasn't reckless!"

"Okay, yeah, that was a mistake. But you *deliberately* joined a demonic cult!"

"It's not a cult! They vote on all decisions." He jabbed his finger in his chest. "I'd have a vote."

"A vote out of how many?"

"Five."

"So what happens when you get outvoted?"

He shrugged.

"You didn't even think this through, did you?"

"I didn't think I should second-guess myself when I was promised that I could bring Chris and Sophia back."

She leaned against the counter.

"Let's pretend for a minute that Zamball and the Pentad *can* bring them back. How do you know he's even going to follow through on his promise? And even if they do, then what? You're stuck in that coven forever."

Josh met her eyes but didn't say a word. She was right. But he couldn't pass up the opportunity to save his brother. If he hadn't taken it, he would go crazy thinking about what would've happened if he had.

"Why don't you start looking for Holly? I'm going for a run. I need to clear my head."

"What do I do once I find her?" he asked.

She untangled her headphones and walked toward the door. "Maybe start searching for a new place to live," she muttered.

* * *

Kathy stood on the front steps and reached down to touch her toes. She normally stretched in the house, but she needed fresh air. Josh had crossed a line. She wasn't sure if she could ever forgive him. The damage he had done was irreparable. She could only hope it would turn out all right.

79

"Where are you off to?"

Just as she grabbed her ankles, she looked over and saw Jeremy approach. Immediately, she stood up straight.

"Don't stop on my account. Please, I certainly enjoy the view."

She rolled her eyes. "I'm not in the mood right now."

"I actually came here to invite you somewhere, but it looks like you're busy."

"I'm going to go for a run." She rested her hands on her hips and let her headphones dangle in front of her.

He smiled. "I've always admired your athleticism."

"What's the party?"

"What makes you think it was a party?"

She cocked an eyebrow. "I thought I said I wasn't in the mood?"

"The Tyler Harris Insurance anniversary party. It's a work thing. I was just thinking that you could come with me."

"Why would I do that?" It came out harsher than she intended. Evidently, she still carried some ill feelings toward him.

"I don't know. A bunch of middle-aged wealthy, intelligent people who might be looking to dive into a fantasy world to escape their mundane lives?" He shrugged. "It'd be the perfect party to plug your new book. Maybe they'll have additional connections throughout the city you can get in touch with." He flashed a smile. "Oh, and you're welcome for dinner yesterday, by the way."

Kathy smiled and softened her stance. He was trying. And the plug at the party did sound like a good idea. But this was tradition-al Jeremy. Veiling his true intentions under something she wanted. "You need a date, don't you?"

He nodded bashfully. "Basically everyone else who works there is married. The Christmas party was brutal. It was the first event I went to solo. If people weren't giving me pity looks, they were trying to fix me up with someone. Spent the whole night downing martinis at the bar."

Kathy rolled her eyes. Of course he'd found the bar.

"I just figured I'd offer the invitation to you, as a friend, to help deflect those comments while giving you an opportunity in the process. I enjoyed catching up with you. I thought this would be another opportunity to get to know the older and wiser Kathy Walker."

She crossed her arms. "When and where?"

He smiled. "This Saturday. Six p.m. At the convention center. It's formal."

"I'll think about it."

"I kind of need an answer by, like, today."

She smirked. "So improvise. It's what you do best."

Chapter Eight

Josh didn't want to consider whether or not his aunt was being honest when she suggested he look for a new place to live. She had never mentioned that before. Despite the fact that he was twenty-seven, the subject of getting his own place had never come up. Their fractured family had been through enough. They were just glad that they still had each other.

He'd known his joining the Pentad would make Kathy mad. Holly would be too. But he thought the outcome would justify the decision. If he had to sacrifice himself for his niece and brother to come back to life, then so be it. They were worth it. Magic had always been a burden to Josh, it was about time it became a resource. Something that could actually help without costing anyone anything else. If he gave up his life, Chris and Sophia's would be restored. That was worth it in his book.

Besides, Zamball needed Josh just as much as Josh needed him. He had leverage. Maybe he could convince the Pentad to resurrect Chris and Sophia before they took care of the Chaos. That way, he could be guaranteed that he wouldn't be double-crossed.

Then what? Kathy was right. What would he do after Chris and Sophia were alive, safe and sound? He was hoping Holly would have some insight with all of her divinity dealings through the years. He needed to find a way to find her now, too.

The magic book was mostly foreign to Josh. He had used it for small things throughout the last ten years, but the potions section had completely changed.

The book was charmed. Whenever they ran out of new pages to add new entries to, another page appeared overnight. Josh's ancestors, the first people to ever create the book, must've placed the charm, because it had been growing for as long as Josh could remember. Only when it needed space, though.

So the pages that had been together were now far from each other after ten years of additions. Kathy hadn't been as active with her magic as she used to be—certainly not as much as when Josh's mother had been alive—but fighting evil was in her blood. She couldn't let some magical terror go unleashed if it was brought to her attention. But she no longer sought it out.

Josh also suspected that she was still trying to right her wrongs for everything she had done while she had been with Will. He didn't know the details, but he had put together enough clues to figure out that she hadn't been a nice witch when she had been with him.

The mystery of the magic book caused Josh to take longer to find the correct spell that would help him find Holly. He knew they had used it before.

Maybe. He wasn't sure. His confidence had been shaken.

It sounded familiar, at least. Chris used to ramble about various spells in the book when they had been younger. He would study the tome every night just for the fun of it.

Josh smiled. He missed his little brother.

Once he found the spell, he remembered that Chris said Drew had used it to take them down to the underworld when they'd killed Will. Drew and Will were two people Josh certainly hadn't thought of in years. They were among the memories he'd tried to push out of his mind when he'd retired as a witch.

The spell needed to be modified. Drew had crafted it to bring them down to Holly, whereas Josh wanted to bring her to him. He set to work. The sooner he found Holly, the sooner she would be home safely. Plus, the sooner he could get back to that mountain of paperwork taunting him from across the room.

An hour later, Josh had rewritten the spell and cross-referenced it with the various candles that would enhance it. Specific colors were required. He only hoped he remembered where they had stashed them.

He thought they were in the attic. But Kathy might've put them in the cabinet in the living room with the scented candles she collected. He couldn't remember. He had come home from work one day while she was cleaning up the magic room. Said they never used it anymore.

And they hadn't. Chris and Holly used to sleep on the pullout couch in the living room when they would come over for holidays. The spare bedroom came in handy. It still did now that Holly was back. But it meant their magical items were no longer in one place.

Not wanting to climb up to the attic and rifle through boxes, Josh found the three candles he needed in his aunt's cabinet.

A birch-scented candle was silver, which stood for femininity. Josh also thought it would help channel Holly's magic to his and create a connection for her to follow back home.

He needed a pink one, too. Pink stood for love, family, and friendship. All essential. Even if Holly no longer considered Josh and Kathy family, they were at least friends. People who aren't friends don't just move in together from a hundred miles away. He found a candle with a watermelon fragrance in the back of the cabinet that was the perfect color. It was still wrapped in plastic. Apparently Kathy wasn't a fan of this one.

Josh was about to close the cabinet when he spotted a weird-looking candle at the bottom of the shelf. It had three layers: brown, white, and more brown. He read the label: Chocolate Delight, a mix of dark- and white-chocolate scent. He grabbed it and skimmed the book. Brown represented home. Hopefully the color that burned was the most effective.

Setting up a small makeshift altar on the kitchen counter, Josh placed the three candles in a triangle, making room for the book in the center. He skimmed the list. He still needed some of Holly's DNA. Back when she'd first joined them, she had used Will's toothbrush to find him. Surely, he could find something of hers that was better than a toothbrush.

Even though it was his house, he felt weird going into Holly's bedroom. She hadn't unpacked much. The bed hadn't been made, and several suitcases sat at the foot of it. One was on its side with the zipper open. She had no intention of staying.

He flipped open the unzipped suitcase and saw a heap of clothes. Rifling through her suitcase would be a last resort. Even if it was for her own safety. He could find something else.

Searching for a hairbrush, Josh remembered that Holly had asked to borrow Kathy's. He went to his aunt's room and pulled a few strands of hair away from the bristles. He couldn't be sure that he had pulled off Holly's hair, but he needed to take that risk.

Now equipped with her DNA, Josh lit the candles and recited the spell:

> *Holly, can you hear my cry,*
> *across the oceans and the skies?*
> *From the place where you have gone,*
> *follow the light to guide you home.*

Nothing happened at first. Josh looked around, wondering if his knack for spellcasting had faded. Then he remembered he was still holding the strand of hair in his hand. He lifted it to the flame of the pink candle and watched it ignite.

Moments later, the air stirred and Holly appeared next to Josh. She was crouched on the floor.

"What's going on? How did—Josh!" Holly sprang to her feet and hugged him.

He squeezed her, relieved his spell had worked successfully. Holding her out at arm's length, he asked, "Are you okay? Where were you? What happened?"

She ran her hands through her hair. "So much. I saw Chris. He's in trouble."

"Chris is *alive*!?" A million thoughts floated through Josh's head: Did Zamball know? Where was Chris? Who had taken him? Had Josh just damned himself by joining the Pentad?

Holly nodded. The smile on her face confused Josh.

"There's more."

"What is it? Where have you been?"

"With the Fire Wizards. The whole thing is a mess."

"What is? Holly, you're not making any sense."

"Sophia's alive, too!"

* * *

Kathy's music faded as her phone began to ring. She was only about twenty feet from her driveway. The big finish. Couldn't the call have waited until then?

She slowed and tried to catch her breath before the call went to voice mail. She hit the button on her headphones to answer.

"Hello?" She forced herself to take deep breaths through her nose. Her chest burned.

"Kathy? It's Greg. How are you?"

"Greg?" Her mind went momentarily blank. "Oh! Hi!" It was her editor at DJ Books. "What's up?"

"I'm at the airport. I'm flying to Erie today."

She nearly choked. "You are?"

"Yeah. Paul thought it'd be a good idea to push the angle of your success story. He thought since I'm the one who discovered you, so to speak, that we would make a good interview team. Didn't you get the email? He updated the marketing plan to include me."

Kathy thought of last night's dinner with Jeremy—could she call it a date?—and how she'd wanted to get her mind off everything, so she'd lost herself in a romance book. Research for the new novel. She hadn't even looked at her email since. "I've been busy."

"Oh. Sorry. Thought you knew. It's just for a couple of days. I'm staying at SpringHill Suites, but I'd like to touch base with you before we have our first meeting."

"You're staying out by the mall?"

"I guess so. I'm taking a shuttle from the airport."

"Oh. All right. Um…" Kathy mentally went through her schedule. She wanted to try to smooth things out so they weren't so weird when it came time to work on her new book. She hadn't really spoken to him since she'd cried like a crazy woman in New York. This was her chance to redeem herself. "Don't take the shuttle. I'll pick you up. The next interview is tomorrow, right?"

"Oh thanks. Yeah, it's tomorrow. I'll see then?"

"Sure thing." Kathy was glad he ended the call early. Even if she had caught her breath, she didn't know what to say to him.

She pulled out her headphones once she was in the door.

"Kathy?"

"Holly?" Kathy followed the sound of the voice and nearly ran into Holly when she turned the corner. "How did you—did Josh…?"

She nodded. "But he left. He seemed pretty pissed."

Kathy nodded. "I imagine he is. I'm not very happy with him myself." Now that the endorphins had kicked in from her run, her anger toward her nephew had eased, but it was still present.

Holly cocked her head. "Why?"

"It's a long story. Where were you? Are you okay?"

"I'm fine, but I was attacked—by both Zamball and the leader of the Fire Wizards. Raven."

Kathy's eyes scanned over Holly. "Did they hurt you?"

"Not really. I'm fine. I found Chris, though. He's alive. But he's not in good shape."

"What do you mean? Is he with the Fire Wizards? Is he okay? Are they going to hurt him?" Kathy reflexively thought the worst. If she had been more adamant about finding him these last two years, maybe he wouldn't have gotten himself mixed up with the Fire Wizards. Maybe he'd be home now, safe and sound.

She remembered the promise she'd made to her sister to take care of her boys. Just because they were adults now didn't mean she wasn't going to keep her promise. And yet she'd failed.

Failed Samantha.

Failed Chris.

Failed herself.

Holly sighed and shook her head. "It's not good. He's in trouble.

We need to save him. And Sophia."

"Sophia?"

Smiling, Holly nodded. "She's alive too."

*　*　*

Now that he was a member of the Pentad, Josh heard voices in his head. If he hadn't already met Zamball and Collie, he would've thought he was crazy, but it was just another sign that he was now officially a part of the Pentad. Members could share their thoughts with one another remotely. Through his anger, it didn't take Josh long to figure out how to contact Zamball through their shared connection.

"You son a bitch!" Josh shouted as he approached the wizard.

Zamball was standing at the edge of the grassy pier, facing the lake. He didn't turn when Josh approached him, and Josh wondered if he had even heard him.

"You lied to me!"

"I did not lie to you. The information about your brother's—and your niece's—survival is news to us as well."

"How do you know already? I just found out." Josh was standing next to Zamball now. He leaned in close to intimidate him. It didn't seem to be working.

Zamball put his hand on Josh's shoulder and pushed him an arm's length away. "That is exactly how we know. Because you know. We're united now. I'm sure you've heard the voices."

"So you didn't know he was alive until just now?"

Now Zamball met Josh's eyes. "This connection of ours works both ways. Read my thoughts. Am I lying?"

Josh tried to focus but couldn't get a solid answer. He didn't get any overwhelming feelings of deceit from Zamball, but he was new to this telepathy connection.

"Okay. Even if nobody knew the state of Chris's life, what about Sophia? Someone had to have known that she was alive. It's been two years."

"That, we may be able to help you with."

Josh took a step forward again. "Can you help me find her?"

"We don't have any of the answers you're looking for. But I may know who does."

"Who is it? Where can I find them?"

Zamball shook his head. "You're not going to like it."

"What do you mean?"

"It's someone you trust."

Josh's heart beat faster. "Holly?"

"No. Her misery for losing her daughter is genuine."

"Then who is it? Just tell me!"

A gust of wind came and knocked Zamball back a step.

"Be mindful of your powers."

Josh crossed his arms. "Who knows what happened to Sophia?"

Zamball met Josh's eyes again. "It's Natalie Quinn."

CHAPTER NINE

"Slim pickings today." Natalie grabbed a fruit cup and placed it on her tray.

"Mmhmm," Josh mumbled. He ambled behind her in the lunch line.

After his chat with Zamball the night before, he told himself that he'd sit Natalie down and get some answers out of her. With the number of patients he had, the opportunity never came up. Now that he had alone time with her, the moment had come. He just didn't know how to start. Or if he was ready.

He didn't really know what he felt about it. Betrayal was obviously his first emotion, but why was he suddenly believing Zamball's word over his own girlfriend's? And he hadn't even given her a chance to explain herself. There might be a completely plausible reason.

No. There was no excuse for kidnapping his niece—*if* that's what Natalie had done. Nothing had been decided yet. He was certainly not going to share the news with Kathy or Holly. His aunt was already furious with him and wouldn't take kindly to the fact that he was sleeping with a potential enemy too.

But that was still to be decided. The first thing he needed to do was talk to her. By the time they found a table, he tried to fill the air and steer the conversation. Their lunch break was only so long and he had enough questions to last them all day.

"So I had an interesting day off," he started.

"You did? Did you get crazy and write in the margins of your journals?" She offered a smile and stabbed a fork into a grape before popping it into her mouth.

"No. It was…magical."

She grinned. "Yeah? Are you actually going to tell me of your own free will, or am I going to have to drag it out of you?"

"Um…" He considered telling her about the Pentad, but he figured that would only muddy up their time with questions about that. Not to mention, it might tip her off if she really was involved with Sophia's kidnapping in some way.

He needed to get some answers. But he didn't want to lose her in the process. She was his first serious girlfriend. Since he'd lost touch with Chris, he'd felt himself slipping into a dark hole. Natalie was beginning to pull him out of that.

He tried a different approach: testing her knowledge. "You know how I have that estranged brother?"

"The one you think is dead?"

Josh nodded. "Right. Turns out he's not."

"What? So, that's good news, right?"

He nodded. "Yes. My, uh, sister-in-law found him."

"That must've been awkward."

He shook his head. "She didn't say. I guess he's in trouble, though."

"Then what are you doing at work?"

"Other people need saving too." He opened the small carton of milk. "Besides, they're coming up with a way to save him while I'm at work."

"Save him from what?"

"I'm not sure, exactly. I'll know more when I get home. Hopefully."

He was drowning. How was he going to test how much Natalie knew if she was only responding to his statements? He needed to get her to say something more.

"What do you think I should do?"

She flicked her plastic fork around. "What do you mean?"

"I haven't seen or heard from the guy in over a year. Do you think it's even worth looking for him? Maybe it's a trap? I mean, it *was* his ex-wife who told me about him being imprisoned."

"Josh, he's still your brother. You're a lifesaver, whether it's as a witch or as a doctor. Don't let Holly's personal feelings toward your brother cloud your judgment."

Josh tried to remember if he had told Natalie Holly's name before. He couldn't remember. So he tried to get her to say Sophia's name instead. He definitely hadn't mentioned her.

"They've got a lot of history. A lot of loss. I don't blame her for being mad at him. I was mad at him for a little bit too. Their only child died." He sat back and shook his head. "I don't know. Maybe he's not the same guy I knew way back when."

"Isn't this the same guy you were nearly balling about two days ago?"

Josh chewed on his bottom lip before answering. "Our history is…complicated."

"Sounds like any other family."

He shook his head. "This is different."

"So what are you going to do?"

"I don't know. That's what I'm asking you. If we get Chris back, there's a possibility their daughter might still be alive—"

"What?"

Josh couldn't tell if her shock was from hearing Sophia was alive or shock from the realities magic provided. Nothing was conclusive yet.

"Yeah. Maybe the three of them can be a family again. My aunt would certainly love that. But I'm not sure. What do you think?"

"Josh, put yourself in your brother's shoes: if you could not only return home but also hold your daughter in your arms again, wouldn't you want any help you could get—even from your ex-wife?"

"Yeah, I guess you're right." He stared down at his tray of half-eaten food. "It's just been so long since they've been a family. She's gotta be all grown up now."

"How old is she?"

"Who?"

"Sophia."

Jackpot.

Josh's heart sank and he tried not to let his face show it. He didn't think he succeeded, though. Natalie did know more than she was letting on. He had never mentioned Sophia's name to her before. But that didn't mean Zamball was right, either. Just because she knew stuff, didn't mean she had bad intentions. Maybe Natalie had been forced into something. Maybe there was some other perfectly good explanation for her knowledge. Either way, he needed to discuss it with Zamball before he made a move.

"Probably about four now." Nodding, Josh added, "You're right. I should think about it some more. Maybe they've already got a plan."

* * *

Zamball was waiting by Josh's car when he went to leave that afternoon. It was perfect timing because Josh wanted to see him before he went home and talked to Kathy and Holly. That was, if he decided to talk to them about his suspicions of Natalie. He had bounced back and forth between telling them or not the rest of the day.

"You've been thinking about me a lot today," Zamball started when Josh walked up.

"That sounds creepy." Josh popped his trunk and tossed his bag in.

"Did you talk to Q?"

"Is that her code name?"

"Actually, it is."

Josh sighed. "I didn't interrogate her, but I did talk to her." He leaned against the car and crossed his arms. "She definitely knows something."

"Like I told you."

"But I feel like you're not telling me everything, either. What *does* she know about Sophia?"

"We're not completely certain, but we're going to need your cooperation to get it. It's good that you're close with her. Now you can use that same connection to play her."

"Like you did with Holly in Salem?"

Zamball lowered his head but didn't say anything.

"You told me the Pentad operate by committee," Josh said. "When do we start voting? This directly relates to me, so how come I don't get a say in how we proceed with Natalie?"

"Because you're inexperienced in our customs. If this were another case, we'd be showing you how we operate so you could make a more informed decision. This situation is different. Meanwhile, we also need to address the problem of the Chaos, although Eleanor has her suspicions that the two are related."

"How do you figure?"

"The parties involved with the kidnapping and enslaving of your niece and brother may also be involved with unleashing the Chaos," Zamball explained. "Now that we're at full strength, we can explore options to eliminate the threat of the Chaos while also instilling your faith in us by bringing your brother and niece home safely."

Josh was surprised. The last time he had seen Zamball, he never would've guessed he would be helping him rescue his family. People really did change. Maybe Natalie could too.

"What happens once they're home?"

"What do you mean?"

"I mean, you're holding up your end of the bargain by bringing them home, but will that make me a free man? Or am I slave to your little power group?"

"The Pentad is *our* group, and it is not little by any means. You should be *honored* that you were asked to join—especially with your recent neglect of magic. You will be a member of this group for the duration of your life. However involved you are on a day-to-day basis is determined by the number of issues that the group as a whole decides to address. We have goals we strive to meet. You were chosen because Eleanor, among the others of the group, thought that you could help us achieve those goals."

"That's not fair! You gave me twenty minutes to make a life-long commitment!"

"The circumstances of your membership were rare, and the rest of the Pentad certainly understands that, but it does not lessen the importance of your role in this group. That begins with Natalie. Keep an eye on her and keep her close. Don't let her know that you suspect. Once she does, we've already lost. She's very powerful."

* * *

The last thing Josh wanted to do when he got home was argue with Kathy. He tried to sneak up to his room before he was seen, but both Holly and Kathy were in the living room. They were huddled over the coffee table with the magic book in the center among candles of various colors, several different herb leaves and branches, and a giant black pot.

"Josh!" Holly called when she spotted him. "We've come up with a plan for Chris."

He nodded and tried to escape up the stairs. He couldn't think about this right now. Natalie and her betrayal were still going through his mind.

Kathy kept her eyes on the magic book. "We're going to need your help."

Now halfway up the stairs, he sighed and turned around. He pulled up a chair at the opposite end of the coffee table. "What do you have?"

"The spell you used on me won't work with Chris because we don't have a recent piece of his DNA to summon him," Holly started-ed.

"Too bad you didn't get any when you saw him," Josh said.

"Right? But we have a different idea. We could use your blood when we all say the spell."

"How would that work? That would summon me, not Chris."

Kathy had decided not to speak to Josh unless she had to, so Holly continued, "Well Kathy's not Chris's biological parent, so her DNA is too different from his. I'm obviously not blood at all, and I think everything is too complicated for me to help anyway. Since you're a full sibling, you're the guy we need. Plus, we all have a connection to him, even if it's not blood. The spell will be worded to hopefully offset a direct DNA sample."

"How can you be sure?" he asked.

Kathy finally looked up at him. "You can't ever be sure with magic. Are you going to help or not?"

Josh didn't know what Kathy had told Holly, so he kept quiet, despite the words on the tip of his tongue. He wasn't a little kid anymore. He could make his own choices.

"Do you have a knife?"

Holly looked between Josh and Kathy a moment before she slid over the small knife.

He held up the blade to his palm. "Let's do this."

Holly spoke a charm and lit each candle with the end of her finger. "As the blood falls into the pot, we all need to say the spell and focus on Chris. Push all other thoughts aside."

"Ready?" he asked. They nodded and he dug the knife into his palm. He gasped a little at the pain. It had been a long time since he had spilled his own blood for a spell.

Making a fist, he watched as the blood trickled into the black pot.

Blood of my blood, answer my plea,
through time and space, wherever you may be.

The trio repeated the spell over and over again. With each repetition, the air moved faster, knocking things off shelves, blowing the ladies' hair in their faces, and making Josh fearful that a small cyclone would erupt in the house.

Just when Holly opened her mouth to wonder aloud if they had cast the wrong spell, the wind ceased.

"Did it work?" Josh wiped his bloody hand on the towel beside the pot.

Kathy began to shake her head, but then they heard a thud from behind the couch.

Writhing on the floor, a skeleton of his former self, was Chris. The spell had worked.

CHAPTER TEN

Chris!" Kathy nearly leaped over the back of the couch. "Sweet-ie, you're hurt!" Her eyes locked on his swollen chest, though she took notice of his other injuries too.

Chris moved his hair out of his eyes. "Aunt Kathy? How did I—" Holly came around the corner. "You summoned me?"

"Of course. I need you, remember?"

Kathy and Josh both gave her curious glances.

"But I thought…" Chris sat up and ran his hands through his matted hair again.

"Look at you! Josh!" Kathy wanted to just wrap Chris up in a hug, but instead she hesitated. None of them were on the same page anymore. She couldn't just assume he would welcome her embrace. Not to mention, she didn't know the extent of his injuries.

Josh came around the couch and knelt next to his brother. "It's good to see you. I wish you were in better health." He looked at the damage: there wasn't much he could do. Not until his brother was cleaned up, at least.

Chris looked down at himself. He was covered in dirt, bruises, burns, scabs. His hair was either matted to his head or standing up on end. His beard had dried blood and dust in it from his last voyage. He couldn't even remember the last time he'd had a shower. Compared to the rest of his family, he looked nearly dead.

He pointed to his chest. "They branded me." Turning to his side, he added, "And burned me. When Holly arrived, they gave up on treating my wounds."

Josh let out a breath of air. He hadn't realized he'd been holding it. "First, you need a shower."

"And rest," Kathy added.

Josh helped him stand.

Kathy squeezed Chris's hand. "You're back!" She stroked the side of his face. The blood and dirt didn't bother her. "You're never leaving me again. None of you are. We'll all live here forever."

"As wonderful—and creepy—as that sounds, we've got some things to discuss," Josh said.

Chris shook his head. "No. First, we need to discuss the game plan so when I go back—"

"Go back?"

"I have to go back."

"Chris, you're not thinking straight," Josh said. "Let's get you cleaned up. You can get some sleep and—"

"Yeah," Kathy added. "We'll figure it out in the morning."

"Guys, let Chris talk," Holly said.

The room was quiet for a moment. Chris was guilty for ruining whatever joy they had from seeing him. They had clearly missed him. He missed them, too. But he'd also made a promise that he wouldn't come back unless he knew what had happened to Sophia. And solved it. He hadn't thought he'd ever come back.

Seeing the worry creep across his aunt's face again killed him. He was a disappointment. He should've waited to announce he was going back until after they'd had a proper reunion.

"Chris…" Kathy started.

He cleared his throat. "They know exactly where I am."

"The Fire Wizards?" Josh asked. "How?"

"Because I'm one of them now."

* * *

Josh knocked on the door to his bedroom before entering.

"It's your room, you don't have to knock," Chris said. He was pulling on one of Josh's white T-shirts. Underneath, wraps covered his body. He felt tremendously better. A long, warm shower did wonders.

"Yeah, I guess so."

"Are you sure you want to sleep on the floor? I really hate stealing your bed." His long hair was still wet, so he pulled it up into a bun. He couldn't remember the last time it had felt so clean.

Josh shook his head. "You're not stealing. Besides, after what you've gone through, you deserve a good night's sleep in a real bed." He smiled. "The hair is going to take some getting used to, though."

Unconsciously, Chris rubbed the back of his neck. "It protected me from the sun and helped keep my face hidden when I needed it."

Josh studied his brother. He was different now. And yet exactly the same. Despite the short awkwardness when he'd first arrived, it felt like he had never left. They were still brothers, through and through.

Chris sat on the edge of the bed. "It's a little weird being back. I've been apart from the real world for so long that all of this," he waved his hands around, "doesn't feel normal."

"Well, as soon as we get everything straightened out, this is going to feel normal again." Josh laid out a couple of blankets on the floor that would serve as his bed for the night.

He said he wanted to be next to Chris in case he needed any sort of medical attention throughout the night, but he just wanted to be there in case *anything* happened to his little brother. Now that he was here and he was safe, Josh wasn't going to let anything happen to him. It was a shame it took the threat of the Chaos to push them to be a family once again.

Josh wondered if they even were a family anymore. Kathy was disappointed in both of them—maybe even disgusted with Josh—and Holly was probably still planning on moving out once everything was smoothed out. Just because they'd learned Sophia was alive didn't mean that she and Chris would get back together.

Things would never be the way they had been.

"Maybe. I don't really know what normal is anymore." Chris lay back in bed and pulled the covers over him. It had been a long time since he had been this comfortable.

"What do you mean 'maybe'?" Josh sat up on his elbow and looked up at Chris.

"I just don't know what the future holds." He kept his eyes on the ceiling.

"It's whatever we decide. We choose our own future. Don't let anyone dictate yours."

"No one is dictating it for me, Josh." He met his brother's eyes. "Circumstances are dictating it for me. It's because Sophia was kidnapped that Holly left me and I left Erie. It's because I was practically dying that I joined the Fire Wizards. It's because Holly was kidnapped herself that I know the truth about Sophia or am even here now."

"But the truth about Sophia and coming back home are signs that things are taking a turn for the better. Take these opportunities to do the right thing. Put your family back together. If Sophia was the only reason Holly left, then getting your daughter back will also get you your wife back."

"Yeah." Chris didn't want to talk about his situation anymore. He had gone over it so much in his head already. Being alone did that to him. "What about you? Do you have a girlfriend? Kids? What have you been up to?"

Josh laughed. "No kids. You know me, I've just been working."

"Still saving lives, even after giving up magic."

"Not always saving lives. More like keeping insurance companies in business." Josh considered telling Chris about joining the Pentad, but he decided to wait. His brother needed rest. He would tell him tomorrow after they both had a good night's sleep.

"Mmm," Chris mumbled.

The sound of his brother's light breaths told Josh that he was sleeping—or on the verge of it. "All right. Time for bed. I have an early shift tomorrow."

He reached up and turned off the light.

* * *

The next morning, Chris lay in bed and stared at the ceiling. Physically, he felt immensely better. Whatever Josh had whipped up had worked better than anything the Fire Wizards had given him. But then, they probably weren't trying to heal him as quickly. They were training a soldier, after all.

Still, he didn't know what he was going to do about the Fire Wizards. They were the key to getting Sophia back—and he would do anything to get her back—but he would be lying if he didn't admit that something clicked when he got back home.

Over the last two years, he couldn't put his finger on it, but something had been off. He didn't feel like himself. He just figured it was because his family had been broken, but the truth was it wasn't. Josh and Kathy had still been there for him after everything had happened with the fire. Chris was the one who'd pushed them out. Now that he was back home, he felt whole again.

Almost.

Something still felt off. Talking with Josh the night before was nice, and certainly reminded him of when they had been kids, but he had this apprehension toward his brother. Josh seemed to be keeping something from him. He'd deflected the "What's new?" question, and it didn't sit well with Chris. As if he couldn't trust him. Not how he used to, at least. Maybe it was his new alliance with the Fire Wizards. Maybe it was the fact that he hadn't trusted anyone in the last two years.

Still, he trusted Kathy just fine. Even Holly.

He pushed it out of his mind. They had enough to worry about. Josh was probably just nervous. It had been a year since they'd last spoken. They needed time to return to the way they had been.

Judging by the amount of light filling the room, Chris guessed Josh had left for work already. It was nice to have the room to himself.

Alone. It was familiar.

He couldn't remember the last time he'd slept that well for that long. It was a nice change—even if it was strange being back in the same bedroom he'd grown up in. So many memories. So long ago.

By the time Chris had pulled himself out of bed and made his way down to the kitchen, it was late morning.

Kathy was sorting through a stack of papers on the counter. She stopped when Chris entered and wrapped him in a hug, trying not to squeeze too tight. She couldn't help it, though. It was like she needed to keep reminding herself that this was real. Chris was home.

"You slept late."

He hugged her back and mumbled over her shoulder, "Yeah."

Even after she pulled herself away from him, she still cradled his hairy face in her hands. "This is going to take some getting used to," she said, giving his beard a gentle tug.

Chris grinned. There was some personal hygiene maintenance that needed to be done for sure. He'd barely recognized himself in the mirror last night.

"Anyway, you're probably hungry." She pointed across the counter. "We've got cereal in the pantry. I think we have some waffles in the freezer—"

"I remember." Chris shuffled over to the tall cupboard by the fridge and looked through their selection of cereal.

Kathy fussed with her papers again. "All right. I have a lunch interview downtown, then I'm having dinner with my editor, so I'm going to be gone most of the day. Josh will probably be gone all day too."

Chris pulled a bowl out of the cupboard and turned to her. "Aunt Kathy?"

"Yeah?"

"I'm sorry I'm not what you expected." He hadn't planned on apologizing—especially for something like that—but it was the perfect moment. Besides, if he was going back to the Fire Wizards, he only had so much time to repair the bridges he had burned.

"Oh, honey." Kathy set her papers on the counter and took his face in her hands again. "I love you. No matter what you do. Am I a little disappointed? Sure. But I'll get over it. We'll make it work.

You and I both know that I've done a few bad things in my time as well." She leaned up on her toes and kissed his forehead. "I'm so happy you're back. And if you think leaving is what you have to do…"

She couldn't say it. She wanted to. Wanted to be supportive and let Chris make his own choices, but she just couldn't condone him for making such a reckless decision. Especially when it affected the lives of so many others.

Instead, she forced a smile and said, "I've really got to get going. Holly will be home all day. I'm sorry if that's awkward for you, but—"

"I'll be fine."

She gave him another quick hug and turned to go.

"Aunt Kathy?"

"Yeah?"

"Thanks."

* * *

As Kathy waited for Greg outside his hotel, she wondered if she should've met him inside. He had told her his room number. But a hotel room was almost like someone's bedroom. She didn't want to cross that line. Instead, she sat in her car under the awning by the front door. A few minutes later, he came out wearing his signature plaid shirt and khakis.

He smiled when he saw her. "So this is what you drive?"

"Yep." It was a small two-door coupe. Nothing extravagant.

She just needed something to get her from Point A to Point B. With a bit of class, of course.

"Nice."

Kathy gave a tight smile but kept her eyes on the road. She didn't know how things were between them after her last visit to New York.

"So how've you been?" he asked.

"Pretty good. My nephew just came back home."

"Oh yeah? That's good."

She nodded. "Yeah, it is."

"Where was he again?"

Clearing her throat, she said, "Out west." She hadn't thought that through. Using her nephews as a topic of small talk used to be so easy when they had been in school. But now that their lives were more complicated, it was harder. She decided to just change the subject. "So are you ready for the interview?"

She mentally cursed herself for being too much of a coward to bring up what had happened at the bar in New York.

"Yeah, I was going to ask you about that. I've only done a handful myself, but they were all solo. I didn't know what kind of dynamic you wanted to showcase."

"Uh…I don't know. I usually just try to be myself and be honest. Stay focused on the books rather than me."

Since Jeremy had interrupted her last interview, that had been skewed to her romantic life. She was hoping today's would be different. It was with *Northeast Literature*, a regional literary magazine that also critiqued popular fiction. Certainly a publication that didn't dabble in the personal lives of the authors it featured.

"Sounds easy enough."

As they drove farther into the city, Greg looked around at the buildings. "This looks like a nice place. How long have you lived here?"

Kathy realized she hadn't been driving through the best parts of the city, but it was the fastest way downtown. This stretch had either drive-through restaurants or empty storefronts. Not Erie's finest. Especially for someone who was used to the big city. She almost wanted to tell him that it was more than it seemed, but he wasn't here to see Erie. He was here to discuss *Spellbinding*.

"My whole life. My family were actually the ones who built my house. Years and years ago, though."

"Hey, just like your characters!"

She nodded slowly, forgetting she had included that detail into her book. "Right."

Luckily, there was street parking when she pulled up to the hotel. The reporter had flown in from Boston and was staying in a suite. Apparently she thought the view of downtown Erie out her window would make a great backdrop for the photo to go with the article.

When they knocked on the door to Suite 825, a small woman greeted them. She had curly blonde hair and a maroon suit that made Kathy feel a little underdressed in her black blouse and jeans.

"Kathy?" the woman asked. There was no sign of a smile on her face.

Extending her hand, Kathy said, "That's me. Nice to meet you!"

The woman looked to Greg. "I didn't think you'd be bringing your boyfriend. But nonetheless, come on in."

"Oh, he's uh—he's not my boyfriend. No. No, this is my editor from DJ Books. Gregory Martin. He's the one who agreed to sign me on my first book."

Greg buried his hands in his pockets and looked down at the floor. Kathy could see that his face was beet-red. She hadn't meant to offend him.

It was going to be a long day.

CHAPTER ELEVEN

Chris didn't have any clothes to wear. He had lost everything he owned in the fire two years ago. Since then, his clothes had mostly been stolen. The few possessions he did have were still back at the Fire Wizards' camp. The shorts he had been wearing when he came back to Erie stank of blood, sweat, and piss. He wouldn't ever put those dirty things back on. So he didn't have a choice but to stay in the T-shirt and shorts his brother had lent him.

Wearing his brother's clothes and wandering around his childhood home without knowing what to do made him feel like an outsider. He didn't belong. He wasn't like Josh, Kathy, or Holly anymore. He was different.

Independent.

A loner.

A Fire Wizard.

THE BLUE MOON

Although everyone—including Holly, it seemed—was grateful that he was home, that didn't stop them from keeping up with the demands of their lives. They all had responsibilities to maintain. So did he.

"Are you going to walk around aimlessly all day?" Holly called to him as he passed by her bedroom—the former magic room.

He stood in her doorway. "I've got nothing else to do."

She ran a brush through her wet hair. She had just gotten out of the shower. "We have a daughter to save."

"Josh told me last night to take some time off."

"Chris, when was the last time you listened to everything your brother tells you?" She smiled at him in the reflection of her mirror.

He shrugged.

"Do you have anything else to wear?"

Chris shook his head. He had grown accustomed to keeping quiet.

"Why don't you find something of Josh's?"

"I don't know."

"Did you want to go to the mall? I have money stashed from when I lived in Lily Dale."

He scrunched his eyebrows together. "You're going to take me shopping?"

It was her turn to shrug now. "You need clothes. We both need to get out of this house and get a taste of reality. Who knows? Maybe it'll help us get past…everything."

"Holly, about what we talked about at the—"

She shook her head. "We'll talk about it later. Right now, let's go shopping. Clear our heads so we can better come up with a game plan to get Sophia back. Don't you want her to be proud of how strong her parents are?"

"She's four."

"Still."

He couldn't help but feel like their efforts were better focused elsewhere. But he had tried and tried and tried for two years to get answers about Sophia on his own. Clearly, his methods weren't working. He needed to listen to Holly and the others and follow their method for a change.

Or, at least, he had to try.

"Okay. Sure."

* * *

After the interview, Kathy considered showing Greg around Erie, but she didn't want him to get the wrong impression. Besides, he said he'd brought work with him that he needed to get done before he missed his deadline, and she wanted to get home to see Chris.

Instead, they agreed that just dinner would be enough. They still had more interviews to do. She could show him around then.

"I think today went well," Kathy said once they had ordered. She had taken Greg to a new pub downtown that she had been meaning to try.

He nodded. "So did I. She definitely wasn't prepared for me, though. I felt like the questions directed at me were sort of an afterthought."

"Yeah, but I think that reflects on her more than it does us—*me*. Paul sent over the updated marketing schedule to everyone. She just didn't look at it before we came."

"It was funny that she thought I was your boyfriend, though."

Kathy's face flushed. She was hoping not to acknowledge that. "Yeah."

Greg studied the label on his beer. They both fell into an awkward silence for a moment.

She cleared her throat. "I was actually hoping to talk to you about that. What I said in New York the last time I saw you—"

He waved his hand. "Don't worry about it. It's fine."

"It's not fine. It's been bothering me ever since and I couldn't figure out why until I saw how my nephew and his ex were together. They both still care for each other, but they're both too scared to do anything about it. Too consumed in themselves."

"Are you saying you want to get back with your ex?"

Shaking her head, she said, "Can't. He's dead."

"Oh. I didn't know. I'm sorry."

"It's okay. It happened after we split up."

"Oh, I didn't mean—"

She put up her hand. "It's fine. What I'm trying to say is that I don't want to be like my nephew and his ex-wife. I don't want to be the reason for my own unhappiness. Giving up on any romantic future is stupid."

"So what are you saying?"

Kathy could see hope in his eyes. "I've decided to keep my options open if anything comes up."

Greg moved his hand a little closer to Kathy's.

She sat back and moved her hands under the table. "I think between us, though, our relationship needs to stay professional. We work well together. Having an editor who understands the author he's working with is so important. I don't want to lose that. I have other books to write!"

He offered a half-hearted smile. "Okay. That all makes sense. But considering your revelation, don't you think it'd be just as foolish to not even *try* to see where things go with anyone who shows interest?"

She smiled. "Just because someone shows interest in me doesn't mean the feelings are always reciprocated. I'd be going on a lot of dates if that were the case."

"Oh." His face dropped.

Kathy frowned. She wanted to set boundaries but she didn't want to break his heart in the process. "Greg, it's not that I…" She trailed off. What was she supposed to say? Greg wouldn't have even been on her radar if he hadn't made his feelings clear. She'd be dating him just because he was a nice guy. Not because she actually felt any attraction to him.

She felt her heart flutter. Something she hadn't felt since…well, since she'd last seen Jeremy. With everything going on with Chris and the marketing tour, she hadn't thought much about him and his confession that he still loved her.

Settling things with Greg made her think of the man she truly wanted to pursue: Jeremy. Hadn't she been down that path before, though? But then, they had both changed so much. Besides, what would Greg think if she turned him down and immediately ran to another man? Best to just end it with him and tread carefully with Jeremy.

"We live in two different cities." She meant to continue but didn't.

Greg's visit to Erie was only temporary. He had a good job in New York City that he worked hard for. He would be a fool to ever leave it. Likewise, she had roots in Erie and had no intention of leaving. Whatever potential relationship they would have had was already cursed to a long-distance one.

Greg seemed to read her thoughts. "Maybe we should just let it be? Neither one of us plans on moving anytime soon. That's not what I want."

Kathy closed her eyes and felt sadness replace the butterflies.

"I'm sorry," he said. "I guess I just got caught up in the moment or something when we were in New York. I shouldn't have crossed that line. You and I are colleagues and that's it."

Her breath shuddered and a lump formed in her throat. She didn't understand it. Before today, she hadn't really put any serious thought into her and Greg's future together.

Deep down, though, she knew what it was. Her heart wasn't breaking for Greg. She was hesitant to open up to someone again. Every close relationship she had had in her life had ended badly. Things wouldn't work out with Greg, which was okay with her, but she couldn't imagine being intimate with *anyone*.

Her fear of isolation was worse than she'd thought.

Sure, she had Jeremy pining after her too, but she could predict how that would go. He had already broken her heart once, and after the disaster that was her marriage to Will, she couldn't risk being that vulnerable again.

"Hey, it's all right." Greg reached for her hand again. She let him take it. "We're more than colleagues. We're friends."

Kathy hadn't realized she was crying.

She shook her head and dabbed at her eyes with her napkin. "I'm sorry. You must think I'm nuts."

He chewed on his bottom lip and studied her. "What are you doing Saturday?"

She shrugged. "I don't know."

"Maybe you could help me with a manuscript I'm working on. It's another work-for-hire and I'm stuck. I could really use your help."

Kathy smiled. She was about to say yes when she thought of Jeremy. His event was Saturday night. She had planned to go, even if she hadn't quite given him an answer. She couldn't ditch him. Karma was a bitch, but she would be too if she stood him up. Besides, she had barely given this new version of Jeremy a chance.

"Uh…Saturday I can't. We're having a, uh…thing for Chris."

Greg nodded. "Okay. Well, it was just an idea."

* * *

"So are you happy with your loot?" Holly dipped a french fry into her ketchup cup.

"Yeah, it beats what I've been wearing. Thanks." Chris only

managed to eat half of his burger before he felt full. His stomach had shrunk too much to take any more food.

"What was it like?"

"What was *what* like?"

"Doing whatever you've been doing these last two years."

Chris shrugged. "Hot. Miserable. Lonely."

"Oh."

"Yeah. That explains the frame of mind I was in when I accepted Raven's offer."

Holly wiped her hands on her napkin. "I know I've said it before, but I'm sorry. I'm sorry for doubting you. For casting you out. For blaming you for Sophia…"

He shook his head. "Don't be sorry. What's done is done. We're moving forward, remember?"

She gave him a faint smile. "Can't help it. I still do."

"You have successfully distracted me today. This is the longest I've gone since the accident that I haven't thought about that night. Thank you." He reached for her hand but dropped his eyes. "It's funny because I never thought in a million years that we'd ever…"

"Me neither. Guess some things are just meant to be."

"Do you really think that?"

"Think what?"

"That we're meant to be?"

Holly sighed. "Chris, one of the things that I realized when I saw you at the Fire Wizards' camp was how much I've missed you." She met his eyes. "I still care about you. That's probably never going to change. But it doesn't mean it's a good thing. We need to prove to each other that being together *is* a good thing. We have too much bad blood already. Let's fix some of it."

Chris grinned. "Good. We'll start with getting our daughter back."

"That's the plan. Speaking of which, we should get going. Kathy and Josh will probably be home soon, and they're going to expect a game plan."

He stood and leaned in and kissed her cheek. Holly blushed and took his hand. She felt like she was fifteen again. Things were drastically more complicated now, though. But still, the feeling was nice.

* * *

Chris was glad that he and Holly made it home before Josh and Kathy did. Even though it had been a while, he knew exactly the kind of questions they would ask about his outing to the mall. Some things never changed.

They hid the bags in Holly's bedroom to further keep their trip a secret.

Josh came home first and made a beeline for the bathroom. Apparently he didn't want to smell like the hospital all night. Kathy, however, made her entrance known.

"I'm probably *the* craziest person in the world. Or at least that's what Greg thinks." She tossed her purse on the empty chair.

Chris and Holly were huddled over the magic book resting on the coffee table.

"What happened?" Holly asked.

"Nothing. I don't want to talk about it." She collapsed on the couch next to Holly. "I just can't make up my mind. First I want to be alone and then I don't. And I come to these realizations while I'm supposed to be giving off a professional appearance and I just look like I'm a psycho."

"Aunt Kathy," Chris started.

"Yeah?"

"I thought you didn't want to talk about it?"

"I don't. You're right. Where's Josh?"

Holly looked to the ceiling. "He's in the shower. He should be out soon."

Kathy nodded. "Good. So what did you guys come up with all day?"

"So far we've come up empty-handed," he said. "But now that we have some inside scoop from someone who has an in with—"

Kathy shook her head. "No, Chris. You're not going back to them."

"Aunt Kathy, I have to. Just long enough to get Sophia back."

"And then what? You're just going to walk away? They have you in their grasp, Chris. By the sounds of it, you haven't exactly been welcomed by them either."

He shot a look to Holly. He hadn't disclosed what kind of conditions he'd been in with the Fire Wizards. Apparently she had.

"Neither you or your brother have thought these things through," Kathy said.

Chris's head jerked up. "What are you talking about? What did Josh do?"

Kathy looked at Holly momentarily before meeting his eyes. "She didn't tell you?"

"No." Chris panicked. Who had he voluntarily let his guard down with the night before? He'd slept peacefully, but what did he really know about his brother anymore? Chris had changed tremendously. Josh likely had too. He had a feeling it wasn't for the better.

Holly reached under her hair and scratched the back of her neck to avoid eye contact with him.

"Josh joined a group," Kathy started. "With Zamball."

Chris's eyes flared. "The Pentad!?" Josh's reluctance to disclose details about his life the night before made sense now. He wasn't the good witch he had been.

"You know about them?" Holly asked.

"I've been keeping tabs on potential enemies."

Holly sat up straighter. "So you knew that Zamball was alive and you never told me?"

"I knew where he was. He was fine." He kept his eyes on Kathy, waiting for more of the story.

"Apparently you didn't." Any affection Holly had felt for him had faded. "He *threatened* me. That's why I moved back here."

"And how was I supposed to know that while Raven had me shackled up? You survived, didn't you?"

They shot daggers at each other with their eyes. Finally, he turned to his aunt.

"So the Pentad isn't a threat?" Kathy asked.

Chris shook his head. "I didn't say that. They've just been dormant for a while. They have the potential to wipe out half the continent. Why would he join them?"

His mind raced with a million reasons. What if Josh had been watching Chris all along? What if he knew that Chris had joined the Fire Wizards and so joined the Pentad in retaliation? What was he hiding? What was he planning?

"To save you!" Kathy shouted. "He didn't do his due diligence and joined them because they promised that you and Sophia would be resurrected. They reneged."

Chris's eyes darted between his aunt and Holly. "You guys thought I was dead?"

"For a little bit, yeah." Josh walked into the room.

Chris recoiled at the sound of his brother's voice. The uncertainty made him nervous. "Still, resurrecting me wouldn't have brought me back. My body, sure, but then you'd have a half-rotted body that you'd need to replace with real parts. That's necromancy. Zamball doesn't specialize in that."

"No, but he said the Pentad can," Josh said.

"And you *believed* him?"

"I had no other choice, Chris! You were dead! I found a way to bring you back and I took it! I'm sorry if I wasn't thinking clearly. Sorry I messed up, but that's *my* choice."

Chris's heart raced and his breaths became shorter. Josh didn't seem broken up about his mistake. Was it a mistake? He suspected there was more to it.

Thunder boomed through the sky, making the house shake.

"What's that?" Holly asked.

"Is it raining?" Kathy added.

They all stood and moved to the windows. The light of the waning moon grew dimmer as a deep purple cloud filled the sky, swallowing up any light on the ground. Thunder boomed again.

Chris shook his head. "I have to go back."

Chapter Twelve

Chris, knock it off. You're not going back." Kathy huddled next to Holly and peered through the curtains.

"What is that?" Holly asked.

"Is that the Chaos?" Josh squeezed next to the women to get a glimpse.

"Yes. And it's very dangerous. I can help end this," Chris said. He mostly wanted to get away from Josh. He didn't trust him. More importantly, he wanted to have the Fire Wizards do some further investigating into his brother. He could use them just as much as they were using him.

"*Why* do you have to go back?" Kathy turned away from the window. "What is it that they're going to be able to help you with that we can't?" She knew she wasn't getting anywhere with him, so she thought she would play along enough to get in his head.

"Well, first off: knowledge. They know more about this thing than anyone I've met. And judging from your confusion, you don't know much more either." He turned to Josh. "What about Zamball and the rest of the Pentad? Can they help us?"

Kathy shook her head. "No. We don't need help from any demonic supergroup."

Josh ignored her and looked at his brother. He considered telling him what he knew about the Chaos so far: that it was created by good and evil to speed up the inevitable apocalypse. Instead, he replied, "No, they can't help us."

Chris hesitated. He knew Josh was lying. "Exactly. Besides, Raven told me after you guys summoned Holly back that she'd hand over Sophia if I cooperated."

"Are you serous?" Hope flickered in Holly's eyes.

He nodded. "Yeah."

"How does that make sense? I thought she kidnapped Holly to persuade you?" Kathy asked.

"She must've been counting on Holly's hatred toward him," Josh said.

Chris eyed him carefully. "That's what she told me, yeah."

Kathy crossed her arms and studied her nephews. She couldn't believe that both Josh and Chris had gotten themselves mixed up with very bad groups.

"Chris, come take a walk with me," Holly said.

"Why?" He pointed out the window. "We need to figure out what to do about the death cloud looming outside."

She nodded and held out her hand. "And we will. But first I

need to talk to you."

"Can't it wait?"

"No! Come with me." She set her eyes on him in a familiar fashion. She didn't think she'd given anyone else that look since she'd last given it to Chris.

He sighed and grasped her hand. They left Kathy and Josh alone and went up to the guest room. Holly's room.

She sat on the bed and patted the spot next to her. "Sit."

"I'll stand, thanks."

"Chris," she spoke through her teeth, "sit."

Dutifully, he plopped next to her.

"I want to talk about us for a minute."

"Holly, relevance? We've got bigger problems right now. The longer we wait, the longer we put off bringing our daughter home. I thought you wanted that?"

She closed her eyes and took a deep breath. He was right. With each moment that passed, she felt like she was a worse mother because of it. "I know. But this is important."

He rolled his eyes. "Okay. What do you want to talk about?"

"Why do you think I left you?"

"Because of Sophia. You told me this."

She closed her eyes. He wasn't wrong, but it wasn't where she intended to go with the discussion. "Okay. You're right. But that wasn't the only reason."

Chris gave her his full attention. "What do you mean?"

"I mean we had problems before Sophia was kidnapped."

"We did?"

"Of course we did! Chris, our marriage wasn't a fairy tale."

He looked down and rubbed up and down his arm. "I know…"

"Nothing bad, I suppose. They were little things that I could see building into something worth leaving over." She tilted her head to the side. "At the time, I didn't know how to bring them up without an argument."

"And you thought now was the perfect time? Holly, we've been divorced for two years!"

"I regret letting you kiss me today," she blurted.

His face flushed red. "Oh."

"Not for the reasons you're probably thinking." She put her hand on his arm, but he pulled away. "A few days ago I thought you were dead. I still thought I hated you. Now…"

"Now what do you think?" He studied his hands, afraid to look at her. It was the same way he'd acted right before he'd asked her to marry him.

"Now I realize I love you. I never stopped, really."

Chris beamed. "Yeah? I love you too."

"But," she watched his face drop, "that doesn't mean that we should be together. Like I said, we've had problems. Sophia's kidnapping was only a distraction from them. An excuse to get out."

"So how is this conversation helping? You love me but you still don't want to be with me. This has nothing to do with the Chaos."

"Yes it does. You're acting the same way you did when we were married. You have tunnel vision. The last two years are proof that you haven't changed—haven't even recognized that there's a problem."

Chris was growing impatient. "What are you talking about?"

"You let magic consume you. You did it back then and you're still doing it now." She pointed to the door. "Your family is downstairs *begging* you to stay and you can't wait to go off on a death march with a woman you barely know. You know you can't trust her. She's holding our daughter over your head. Why don't you pull your head out of your ass and start thinking about what everyone else wants!"

Holly let out a huff of air and looked to the floor. She hadn't intended for it to all come out like that, but it did. It had been building up while they were married, only dormant in the time that they were apart. Now everything was rushing to the surface.

She felt the same push and pull in her heart. She wanted him, but not the way he was acting.

They sat in silence for a moment. Chris didn't want to admit that she was right. Nobody liked to accept their own faults, especially when someone else needed to point them out. The last two years had been his pity party to an extent. If he was going to make things right with Holly, then he needed to man up and be there for her and everyone else.

Still, he couldn't help but think he wasn't doing his part as a father if he stayed. His only chance to get Sophia back would be to give himself to the Fire Wizards.

He glanced over at Holly. "What about you?"

"What *about* me?"

"What do you think I should do?"

She sighed. "We'd be stupid to not at least play with the idea that Raven might be telling the truth, but I don't expect her to deliver on her promise. How many times is she going to keep raising the bar for you before we get Sophia back? And even then, how will you get out?"

Chris shook his head. "I might not get out. If that's what it takes to—"

"You haven't listened to a word I've said."

"I have, Holly! But I don't see any other way. The Fire Wizards are too powerful. Drew was fearful of them, and he was one of them."

"The Fire Wizard coven Drew joined was a different coven then. They've changed since they cast Drew out. We've changed. We're stronger now."

Chris shook his head. "We're still no match."

"Then what are we going to do?" Her voice broke.

He'd never liked to see her cry. She had him under her spell when she did. He stood and kissed her forehead. "I swear on my life that you will hold your baby girl in your arms again." He wrapped his arms around her.

Holly wiped her eyes on his T-shirt. It felt nice to be in his embrace again. "It won't be the same without you."

"It's the best I can offer."

"Then it's not good enough."

He ran his hands down the sides of her arms, smiling at the fact that he still gave her goosebumps. "If that's what needs to happen—"

"Don't you get it, Chris?" She pulled away and looked up at

him. "Nobody can ever replace you. Despite everything, you're still the one I want."

Chris kissed her on the mouth. It was better now that they were home rather than at the mall. He fought the urge to push her down on the bed like he used to, but then he felt her pulling at his shirt, leading him.

It was as if no time had passed. Both of them finally giving in to their desires. Both of them missed the familiar touches, the loving embraces, the way their lips seemed to fit together like two pieces of a puzzle.

Together, they would move forward.

Together, they would get Sophia back.

Together, they would become a family again.

* * *

Kathy flipped through *The Art of Magic* in the living room. "I can't believe there is nothing in here about the Chaos."

"I'm not surprised." Josh was looking through the curtains, studying the sky. He hadn't seen anything like it. It was like a dark storm cloud but thicker. And with color.

"Yeah, yeah. Our ancestors hadn't come into contact with it. But they must've heard rumors," she droned.

"What about the Pentad? Did you ever hear about it?" He stole a cautious glance at Kathy. He was already on thin ice with her and the question didn't help. But still, he was curious.

"They definitely sound familiar. I think your mother might've mentioned something a long time ago. But then she got pregnant with you guys, and it must've slipped off her radar."

"She did?" Josh was surprised. From his telepathic connection with the other members of the Pentad, he knew it had been around a long time, but how would his mother know about it?

Kathy nodded as she flipped through the pages of the magic book. "Uh-huh. Your mom was constantly hunting down leads. The two of us took out our share of bad guys. She only really semi-retired when you guys came along."

"Oh." Josh didn't know that. He knew his mother had been more involved with magic and hunting evil when she had been younger, but he didn't know to what extent. He thought he and Chris had their own reputation, but it likely didn't compare to that of his mother's or his aunt's.

"She didn't write anything down about them, though, so I could be wrong." Her phone began to ring. It was Jeremy. She'd texted him earlier asking for details about his work party. She knew it gave away her mystery, but she needed to stop playing games. If she and Jeremy were ever going to have a second chance, she needed to show her cards once in a while.

"Jeremy, hi." She walked into the kitchen for some extra privacy.

"I was surprised to get your message."

"I was surprised to send it." She giggled nervously.

He laughed. "Well, I'm glad you're coming. I'll pick you up. It's not like I haven't been to your house before."

Kathy smiled because she knew he couldn't see. "Actually, I

want to make an entrance. I've been thinking about it since I texted you."

"There isn't exactly going to be a red carpet. I don't know what kind of Hollywood author parties you're going to—"

"Authors don't have red-carpet premieres, Jeremy." She rolled her eyes and grinned. "No, I was talking about you. You show up alone, and when everyone starts to pity you—BAM! I show up looking amazing, as always, and tell them you're not as lonely and miserable as you look."

Kathy hated reverting back to the girl she had been thirty years ago. But she had to admit, it was nice to be in familiar territory for once. And even though it made her sound like a lovesick schoolgirl, the mutual infatuation was nice.

"I like it—except for me looking lonely and miserable. Could we change that?"

She shook her head. "Nope, it's an essential part of my plan. If I'm coming to this party, we're playing by my rules. Oh, I forgot to mention that after you introduce me to everyone, you should gush about my book. Maybe even suggest buying a few copies as gifts."

"This is going to be an expensive night, isn't it?"

"I'm not a cheap girl."

"That you aren't."

Thunder boomed again. Kathy had almost forgotten about the Chaos looming overhead. Would she even be able to go to the party Saturday? Would there even be a party if the Chaos rang true to its name? She couldn't think about that now.

"Look, I've gotta go. Text me if anything changes. I'll see you

Saturday." She hung up and returned to the living room. Josh watched out the window as the cloud began striking toward the earth.

"Uh, Aunt Kathy! Something's happening!"

She rushed to the window beside him. "That's exactly what happened in New York! Right before the guy started choking me." She touched her throat absently.

"We should go upstairs and get them."

"We're right here." Holly bounded down the stairs with Chris in tow.

"Did you see the sky?" Josh asked.

"Yeah," she said.

Kathy turned to them. "Was it a good talk?"

Chris and Holly exchanged glances.

"I'm going back," Chris declared.

"What!?" Kathy shot a look at Holly. She'd thought they were on the same page. Holly's was supposed to have been the convincing argument.

"Kathy, he needs to go," Holly said. "I don't want him to, either, but we can't just ignore Raven's promise. My family did that with Toxanna and look what happened."

"This is different," Kathy retorted.

"How do you even know Raven still wants you?" Josh asked his brother. "You *did* just disappear for two days."

"We don't." Chris refused to look at him. Josh was being a hypocrite. Didn't he join the Pentad under false pretenses? "But we can't just ignore it."

"What happens if she's lying?" Kathy asked.

Chris shook his head. "She's not. Finding Sophia was one of the stipulations of me joining."

"So was you leading, and look where that's gotten you," she countered.

"I'm open to suggestions. Right now, going back to the Fire Wizards is the best option." He grasped Holly's hand. "I have to."

Josh raised his eyebrows in surprise. Kathy's looked worried. They had reunited so fast. Things had escalated faster. She didn't want either of them to get hurt.

She worried how bringing Sophia back into the picture would work with their reunion. You don't have a baby to save your marriage. These were different circumstances, but the basic principle still applied.

The front door crashed in and the witches jumped. Chris and Holly saw him first: Ray Yates, their next-door neighbor. Something was off. His eyes didn't seem to focus. He acted like the house was a strange place. Chris figured it was the Chaos.

"Ray, you scared me." Kathy was unable to see the maroon glow of his eyes. She noted Chris's and Holly's nervous looks and asked, "Are you okay?"

Ray turned and growled.

"That's not Ray," Josh said.

In a second, Kathy was on the ground. Her arms pinned to her chest. Ray raised his fist for a punch.

Chapter Thirteen

Josh tried to pull his neighbor off, but the Chaos supernaturally charged him. Chris's hands lit up with flame, but Holly tugged at his shirt.

"Chris, don't! He's still human!"

"He's going to kill her!" he shouted.

Ray threw his elbow back and knocked Josh in the jaw. The witch fell to the floor, grabbing at his face.

Chris quickly took his place, pulling first at his arm and then his neck. Ray raised his elbow again and got Chris in the ribs. It certainly stung his damaged skin, but Josh's medicine seemed to be working. He moved toward Ray again, but Holly slammed one of the dining room chairs hard against the intruder. He grunted but held his grip on Kathy's throat. Using what was left of the dining room chair, Holly continued to swing, hit after hit, against

Ray's back. Finally, with the sound of a crack, he collapsed on top of Kathy.

Grabbing ahold of his wrist, Chris rolled their neighbor off his aunt.

"Are you okay?" Holly knelt next to her.

Kathy rested her head against the floor and took deep breaths. Finally, she nodded. "Yeah." She rubbed the back of her neck. "I wasn't ready for that."

Holly inspected her injuries. "Your neck is pretty red."

"Well, I suppose that's better than being dead." Kathy met Chris's eyes and then Holly's. "Is the Chaos gone?"

Chris looked to their neighbor. Ray lay still. He reached over and checked for a pulse. "The Chaos is gone."

"Is he...?"

Chris nodded. "Dead."

Kathy rubbed her face. "Oh no. Where's Josh?"

"Right here." He walked over holding the side of his face. He worked his jaw by opening and closing his mouth. "That sucker got me good. What's his deal?"

Kathy looked behind her and out the window. "Do you see the way the cloud is striking the ground?"

Chris pointed to Ray. "Is that what happened to him?"

"The Chaos must've infected him. He's not the only one. I don't think it's a coincidence that he chose this house to come to, either. He's got a family—*had* a family. If the Chaos only caused rage, he would've been hurting them. Not me."

"So someone is targeting us specifically?" Holly asked.

Kathy waved her hand between her nephews. "With these two joining groups left and right, we can't even narrow down our list of threats."

Chris shook his head. "I don't think it was the Fire Wizards."

"How can you be sure?" Josh asked. "I imagine they've gotta be looking for you. You're a runaway."

"They don't want to kill me, Josh." Chris folded his arms across his chest. "They want to use me for something."

"And what is that something?"

Chris diverted his eyes to the floor. He wasn't going to admit he didn't know. This was another reason he liked being on his own. "What about Zamball? He could've released it too."

"It wasn't Zamball."

"How do you know?"

"Because he told me."

"And you believed him? He also told you I was dead and he could resurrect me! He's a liar, Josh."

"And Raven and the Fire Wizards aren't?"

"Enough!" Kathy shouted. "You two are acting like a couple of brats. You're both grown adults. Quit the bickering and let's solve the damn problem. Now we have a neighbor's dead body here. As bad as it is, the best thing we can do is drop him off somewhere without anyone noticing."

The brothers studied one another. Both of them were too proud to acknowledge their aunt's scolding. But she was right. Better to make it look like a random assault than try to explain it to the police. That would save them from being incriminated and wouldn't build up any resentment from Ray's family. Suddenly losing him would be hard enough for them.

"Kathy and I can move the body," Holly suggested. She knew the older witch's time specialty would be perfect for dropping him without being seen.

"Josh, why don't you go talk to Zamball if you think he can help—don't tell him what we know, but try to figure out what he knows," Kathy delegated. "And Chris, if you think going back to the Fire Wizards will help, then maybe you should go." She couldn't stand the idea of both of her boys leaving to play a demonic game of roulette, but at the moment those were their only leads.

"Be careful, though," Holly added. "Both of you."

"So you're okay with me leaving again?" Chris asked.

"We don't really have a choice, do we, Chris? You both made stupid decisions, and now we've *all* got to live with them. We have a family to put back together."

Chris nodded. "I'll figure out a way to get in touch with the Fire Wizards." He turned to leave, and Holly followed him.

"Chris." She tugged on his arm when they were out of eyesight of Kathy and Josh. "Promise me you'll be careful. I want Sophia back, but I want you too."

He was quiet. He couldn't promise his safety. Not after the way they'd treated him the last time. He could very well be marching to his own death. Holly didn't need to be reminded of that.

He took a deep breath and slipped his arms around her in the familiar way they used to. Their reunion was exactly what he'd hoped for, but they weren't complete yet.

"I'll try." His voice was thick.

"I don't want to lose you." She spoke against his chest. "Either of you. Not again."

"Holly, I'm going to do my best, but you have a part to play too. You're needed here. Don't run away this time."

* * *

"Josh, what are you doing here? I thought you worked this morning?" Natalie was at the nurse's station on the third floor. "Did you get called in?"

He shook his head. "No. I need to talk to you."

She gestured toward the desk. "I'm kind of busy right now."

"It's important."

She noted the look on his face and nodded. "Okay. Sit."

"Is there anyone else around?"

"It's a hospital, Josh. Of course there are other people around."

"I know that. I just…" He lowered his voice. "Something's happened."

"What? Is it…?"

He nodded.

"Are you okay?"

"I'm fine. But look, it's not safe anymore. For me. For my family. Or anyone we…have contact with."

"You mean anyone you're sleeping with?"

"Anyone I might care about."

"Josh, you're scaring me. What's going on?"

He wondered if this was all a show. He knew she knew more than she was supposed to, but that didn't change the fact that he cared about her. A lot. Maybe she actually cared about him like she said she did.

"Just promise me you'll get somewhere safe."

"Now? I can't go now. I'm at work. I've got patients."

"You're a target."

She gripped his hand. "I'm not leaving, Josh. Whatever it is, I know you'll figure it out."

"How? You only know about me and my family because I told you."

"Because you protected me at the Downs."

"I told you to run. You listened that time."

"But I could only run so far." She took both of his hands now. "Josh, if I'm a target, I'm a target here just as much as I am anywhere else. At least let me help people in the process."

He met her eyes. She had a point. Since she wasn't magical, she could be just as easily traced. Summoned even. If they were going to use Natalie to get to him, it didn't matter if she was working or hiding under her bed, she could be found. He knew whom he had to talk to.

"Okay. Stay here. Just be mindful."

She put up her right hand. "Always."

Josh grinned. "Yeah, okay." He leaned forward and kissed her. He only intended for it to be a quick good-bye, but he couldn't stop himself. They didn't know anything about the Chaos. It could possess him and, with his powers, he could do unspeakable things. They might have to put him down. This might be his last kiss with Natalie ever.

* * *

"You realize we have a regular meeting space that's much more private than this pier, right?" Zamball asked. He was facing the lake once again. With the purple cloud looming overhead, the glow from the city lights was the only thing offering light.

"I don't care. I needed to talk to you, and I was just at the hospital." The pier was across the street from the hospital. It was a short walk over from his visit to Natalie.

"Did you find anything else out about our special friend?"

"No. I'm here about the Chaos."

"As am I."

"What do you know?"

"Don't you know?"

"I'm not here to play games, Zamball. I want answers. I want *action*. We haven't done a single thing about the Chaos—or Sophia—since I joined. You told me it was *imperative* to join when I did."

Zamball turned and met Josh's eyes. "I told you to join then because of the blue moon. I didn't say you would be given an assignment straightaway. The rest of the Pentad needs to measure your abilities—your loyalty."

"Then why didn't you tell me that!? I thought I was going

to be an equal member immediately. I don't like being fooled." Kathy's warnings rang in his head.

"I'm sorry if you felt fooled, but there's nothing you can do about it now. You're a member of the Pentad, whether you like it or not."

Josh crossed his arms. He had gotten himself into this. He had allowed himself to be peer-pressured until he'd given in. He could've walked. He hadn't. All he could do now was work with them. For the time being, they had a common enemy.

"What are we going to do about the Chaos? My aunt was nearly killed today. By our neighbor. How are we supposed to use magic against innocent people?"

"I know, we read your thoughts."

Josh's mind flashed to Natalie and their good-bye kiss. "Stay out of my head!"

"I don't have control. Your memories are now shared with the rest of us."

"Is there a dispossessing spell or an exorcism we can do to get rid of the Chaos? Maybe we can amplify it enough to dispossess anyone in the city who has been infected?"

Zamball shook his head. "Impossible. There isn't a spell strong enough to do that—least of all cast by either one of us. We're powerful but not that powerful."

"Then what are we going to do? This is my vote on what we should do next as a group."

"*Don't* make demands. We vote as a group." Zamball's expression softened. "Lucky for you, the rest of the Pentad is in agreement that this problem needs to be solved. We may have a solution."

"Yes! Anything. What is it?"

"You remember Eleanor's theory about eradicating the Chaos in the same fashion as it was formed?"

Josh nodded.

"Eleanor has been crafting a spell for that."

"Great, where is it?"

Zamball held up a finger. "It's not that easy. It needs to be cast by good and evil with the same intentions."

"You and I. Done."

He shook his head again. "No. Since we're both members of the Pentad, we're allies. Not enemies. It needs to be someone with no affiliations to the dark side."

Josh felt a twinge of guilt. Kathy was right. He had joined the dark side. Which meant Chris had done the same. The spell would have to be cast by either Kathy or Holly.

"Okay. So that's one of us then and my aunt."

"Would she agree to help us?"

"To defeat the Chaos? Sure. Afterward? I don't know."

"Okay…" Zamball said cautiously. "The spell also needs to be cast on neutral ground."

"What qualifies as neutral ground?" Josh asked.

"Anything the good and evil sides don't claim to be theirs. Your house, for instance, is off-limits. Even this pier wouldn't work. We've had too many discussions here."

Josh shrugged. "That's anywhere in the city, really."

"No. Erie is your home. You claim that. It needs to be somewhere unfamiliar to you. Preferably, somewhere without people nearby. There's no telling how big the blast could be."

"Wait a minute." Josh took a step back from Zamball. "If the blast is going to be huge, how are the people casting the spell supposed to get away?"

Zamball turned back to the water. "It may be a sacrifice."

"Then how do we even know it's worth it?"

He whipped back around. "Because otherwise the Chaos will destroy us all! Do not underestimate its power! You have only seen a small preview of it. Paranoia is a silent killer."

Josh sighed. "Okay. So I've got to convince either my aunt or my sister-in-law to potentially give up their lives to save mankind?"

"Yes, that is your first step."

"What's my second?"

"That will be determined soon. I'm sure it won't be easy convincing your family. Your aunt in particular doesn't seem to like your connection with us. Understandably, of course." Zamball tapped a finger to his temple.

"I hate this telepathy thing we have."

"You haven't been using yours. I'll have to show you once we rid ourselves of the Chaos and we're back to full strength."

"Full strength? What are you talking about?"

Zamball looked to the sky. "When the moon is hidden behind this much darkness, our powers aren't what they should be."

"So this is it. The Chaos is here and unless we're willing to sacrifice ourselves, it's going to make us go crazy."

"The Chaos is here, yes. But we still have time before it strikes everyone."

"What do you mean?"

The wizard indicated the cloud. "You can already see it beginning to clear up. Whoever is controlling it is just letting us know they're around. I'm sure there will be other isolated attacks like tonight's."

CHAPTER FOURTEEN

As far as face-to-face interviews went, Kathy was done with everything DJ Books had lined up, unless another publication showed interest. She didn't have access to the sales, so she couldn't be sure, but she doubted there would be more interviews. DJ Books had spent most of their marketing budget on this launch and they'd be reluctant to spend more. From here on out, she was doing podcasts until her small book tour next month. Everything within driving distance of Erie. The publisher couldn't afford to put her up in a hotel for even one night. Even Greg had to pay for his trip to Erie out of his own pocket.

Kathy and Greg only had one more interview to do together before he went back to New York City. He had a job and a life, and Kathy was sure he was behind on deadlines.

Still, she was going to miss him. Even with the lines that they'd blurred and then redrawn, he was important to her. Especially to her career. More than that, he was a friend. Which is why she thought it'd be okay to meet him at his hotel room for their last promo. Plus, it was a nicer backdrop for a video podcast than the cluttered and noisy house.

"Welcome to my home away from home." Greg stepped aside to allow Kathy to enter the suite. It was small, but cozy. The small living room and kitchenette were separated by a short table. The large window overlooked the mall parking lot but let in a lot of natural light.

"Oh, this is nice. I've never been inside before. I try to stay away from the mall as much as I can. Crowds drive me insane." She kept her thumb hooked on her purse and tried to act casual. This was more awkward than she'd thought it'd be. Luckily, the bed was in a whole separate room, so it felt more like a small apartment.

"I would say me too, but when you live in the most populated city in the country, you kind of get used to crowds."

Kathy smiled and nodded. "True. But that's not something I can get used to."

He smiled at her for a moment longer. "Anyway, I thought we should go over a few notes while I set up the connection."

"Thanks again for agreeing to do it here—the podcast." Her cheeks blushed. With everything going on with Chris and the Chaos, she wanted to get out of the house. She needed to focus on something else for a bit. Like her job. That was important too.

Greg smiled as the computer screen illuminated his face. "No problem. I was a little surprised you didn't want to show off your house. From the few pictures you have up on Facebook, I can tell it certainly fits the tone of your story."

Kathy kept her head down. So Greg had been doing a little online stalking.

"The house is too noisy nowadays. If you would've asked me two weeks ago, my answer probably would've been different."

"That's a good thing, though. Isn't it?" He hit the trackpad with his middle finger. "I think we have a connection."

"It is. It's just not very conducive to getting work done."

He nodded. "Sometimes you just have to get away."

She raised her eyebrows. He was spot on.

* * *

Once Kathy got into the discussion of her book, she and Greg slipped back into their collegial relationship—more easily than the last interview they'd done—and she was completely consumed by the world she had created.

Despite her problems in her personal life, her career was exciting. It was something she could mold herself. Something she had direct control of. Control was not always something she had had throughout her life.

She had found her purpose and she pursued it fervently. Not only because she loved it, but also because she knew Samantha would be proud. Kathy remembered all those arguments they'd had about her finding a real job and the time Samantha had put in trying to help her prepare.

The woman Kathy was now was completely different than when she had been her nephews' ages, and it showed in her work. It had taken some time, but she was finally where she wanted to be.

They signed off and Kathy slumped back in her chair. "Well that was fun, but the proper posture was hurting my back. How do people sit like this all the time?" She twisted and her back popped.

"People who sit a lot find a way—trust me. I'm usually hunched over a desk." He looked down at her phone. "You're just going to let it ring?"

Kathy saw Holly's name displayed across it. She was immediately reminded of her magical duties. Whatever relief she had from the escape of the interview was wiped away just like that. She knew she should answer, but she was at work. If she worked a regular nine-to-five, a phone call would be off-limits right now. It could wait.

"No. I can get it later." Kathy gathered up her purse. "Thank you so much for coming to Erie and sitting in on a few interviews. I'm sure it helped give me and my books more depth for the reader." Thinking back, Greg had certainly helped fill a couple of voids in moments when she'd needed help. Video interviews were a new thing for her. She needed better practice.

"No problem." He stood with his hands on his hips. They both stared at each other, unsure of how to properly say good-bye. "Would it be weird for me to give you a hug?"

She looked down and scratched her forehead. "Uh, Greg, I don't…"

"Oh, yeah. No, I understand."

When she looked back up at him her eyes immediately went to the window. The sun had vanished, replaced by the familiar dark purple cloud. It was appearing more frequently now.

The cloud continued to fill the sky until the whole building was swallowed up in it.

"Weird," Greg commented, stepping closer to the window.

The purple mass pressed against the glass. They could hear the soft sound of the glass reaching its breaking point.

"Greg, come here. Get away from the window."

He placed his hand against it, snatching it away when the window began to crack.

"Come here!" she barked, stepping forward to grab him by the hand and pull him away. He nearly tripped on the couch as she ushered him into the hall.

The door slammed shut behind them.

"Hey, my keys are in there!" He pointed to the door.

Kathy heard the glass shattering from inside and pulled Greg down to the floor with her. They leaned against the wall and waited. They were stuck. Leaving the building wasn't an option and anywhere they went inside wouldn't matter. The Chaos was going to find them. Find her.

"What's going on?" he asked.

She made the shushing face and put a finger to her lips. Leaning her ear closer to the door, she listened for the sound of anything approaching. Was the Chaos harmless by itself? Maybe its power only worked when it had infected someone? Would they be safe if they kept quiet?

Greg leaned against the wall. "How long are you going to make us sit out here before I call the front desk? I still have another night here."

Kathy opened her mouth to answer, but the cloud began to slip underneath the door, pooling at the floor before slithering up toward them.

"Get away from the door!" She skidded farther down the hall on her butt, kicking at the floor with her feet.

He looked at her, confused. Then the cloud hit him, and he collapsed to the floor choking.

"Greg!" She raced to him, swatting in the air to try to clear the influence of the cloud. She held her breath but quickly grew tired. Her heart pounded in her chest.

A couple of doors opened down the hallway as people peeked their heads out.

Suddenly Greg lunged at her, his hands around her neck. Kathy swatted and kicked at him, but he had her pinned to the floor with a firm grip on her throat. The room started to spin as she gasped for breath and he pressed against her sore skin.

One of the other hotel guests tried to pull Greg off, but like Josh the night before, he couldn't. Another guest ran up with a steak knife—the greasy A1 sauce dripping from it indicated he'd gotten it from room service—but Greg elbowed him in the jaw. Almost in the same fashion as the night before.

Kathy saw the knife land just outside her reach. She stretched and wiggled toward it. Her vision was fading. Grasping the blade, she swung it into Greg's side until she felt the fabric of his shirt wet with blood. He let out a breath, and with it the Chaos escaped. Once it was gone, he collapsed on top of her. She gasped for breath, clutching at her throat as one of the hotel guests rolled him off her. She lay covered in his blood.

"Someone call 9-1-1!" the guest shouted.

"They're on their way!" a woman called.

Kathy pulled the knife out and put pressure on Greg's side. The first guest handed her a towel, and she used that to cover his wound. It was immediately stained red.

Focusing on inhaling and exhaling, she tried to remain calm. She had stabbed Greg. Her friend. Someone who would never actually hurt her in his right mind.

This was different than the attack last night. There had been witnesses. There had been blood. While she hoped he would survive, she knew the outcome wasn't good either way. There would surely be an investigation. Even if she wasn't convicted, Greg would be. He had been the one to attack her.

"Are you okay? Did you know him?" The guest who had brought the towel sat by her side.

Kathy bit her lip and nodded. She may have just killed him. Words were impossible right now. Her throat burned from two attempted strangulations in a matter of twelve hours. Besides that, the attention on her breaths was the only thing keeping her from completely losing it.

The guest took her place, and Kathy stood and leaned against the wall, her hands bloody and shaking. Everything seemed to be happening in slow motion. The people rushing out of their rooms.

The sounds of sirens in the distance. She sank to the floor and buried her face against her legs and finally let herself cry.

* * *

Josh was too distracted to work a single shift let alone a double. With everything going on at home, he was barely sleeping. The first night Chris was home, Josh sat up for almost two hours just listening to his shallow breaths. The sound reminded him of being a kid. When things had been simpler—even if they didn't seem so at the time.

Of course, now that he was an adult—and a doctor, no less—he couldn't afford to miss sleep. He didn't know how some of his colleagues were getting married and having babies. He couldn't imagine that. He and Natalie hadn't been on a proper date since their first one at Presque Isle Downs. That had almost ended disastrously.

What passed as a date nowadays were a movie night and maybe a quickie before bed. If they were lucky. Some nights neither one of them even wanted that. Just sleep. The nights they stayed up and enjoyed each other's company meant he had a long day the next day. Even when he took some time for himself, he ended up paying for it later.

"Dr. Harper? There's someone here to see you." One of the new med students from Gannon stopped him on his way to the only saving grace of the night: the sleep room. He hadn't heard her calling his name.

He sighed, annoyed. It wasn't the student's fault, though. "Okay. Thanks. Who is it?"

She shrugged. "He didn't say. I don't think he's a patient, though."

"Well then I don't have time." He turned to walk away but spun back around. "Wait!" He knew who it was. "Never mind. I'll see him. Where is he?"

"He's in the waiting room."

Josh walked down the long hallway and saw him. He was in disguise as his Elliott alias: blond, smooth-faced, and wearing a gray jacket over his plain blue T-shirt. Very generic. But then, Zamball only used his alias nowadays to go places where his natural blue skin would draw too much attention.

"This couldn't wait until after I was out of work?"

Zamball shook his head. "You weren't answering my probes."

"Your *what*!?" Luckily, the waiting room was empty.

"Probes," he repeated. "I've been trying to contact you telepathically."

Josh thought his day over. His mind was filled with so many other things that he couldn't remember if he had felt any probes. But then, it had been difficult to concentrate for a while.

"Whatever. What do you want?"

"Eleanor is calling a meeting."

"Now?"

Zamball nodded.

"No. I can't go now. I'm not even halfway through my first shift! I'm here until seven in the morning!"

"You don't get any breaks?"

Josh dug his hands into his pockets and raised his shoulders. "I guess I'm kind of on a break right now."

Zamball nodded once firmly. "Great. Let's go."

"How long is this going to take?"

"As long as it does. These are important matters to discuss."

"So is my job! Twenty minutes, tops."

Squeezing Josh's shoulder, Zamball leaned in close. "Remember that you are still a new recruit. You haven't done anything to build the reputation of the Pentad, therefore you are not in a position to doll out orders—especially to Eleanor."

"I thought you said we were all equals? Why is Eleanor so special?"

"Because her power is the strongest. I guarantee you that she's listening in right now. Don't give her a reason to be upset with you. You still have favors to ask of her."

Josh let out a frustrated breath of air. He had a point. But Josh had been fooled before. He didn't want to have to cooperate anymore. Chris was safe. Sophia was alive. The Pentad's bargaining power had vanished. Yet, here he was in the thick of their operations.

Zamball looked off into the distance and then returned his gaze to Josh. "Eleanor says that we'll wait for you. However, the meeting is still urgent. Meet me at our usual place as soon as your shift is over."

Chapter Fifteen

Chris knew his return to the Fire Wizards wouldn't be easy. Especially since he needed to ask a favor of them immediately after he returned. But he hoped that they would see the Chaos as a threat to everyone, including themselves. If he pitched it as helping the group rather than himself, they'd be more likely to help. At least, he hoped.

The spell he used to return to the camp put him just outside the circle of tents. He reckoned it was only because he was a member of the coven that the spell worked. As he slowly crept into the inner circle, he was distracted by who was surrounding the central fire and he didn't notice the two guards in the shadows. Next thing he knew, his hands were bound behind his back.

"Mr. Harper," Raven greeted him as she emerged from around one of the tents.

The guards dragged Chris to a nearby tent. Raven followed and stood over a table holding some sort of map. He couldn't make out what it was of, though.

"He walked in voluntarily," one of the guards told her.

"Is he bound?"

The other guard nodded. "Yes, ma'am."

"Then leave us. Mr. Harper and I have some things to discuss."

Chris waited for the guards to exit before he spoke. "I didn't leave on my own. I was called away." Even though he didn't want to pin blame on his family, the negotiations would go better if Raven believed he had loyalty to the Fire Wizards.

She crossed her arms and stared at him. He could tell she didn't believe him. What else she was thinking, though, was a mystery.

"Obviously, I came back," he continued. "There has to be some merit to that."

"Mr. Harper, do you think I'm stupid?"

Chris kept his eyes on the table. "No." Then, as an afterthought, "Ma'am."

"Just because I didn't send troops after you doesn't mean I didn't know where you were. You were being chummy with the rest of the Harpers. The ones you led us to believe were no longer a part of your life." She shook her head slowly. "Apparently I misunderstood your relationship with Holly Bowen."

"They're not a part of my life. That's why I came back."

"After two days? Pardon me if I don't believe you."

"They were treating my wounds. I needed my strength back. Something *you* promised me." He looked down. That last bit didn't help. "Once I was healthy again, I left."

"We were treating your wounds just fine. We don't baby our soldiers here, Mr. Harper."

Chris bit his tongue. Telling her what she already knew—that she had been the cause of his injuries—would only infuriate her.

She stood next to him but peered through the opening of the tent. "There's another reason you came back. It certainly wasn't loyalty."

"Well, you have my daughter."

When she turned back to him, she had a sly grin that only made Chris hate her more. "The terms I laid out for you were clear: cooperate and your ex-wife gets the girl back."

He shook his head. "That's not good enough."

She leaned in close to him. "That's exactly what it is, Mr. Harper. Enough." She stood straight again. "It's as good as you're going to get. The other option is death. For you and your daughter."

Chris released a long breath of air. He had to let Raven's threat of Sophia go. "There's another reason I came back. It concerns you and the rest of the coven."

"I can assure you that nothing you say will be news to me."

"The Chaos has been released. Just like you said. And it's active in Erie, maybe even other places too. My aunt said she saw it in New York City."

Raven nodded. "I'm aware. It's exactly the reason I asked you to join. You have been less than helpful, however. Besides, we no longer fear the Chaos."

Her apathy was surprising. "The Chaos will cause anarchy! Innocent people are dying. Even if that's not a concern to you now, the strength whoever released it will gain from it will be. It'll only be a matter of time before the Fire Wizards are targeted too."

"At that point, we will have recruited the person controlling the Chaos to our cause. As you have seen firsthand, we can be very persuasive."

"You're—" He held back his words. "You're going to want to act now. We need to figure out who or what is in charge and convince them to stop."

She smiled. "My, how the tables have turned. Mr. Harper, why do you think no one from the Fire Wizards chased after you?"

He shook his head.

"We were working. Searching for the one who controls the Chaos. We are in negotiations with her. What we anticipated would be a bloody fight will be a rather simple business deal. This sorcerer will help us achieve our end goal."

"What is that exactly?"

She flashed her teeth again. "Two days ago I would've conveyed our plan without hesitation. After some time being treated as a prisoner, I find that most recruits are more than eager to cooperate. After all, it's a choice between us or death. You, however, bucked the system. And for that, you aren't awarded certain privileges—such as our main objective."

"If I've shown I'm no longer loyal, then why don't you kill me?"

"You still have value to us. Therefore, your death wouldn't advance our position at all. Some people are worth sacrificing. At this moment, you're not."

* * *

The first-response team didn't allow Kathy to ride in the ambulance with Greg. Instead, she trailed them all the way downtown. She called Josh on the way.

"Honey, I'm on my way to the hospital." She tried to keep her voice even, but she could hear it shaking.

"What's wrong?"

"I stabbed Greg."

"Your editor? What!? Why?"

"The Chaos. Look, I'll tell you more when I get there. They're probably not going to give me any details. Could you find out what room he ends up in?"

"Depending on the extent of the injury, they'll probably take him across the street to the surgery center first. Just go there now. I'll keep a tab on him to see if and when he's moved."

"Thanks."

"Are you okay?"

"No," she admitted, trying to focus on her driving—anything other than the man she'd just stabbed. "It's just another day, right?"

"Let me know when you get here. I'll come see you."

Kathy splurged for the valet parking once she got to the hospital. She just wanted to get inside. She needed some sign of hope. Greg was hurt and it was her fault. She hadn't seen that much blood since Samantha had died. It brought back too many bad memories.

Josh met her in the surgery center waiting room and pulled her into a hug.

"Is there a place we can talk?" she asked.

He ushered her down a hallway and into one of the small staff lunchrooms. It was empty.

"It doesn't look good." He squeezed her hand.

Kathy shut her eyes tight and rubbed them with her thumb and forefinger. She let her hair fall to help shield her face.

"But they just started the surgery," he continued. "Once they get in there, things might turn out differently. We've seen our share of miracles."

"We've also seen our share of bad things."

Nothing he could say at that moment could offer her comfort, so he wrapped her into a hug instead.

She pulled away a few moments later and dabbed at her eyes with a napkin. "Did you get anything out of Zamball?" Despite her emotions, they still had work to do. Besides, there was nothing she could do about Greg at the moment. She needed a distraction.

Josh shook his head. "Not really. I guess the Pentad is having a meeting as soon as I'm done with work."

"Have you met them all?"

"Once. When I was initiated. But the five of us haven't been together since."

"Do you think it's a good thing?"

He shrugged. "Well…Zamball did say something else…"

"What? Josh, we can't keep secrets from each other."

She was right, but he knew she wouldn't agree to help. And he wasn't sure he wanted her to help, either. That would only send her to her grave. "The Chaos can be destroyed by joining white magic and black magic together."

"Great, so that's you and anyone else in the Pentad—or even any of the Fire Wizards. Chris might be able to—"

"I can't do it. Neither can Chris. We're both white magic practitioners in," he didn't want to say it, "black magic groups."

Kathy blinked at him. "So what does that mean?"

"It has to be you or Holly and someone who practices black magic. Anyone else in the Fire Wizards or the Pentad can help."

"Okay. So we flip a coin. It's just a spell."

"Not exactly. According to Zamball, it could be a deadly spell for the casters as well."

"What do you mean?"

He couldn't meet her eyes. Instead, he studied the floor. "The ones who cast the spell will likely die."

"So what did *you* say?"

Josh shrugged.

"*That's* the best you've got!? Why do you trust him so much? He's telling you to sacrifice your family for a force he very well could've released himself!"

"He's not controlling it! And I believe him because he volunteered to cast the spell. If he's willing to sacrifice himself, why wouldn't I trust him?"

"Because he hasn't given you any reason *to* trust him!"

"What do you want me to do? First you tell me to cut them out, then you tell me to use them, now you're saying I shouldn't trust them. Make up your mind!"

Kathy folded her arms and studied him a moment. "You have a meeting soon, right?"

"When I'm done with my shift in the morning, yeah."

"Go to the meeting. Tell them that some suicide spell is not going to work."

"Then what do you suggest we do?"

"I don't know. Just get a better answer."

* * *

After the unsuccessful meeting with Raven, Chris found himself back in familiar territory: his cage. The only difference this time around was that he felt better. His skin no longer ached from burns. His stomach no longer churned with hunger. And his mind no longer faded from sleep deprivation.

Now that his plan had failed, he needed to figure out a new way to help. It was very foolish not to have a Plan B.

His brief trip home helped give him a sense of where everybody's heads were at and what problems were afoot. The Chaos was very much a threat, but hopefully Josh would have a better outcome with the Pentad than he did with the Fire Wizards. Not that Chris was too keen on the idea of asking Josh or the Pentad for help, but Sophia was the top priority.

In order to get any new information on her, he needed to prove his loyalty to Raven. His time in the cage would allow him to figure out a new plan. He needed something that would show her that he was serious about being a Fire Wizard, but it couldn't be something that would hurt anyone or cause irreparable damage.

Helping the Fire Wizards get a step closer to achieving their top-secret goal would certainly help his case. At the moment, Raven didn't seem too concerned with the Chaos. But Chris had witnessed its power. He knew what it was capable of. Someone like Raven wouldn't be able to stand by and let this mysterious sorcerer have it. Raven likely wanted it. Helping her get better control of it would help him.

But he couldn't just let her have it. He needed leverage. He needed control.

Chris wondered if someone who was already a member of the Fire Wizards could take the power from the person who had it without strengthening the group as a whole.

The conversion of power wouldn't be simple, and there was no guarantee that just anyone could contain it, but whoever did would have control. If Chris could take power, the Fire Wizards would be forced to listen to him. He could use them long enough to get Sophia back. Then, once his daughter was home safe, he could use the Chaos to wipe out the Fire Wizards.

But what consequences would that have? Chris didn't even know the extent of the Chaos's power. How would he be able to control it? And what would happen once he returned it back to its resting place? Would he be the same or would he have some side effects? Worse, what if he couldn't even control it? What if it only consumed him? He'd seen what it had done to Ray. What kind of effect would it have on a witch?

Regardless, he had to try. Whoever was controlling it now was not using it for the greater good. They were trying to kickstart an apocalypse.

* * *

The Magician.

The High Priestess.

The Lovers reversed.

The Hermit reversed.

The Devil.

The Moon.

Death.

The cards Holly drew for the situation with the Chaos didn't look good. They'd once had skill and self-confidence, they now had secrets and mystery, and soon they would have failure. The Hermit reversed showed that something was still hidden from them. A person or their intentions, Holly couldn't determine. Clearly, violence and fatality were influencing the Chaos.

What concerned Holly the most were the last two cards. Showcasing their hopes and the overall outcome, the cards showed hidden enemies and destruction.

She studied the spread further, trying to come up with different theories on how their future would turn out.

The Hermit reversed bothered her. Somebody must still be hiding their true intentions. Judging by The Moon's symbol for hidden enemies and destruction, Holly wondered if it was Chris who hadn't been the one showing his hand. What did they really know about him and the time he'd spent away from Erie?

Holly pushed the thoughts from her mind. She'd seen with her own eyes that Chris was a prisoner of the Fire Wizards. Besides, she needed to hold on to the hope that Sophia was alive and that Chris was going to do everything in his power to get her back. He was her only connection to her now. He was her last bit of hope.

But who else could it be? She hadn't been back in Josh's and Kathy's lives for long, but she couldn't think of anyone who would be a potential threat. Josh had a girlfriend, but as far as Holly knew, she wasn't magical. Kathy had alluded to having a man-friend, but she would've mentioned it if he was magical. Besides, none of these outsiders had any curiosities about them that made Josh or Kathy wonder about their intentions. At least, none that they shared. Meanwhile, Chris's history was shrouded in mystery.

She scooped up the cards and reshuffled. There had to be another explanation. Chris would not betray them…unless he had. Hadn't she once thought that before? It had only been within the last few days that she'd forgiven him and acknowledged her continuing love for him. But that didn't mean he was good for her. At the end of the day, she still couldn't trust him. Not until he proved he *could* be trusted.

There was a surefire way to find out. Holly had seen a talisman design in Lily Dale that allowed the wearer to know when someone was being deceitful. She had written down the parts necessary to recreate it. She just needed to find her notes and the proper supplies. Then she needed to find a way to see Chris face-to-face. That was the only way to tell if he was lying.

CHAPTER SIXTEEN

Josh was able to sneak out to his locker long enough to text Holly to come to the hospital. He knew Kathy shouldn't be alone, but he was too busy with work to be with her himself. Even if he did have the time, she'd made it pretty clear that she didn't want to see him. Besides, everyone needed to be on the same page. If only there were a safe way to get in touch with Chris, too.

The rest of Josh's shift went by quickly. He had so much to do that he didn't pay attention to what time it was—or that the sun had risen—until Natalie came in.

"What are you still doing here? Go get some sleep! You look exhausted."

He pulled back his sleeve and looked at his watch. "Shoot. I've gotta get going."

"Well, nice to see you too."

"No, it's for…other things." He pointed out the window to the building across the street. "My aunt is over at the surgery center with…" He hesitated. How did he describe Holly now? Natalie was still stuck on the fact that she and Chris were exes. "…with a friend. If you get a chance, see if you can check up on them. You remember my aunt, right?"

"Well, I mean I only chatted with her for a hot second when we first started dating but—is she okay?" She hurried after Josh, who raced to his locker to get his things.

"Not really. Her friend was stabbed."

"Oh."

In the locker room, Josh pulled out his bag. "Yeah. When I checked when she first came in, it was pretty bad."

"I don't know how I'll be any comfort—"

"Please? For me?" He stopped long enough to plant a kiss on her lips and then moved to the door. "I'm already late. I'll talk to you later. Text me if anything comes up with my aunt."

* * *

"You're late, Windy." Collie leaned against a parked car at the end of the pier with her arms crossed. The other three, who stood nearby, all looked up when she called to him.

"Sorry!" He jogged over to them. "It was a long night."

"We're not here to listen to your excuses, newbie." Ignatius O'Reilly was the fire branch of the Pentad. He had the biggest bark out of all of them and, likely, the biggest bite. He wore the same khaki jacket with holes at the elbows as he had during the initiation ceremony.

Josh hung his head and waited until someone started the meeting. He hated feeling like a child, but he had no seniority in the group. More importantly, he needed their help. There was no use in standing his ground if it would only hurt his chances of getting his niece back. And his brother.

"How long has it been since the blue moon?" Eleanor was the only one not facing the circle. She looked out into the lake. The ends of the bandana she had wrapped around her head blew in the gentle breeze. The pattern was a mix of greens and pinks.

No one answered her. Josh looked up, and Zamball pointed to him.

Clearing his throat, Josh said, "Almost a week."

"And in that time you've managed to put the group in more danger. What do you have to say for yourself, Joshua Harper?"

He looked to Zamball for help, but the other three had their heads bowed.

"To be fair, joining the Pentad was never my intention. My membership is something that *you* requested."

She lifted her head slightly, her heavy earrings jangling with the movement. "I saw great potential in you—still do—but the interference of the Chaos may have set us back from our final goal. How do you think we should proceed, Joshua?"

"Well, I don't know what the final goal of the group is, but I think the Chaos is certainly something that needs to be handled as soon as possible."

"He just wants us to fight his battles for him!" Ignatius shouted.

"The Chaos is a threat to everyone—good and evil, magical and nonmagical," Josh argued. "Yes, eliminating the Chaos will help my family from having to deal with our neighbors attacking us—having to hurt our friends—but it will also ensure that all of you survive. The only way we're going to get rid of this thing forever is through cooperation."

Eleanor paused for a while before she finally turned to face them. "Lovely speech, Joshua. I do agree with you that currently the Chaos is a threat. However, I'm reluctant to eliminate it completely."

"What? Why?"

"I see potential in it as well. If, as a group, we gain control, we will be the ones who delegate who lives and who doesn't. A powerful position that will certainly bring its own risks. However, I am certain that the benefits will be far superior."

Collie looked up quizzically but didn't say anything. Nobody seemed to challenge Eleanor, and Josh didn't like it.

"Thoughts?" Eleanor asked.

"I think it's dangerous." Josh did not want to gain control of the Chaos, nor did he want to be the only one in the Pentad who didn't have control. He just wanted it gone.

"As I said, it comes with risks."

"I'm not just talking about the threat of people trying to kill us, I'm talking about the power of the Chaos itself. What do we really know about it? How do we know any one person can control it? What if only *one* person can control it? How do we keep the balance of power in a group of five?"

Collie held up her hand nervously. "I've gotta agree with

Windy. I don't know if we're ready for that much power just yet. I know I'm not. I don't want to be the weak link for the group."

Eleanor nodded. "That is true. Our newest recruit still needs to be conditioned."

"The idea is tempting, though," Ignatius said. "It'd be a shame to throw all of that power away."

Eleanor turned to Zamball. "What do you think?"

He looked to Josh briefly before turning to Eleanor. "We've all made some good points. My suggestion is we reseal it back to where it was, but guard it. We all have territories to maintain. We'll move the captured Chaos from territory to territory to keep anyone else from finding it. Then, once we're ready to take power, we use the magic of the Chaos to strengthen us. Nobody would be able to stop us. Especially if we make it out that the Chaos is gone."

"How are we supposed to keep that a secret?" Josh asked.

"You'll have to keep it from your family," Ignatius said.

Eleanor nodded. "He's right. Your first allegiance is to the Pentad. That's what you agreed to during the blue moon at your initiation. But we are also going to need the help of a white witch to cast the concealment spell. At this time, the best chance we have to get the Chaos bottled up sooner than later is to work with the Harpers."

"But Zamball said it could potentially kill them!"

Everyone looked to Zamball.

"That's only if we destroy it. Our plans have changed. Your family will be fine."

Josh's mind raced. Kathy had already lost his trust, how would he ever get it back if he kept flip-flopping? He didn't want to lie to her again.

"But the Chaos shouldn't have ever been created! It's too dangerous for anyone!"

"As right as you are, the reality is that is has been created. Now let's use it to our advantage." Eleanor glared at him. He had spoken out of line too many times at his first meeting. With the exception of Zamball, they all questioned him and his position in the Pentad. "Final vote: all in favor of sealing the Chaos away until later, raise your hand."

Everyone's hands went up except Josh's.

"Sorry, Joshua, you've been outnumbered. The decision is final. I don't want to hear anything about the subject again. Understood?"

He opened his mouth to protest but Zamball glared at him, sending a warning through his eyes. Josh shut up before he dug himself a deeper hole.

"The first step we need to take in executing this plan is to get close to the person who currently controls the Chaos," Eleanor said.

Josh looked around at the rest of the group, but they all averted their eyes. "Don't we need to figure out who it is first?"

"We know who it is," Zamball said. "It took us a while. I even had to expose my position to your former sister-in-law in Lily Dale just to confirm that it wasn't her. Plus, I needed proof that the Chaos had, in fact, been released. We had it narrowed down to two people. Holly wasn't it."

"Then who are you talking about?" Josh asked.

"You know who it is," Zamball said with a bit of an attitude that Josh didn't care for. "I told you to get close to her."

He could tell that Zamball was fearful about not following orders. "Natalie!? No! She's not even magical!" He knew she was familiar with magic—more than she let on—but that didn't mean that she *was* magical. She was certainly too inept to control something like the Chaos.

"Don't be fooled by lust, newbie." Ignatius looked him up and down.

"While you've been celebrating the return of your brother, the rest of us have been looking into Natalie Quinn, or Q, as she's called," Eleanor said. "She is definitely magical—what kind of magic she possesses remains to be seen. That's your first job."

"Good thing you're already sleeping with her," Collie added.

Josh's cheeks flushed. Had his private life ever been private? It didn't seem so. Lately, everything he did in life was dictated by someone else's decisions. He felt helpless, but he only had himself to blame for that.

"How do you expect me to get her to not only tell me that she's magical but also tell me her master plan?" There was no way his relationship would survive this. He wasn't ready to let her go. There had to be an explanation for her controlling the Chaos. He couldn't believe that she had bad intentions.

Eleanor shook her head. Her earrings jangled once more, bouncing against her neck. "You need to maintain her trust. That is crucial."

"How do you expect me to do that?"

She smiled. "You're a witch. Use your resources."

* * *

THE BLUE MOON

Holly didn't get Josh's text until the morning. Once she read it, the empty house from the night before made sense. She knew Josh would be working, and obviously Chris was gone, but Kathy was usually home before it got too late.

The benefit of not having a job meant that Holly could race down to the hospital first thing in the morning. It wasn't until she was halfway there that she realized it was Saturday. Even if she had had a job, she wouldn't need to call in.

That reminded her of money. She had just dropped three hundred dollars on her ex-husband two days ago at the mall. She would need to find something soon. The future was still a mystery, though. A week ago she'd had no intention of staying in Erie. Now, a part of her wanted to regain the life she had had. With Chris.

The night before, Holly had finished the talisman. It had been easier to construct than she remembered. Blue thread wrapped around a circular piece of vine—something she picked up from a craft store down the street. Black thread spread across the center of the circle like a spider web. The backing required a piece of metal, but the only thing Holly could find was a piece of aluminum foil. For what she had to work with, it turned out pretty well.

After she recited the proper incantation, she slung it around her neck and wore it as a necklace. It was intended for Chris, but she figured the more people she surveyed the better. There was no telling who was the betrayer among them.

Josh's text was vague. He just told her that Kathy was at the hospital and she should come. It didn't sound urgent, but it was still suspicious.

With the way the hospital complex was laid out, Holly needed to walk two blocks after she parked to get to the surgery center, so it took longer to get there than she'd thought it would. In the waiting room, she found Kathy. She was leaning on her fist drifting in and out of sleep.

Holly filled a Styrofoam cup with water before she took the seat next to her and shook her shoulder.

"Have you been here all night?"

"Oh. Hi." Kathy shifted and sat up. "Yeah. I'm not family, so they won't tell me anything. Josh was supposed to let me know if anything changes, but I haven't heard from him since I got here." She took the water Holly offered and took a sip.

"I'm sure he just got busy with work," Holly said. "What happened, anyway?"

"Josh didn't tell you?"

Holly shook her head. "Just told me to come down here."

"I stabbed Greg."

"What!" She was louder than she intended. "Why?"

"The Chaos." Kathy took another casual sip.

Holly leaned in and lowered her voice. "It possessed him?"

Nodding, Kathy said, "Just like Ray. Nobody could fight him off. Once I…did it, the Chaos just slipped out of him, and he was left with very real injuries. Whoever is possessed is the one suffering the injuries. Not the Chaos."

"Did you see anyone around? Maybe there was somebody controlling it?"

Kathy shook her head. "We were alone when it first showed up. Luckily, I got us out to the hallway before he…" She sipped her water. She had replayed the events from the night before over and over and over again. "Anyway, afterward I just wanted to get him help as soon as possible. I wasn't even thinking about the Chaos. He was…it was a mess."

Holly nodded. "Of course, yeah."

They sat in silence for a moment. Holly felt foolish for having gone to bed while Kathy was dealing with the pain of stabbing a friend. The Chaos certainly lived up to its name. Somehow, it had impacted their lives and brought about major consequences without a clue as to who was controlling it. Holly worried what circumstances Sophia was in because of it. And Chris.

"What's this?" Kathy reached for Holly's talisman and inspected it.

"Oh, I made this last night. I drew some cards, and they showed that the Chaos is being controlled by someone we trust. So, I made this to alert us to who it is."

Kathy circled the top of the Styrofoam cup with her thumb. "Do you think it's Chris?"

Holly sighed. It was as if Kathy had read her mind. "I really hope not, but I'd be lying if I said he's not the reason I made it. Is that bad?"

"No. Something has drastically changed with both of those boys. I feel like I've lost control."

"Well, I mean we're not kids anymore. Independence kind of comes with the territory."

Kathy shrugged. "Maybe that's it. I don't know. With the groups they're a part of now…it just makes me wish that I had had more of an influence. A *good* influence."

"Those boys love you. You're like a mother to them." She

shrugged. "Even if they try to explain it, you don't always know what kind of circumstances they were in when they made those decisions. Everyone makes a bad one now and then. I know I have. Just trust them."

Holly felt like a hypocrite. The talisman draped around her neck was proof that she didn't trust Chris herself.

Will flashed into Kathy's mind. She now knew what Samantha had felt like all those years ago. Only she had been worse. She had actually turned to the dark side. Josh and Chris were only trying to use the dark side for a positive outcome.

"Kathy?" A small blonde woman in blue scrubs approached them. "Hi, I'm Natalie Quinn. I'm…a friend of Josh's."

"Oh, yeah. I remember." Kathy stood to shake her hand. After spending the night in the hospital, she was sure she looked like a mess.

"Josh just wanted me to drop by to see how you were doing."

"I'm better, thanks." She tossed her thumb over her shoulder to the reception desk. "They just won't tell me anything."

"Oh, I'll see what I can do. What's his name?"

"Gregory Martin."

"I'll be right back." With a smile, Natalie wandered off through the side hallway Josh had led Kathy through before.

Holly gripped Kathy's arm and pulled her back into the chair. "I've met her before!"

"You have? Small world. I've only met her once. She seems nice, though."

The talisman around Holly's neck began to glow. Her eyes grew large and she stared at Kathy.

"What is it?" She pointed to the talisman. "What's it doing?"

"She's the one!" Holly declared. "She used to be mine and Chris's neighbor."

CHAPTER SEVENTEEN

"You want me to cast a spell on her?" Josh was incredulous. Even if he wanted to, he wouldn't be able to pull it off. Especially if Natalie *was* magical. Besides, if what the rest of the Pentad suspected was true, she had placed herself in Josh's life on purpose, which meant that she'd be on the lookout for anything suspicious.

It also meant that she didn't actually care for him. He had been just a pawn. A way to get close to her biggest enemy in Erie. He had let his guard down for someone who was just playing him. Fooled once again. He was nothing but a way to gauge the Harpers' knowledge of the Chaos. Meanwhile, she had been his escape ever since she'd started working at the hospital almost two months ago.

Josh suddenly felt sick to his stomach, and he crouched down and leaned forward, rocking on the balls of his feet. He was almost sure bile was rising up, but luckily it didn't. The last thing he needed was to give the other members of the Pentad—especially Ignatius—a reason to think he was weak.

Natalie might not be who he thought she was, but he still had a job to do. Regardless of whatever group he was aligned with, he would always strive to do what was right. If Natalie intended to let the Chaos ruin the world, then he needed to stop her. But he still couldn't do that to the only woman he loved. He needed more proof.

Eleanor's voice broke into his thoughts. But be mindful of her abilities."

Josh kept his eyes on the pavement. "And what are those? What exactly do you know about her?" His voice was weak. Defeated.

"We know she's dangerous."

He picked up his head. "I need to know more than that if you expect me to get anything out of her. I need to know what I'm up against." He stood, regaining his composure. "Clearly, my emotions are involved here. I need to know everything. What else aren't you telling me?"

"You don't know how deep this runs, Josh," Zamball said.

Eleanor put a hand up toward Zamball to stop him. "No. He has a right to know like the rest of us. Natalie Quinn is the one who kidnapped Sophia Harper."

Josh crumpled to the ground again. Although he tried to brace himself for the worst, each new piece of information was still shocking. He couldn't believe it. How could Natalie—*his* Natalie— do something like that? That wasn't the woman he knew. But then, apparently he didn't really know anything about her.

He wondered briefly if Eleanor was telling the truth. But she had no reason to lie. His allegiance to the Pentad was already forced.

"We were the ones who hired her," she continued.

Josh's eyes snapped to hers. He stood and stepped toward her, fist raised. Zamball and Ignatius blocked his path. "You did what!?"

"Your niece showed great strength. Her specialty was already developing at such a young age. Combining two powerful witch lines produced a very powerful child. We wanted to make sure that that power was contained until she could control it."

"So you *stole* her from her parents!" Zamball and Ignatius each put their hands on his chest to hold him back. The air around them began to stir, but he tried to keep it under control. It was all he could do not to lunge at Eleanor and rip out her throat.

"We had every intention of returning her just as soon as her powers were rightfully bound," Eleanor continued.

"Why didn't you talk to my brother or Holly? Shouldn't they have a say in what you do to their daughter?"

"Christopher Harper has quite the reputation for having a temper. He blows things up first and asks questions later."

She had a point.

"We couldn't risk him mistaking us for a threat."

"Then what would you call yourselves, exactly?" Josh lowered his fist.

"We were simply doing a public service."

"You were covering your bases," Josh corrected. "Making sure nobody would ever be able to stop you in the future."

"And clearly that was required." Eleanor raised her voice for the first time. "We were never able to administer the binding potion. The Fire Wizards attacked while Q was at the house. It burned to the ground. Everyone assumed Sophia was dead. So did we. It seems that the Fire Wizards were wary of the threat of her specialty as well, so they took her. *They're* the ones who kept your niece away from her family all this time. Not us."

"And yet they were the only ones with enough balls to do the job themselves." Josh wondered what Sophia's specialty was that made both covens so fearful, but it wasn't the time to ask.

"You'll understand after you've spent some time in this group that it's best to outsource some of our more dangerous operations."

"You mean keep your hands clean?"

"That's *exactly* what I mean." Her voice rose again for a moment. "Because we hired Q, your brother spent the last two years on a wild goose chase looking for her. Meanwhile, her true captors were the ones chasing him. And now, as I understand it, he is one of them. That makes him an even bigger threat to us."

"No, Sophia's true captor was you!"

"I've never laid a hand on the girl. Never even laid eyes on her. She was plucked from her home by your beloved Natalie Quinn."

Josh put up his hands and backed away from Zamball and Ignatius's blockade. "No. That's it. I'm done. I'm out. I can't be a part of a group that would sink so low as to kidnap a baby from her home. My *niece*, no less. And then you recruit me? No." He knew that wasn't a coincidence.

"Let me remind you, Joshua, that whether you cooperate or

not, you are a member of the Pentad until your death." She spoke to his back. "Despite your personal feelings toward us or our operations, your powers are forever linked with ours. We are your new coven. If you choose to fight against us, know that we will always have the upper hand in our unity. This path you're looking down doesn't end in your favor. Don't end your life prematurely."

Josh gritted his teeth. The only reason he was a part of them was because of empty promises. And he had fallen for it. Eleanor, Zamball, and the rest of the group were connected not only to his powers but also his mind. Josh had no idea how to control that telepathy yet. The only ones who could show him were members of the Pentad, but he would much rather die than aid them in any more operations. Especially knowing that they had been the ones to order Sophia's kidnapping.

Chris would never forgive him if he stayed.

But there was still a silver lining to all of this: Josh now knew who was responsible and where Sophia was. *That* was their main goal now. If Sophia was as powerful as Eleanor feared—and hopefully her powers hadn't been bound—then maybe simply her presence would be helpful enough to eliminate not only the Chaos but also the Pentad and the Fire Wizards altogether.

* * *

"What do you mean?" Kathy looked to the hallway where Natalie had just gone.

"Josh's girlfriend used to live next to me and Chris when we were married." The glow from the talisman subsided. Still, she tucked it under her shirt. "Judging from this, I don't think it's just a coincidence."

"Wait, so what does this mean?"

"The cards I drew said that someone we trusted was hiding their true intentions. I made the talisman to find out who that was. Now we know that it's Natalie. Someone Josh trusts."

"That doesn't mean her secrets have anything to do with magic." Kathy didn't want to blame anyone until they knew for sure. The accusation alone could sever any ties between them and Josh.

"Kathy, the reading was directed to our problem with the Chaos. Besides, I don't even know Natalie. Why would I be drawing cards for her unless her actions somehow effect me?"

"How do you think she's involved with the Chaos?"

"She may even be controlling it."

"Then we've gotta stop her." Kathy wondered if Josh knew. She hoped he didn't, but he had done some unexpected things lately. She couldn't be sure.

"We're going to need to come up with a good plan first, though." Holly's eyes darted to the hallway Natalie had just passed through. "We've gotta just play along for now."

Kathy nodded. "You're right. We'll need to tell Josh and Chris, though."

"How do you expect we tell Chris? He said he was going to try to check in with us once he knows something, but that might be too late. And what if he can't get away long enough?"

"Then what do you think we should do?"

Holly shook her head. "I don't know. We still need to tell Josh, though."

"How do we know he won't tell the Pentad?"

"We have to trust him. Even if he does tell them, Natalie needs to be stopped." She saw Natalie return and muttered, "Here she comes."

Natalie smiled and sat opposite Kathy. "Well, the surgery went well. Surprisingly, the knife missed major organs. He's still in recovery. It's hard to tell where he'll go from here, though. There will likely be permanent damage, but I personally think he'll be fine."

Kathy nodded. Despite her personal feelings toward Natalie in light of recent news, she felt like she wanted to hug her. Greg was going to be okay. Hopefully he wouldn't remember anything and she could make up an excuse, but she doubted that was going to happen. If she had to, she would have to tell him the truth. He was trustworthy.

"Natalie, I can't thank—"

"Kathy Walker?"

She turned and saw a man looming over her. He pulled a badge out from the inside pocket of his blue blazer and flashed it. "I'm Detective Wendel. If you have time, I'd like to ask you a few questions about last night."

Holly's jaw dropped and her heart raced. In her experience, the police had never gotten involved with anything rooted in magic. Well, besides the fire. But she'd had a solid alibi then. She really didn't know what had happened. Still didn't.

Kathy, however, had been through this before. Still, the fear of being exposed terrified her. This instance would likely turn out better for her than Vepar's death had, but it might end up in Greg's incarceration. She couldn't do that to him. *She* had been the one to hurt *him*.

"Is there a problem?" Holly asked before Kathy could answer.

"I'm just following up on a skirmish from last night. Ms. Walker, if you wouldn't mind, I'd like to speak with you."

She cleared her throat. "Uh, yeah. Sure. Did you want to step outside?"

Wendel nodded. "Sure."

They went into the breezeway between the waiting room and the parking lot. Kathy leaned against the wall away from the doors.

"So what exactly happened last night?"

Kathy took a deep breath. "Uh, Greg and I—I wrote a book. Several, actually. My new one just came out and we were doing promos—a podcast." She stuttered. Apparently she was more nervous than she thought. Talking to the police when she knew she was guilty was something she'd never get used to. "Last night we did a podcast from his hotel room."

Wendel nodded. "Right, I thought I recognized you from the paper. Congratulations, that's great."

She offered a small smile. If this ended up in the paper, the publisher would probably put an end to the rest of her marketing schedule. Maybe even reject her next book.

"How long have you known Mr. Martin?" he continued.

"Uh…since my first book was acquired. That was…five years ago?"

"And has he ever visited Erie before?"

She shook her head. "No, this is his first time. Like I said, he's been doing a couple of interviews and stuff with me. It's kind of new territory for me, and he's been a part of my career from the beginning."

"How would you describe your relationship then?"

Letting her bottom lip slip between her teeth, Kathy said, "Um, I wouldn't say we were best friends, but we were close. He's been my editor for my whole career."

"Do you have any idea why he might try to hurt you?"

She shook her head. "No. He just started out of the blue—I don't think it was completely his fault, though. He seemed off." She wanted to try to provide an alibi for him as well, but she was having a hard time. Short of a magical explanation, nothing in the nonmagical world would make sense.

"Off how? Did you suspect substance abuse of any kind?"

"No, nothing like that. He was just…not himself, I guess. But not so much that I thought I was in danger. We made it out to the hall before…"

"Was that before or after the windows in Mr. Martin's hotel room crashed in?"

Kathy's stomach lurched. She had forgotten about the windows. "Uh, that was after."

"Any idea what caused it?"

She shrugged again. "It looked like a big storm cloud. We were on one of the upper floors, so I just thought we were in the midst of it. Maybe lightning or something? I don't know."

Wendel's face was expressionless. "So the windows crashed, you went out to the hall, and then he attacked you?"

"Yeah, that sounds right."

"What were you guys talking about?"

"Oh, I don't know. The window, probably."

"So there was nothing evident that provoked him to attack you?"

Kathy bit her bottom lip. She didn't want to go this route, but she had no other choice. "Greg…had shown interest in me. Beyond a working relationship."

"He had feelings for you?" His eyebrows rose with interest.

She nodded. "I turned him down. I'm…sort of seeing someone." Whether Jeremy was technically her boyfriend was a question to wrestle with another day.

"When did you discuss that?"

"It's sort of been floating around since the last time I went to New York. Maybe a month ago? I tried to let him down gently, and I thought he took it well, but I guess he didn't."

"So that's when he became aggressive with you?"

He was testing her story.

Kathy didn't take the bait. "No, I thought he was fine with it, but…" Her hand instinctively went to her throat. It was still sore and she knew it was likely black and blue, but at this moment it was only helping her case.

Wendel nodded. "Okay. The other guests in the hotel said they heard a scuffle and came out and saw him choking you."

Kathy nodded. "Yeah."

He pointed his pen at her neck. "Are you okay?"

"As okay as I can be. I'm still kind of shaken up from it."

"Of course, yeah. So where did you get the knife?"

Kathy crossed her arms and buried her hands in her armpits. She had tried washing Greg's blood off in the bathroom, but her skin still had a pink tint to it.

"The other guests tried to pull him off me. I guess when they couldn't, one of them brought out the knife. I don't know how exactly—I was in and out for a bit—but next thing I knew, the knife was beside me and I stabbed him." Her eyes welled up, and she covered her mouth. "I'm sorry." The smell of his blood was still all over her. She needed a shower.

Wendel nodded. "Okay. That's enough for today, Ms. Walker." He pulled a business card out from his inside pocket. "One other thing that I'd like to see is the podcast you two filmed yesterday."

Kathy tilted her head to the side. "The podcast? Why?"

"Just want to gauge his demeanor with you just before the attack. Send me a link or a contact for the person who has it. If you think of anything else that could be useful, please call us. We'll be in touch if we need anything else."

When Kathy returned to Holly, Natalie was gone.

"How'd it go?" Holly asked.

"All right, I guess. I think I should be okay. Greg is probably screwed, though."

Holly rubbed Kathy's shoulder. "That's too bad. Do you think we could…?"

"No. I've been down that road. Messing with police evidence

wouldn't work. Last time we did it, my sister could erase their minds as well. None of us have that ability, and creating a spell or a potion to do so wouldn't be precise enough."

"Oh. Well, hopefully everything works out. Who is even pressing charges?"

Kathy shrugged. "No idea. How'd it go with Natalie?"

"Josh texted me. He said he has news about Natalie. He probably just found out too."

"How?" Kathy asked. Then she remembered. "Oh, the Pentad."

"Probably."

"Did he say anything else?"

Holly shook her head. "Not really. Just that he's got a plan. I guess he and Natalie are doing date night tonight: stargazing outside the city."

"That's good. Get her away from as many people as possible. But what does he plan on doing with her?" Kathy knew what Josh must be going through. The love of her life had once betrayed her as well. She wondered if she had been too hard on Josh. He needed support right now.

Holly shrugged. "I don't know. He didn't say. The way I took it, I think he's going to kill her."

Chapter Eighteen

Holly spent the rest of the day concocting a potion that she hoped would protect them from the Chaos's influence. They couldn't afford to be turning on each other if Natalie became aware that things weren't going her way. There was no telling what she would do—or what she was even capable of. Holly was certain things would get ugly. They always did.

Kathy had spent most of the day resting. The spurts of sleep she'd gotten in the waiting room of the hospital were not enough. With the eventful night they were planning, she needed as much rest as she could get.

The buzz of her phone, however, woke her. She glanced at the clock on the wall: 7 p.m. The display on her phone showed Jeremy's number.

Shit.

She had forgotten all about his work party.

"Hey, Jeremy." She sat up in bed and ran a hand through her hair. Even if she had the night free, there was no way she would be ready in time.

"I'm about to head in now. I don't know when you were expecting to show up. I just don't want to play the loser card for longer than I have to."

Kathy bit her lip and closed her eyes. The tables had turned. She was the one letting him down now.

"I'm not going to be able to make it tonight. Jeremy, I'm so sorry."

"Oh."

She could hear the disappointment in his voice. It surprised her how much it hurt. She hadn't realized how much she truly cared for him. If she had it her way, she would find a way to be at the party. But it was out of her hands.

"There's just a lot going on right now. Maybe next week we can get some coffee and I can tell you about it."

The past forty-eight hours had been so unusual. Well, unusual for her lately. Ten or twenty years ago, this would just be another Saturday.

He sighed. "Uh, sure. Yeah. Sounds good. I'll call you."

The call ended before she could say anything else, and she sat a moment longer with the phone still pressed to her ear. This put whatever possibility they had of getting back together ten steps backward. She wasn't expecting a phone call, and she couldn't blame him. Thinking back to their dinner at the diner when Jeremy had laid it all out for her, Kathy knew it had taken courage. She hadn't exactly been the most welcoming to the idea, either. Not until Greg helped her see how much she actually missed Jeremy. But promising to go to his work party and then pulling the rug out from under him just wasn't fair.

* * *

"Are we sure this is a good plan?" Holly asked. "We haven't even really talked to Josh about it yet." She was nervous about attacking someone they didn't know much about.

"We don't have a plan yet," Kathy responded. "Josh told me he was going to meet us here before Natalie showed up."

They were a half an hour outside of the city in a wooded area along a narrow country road. The driveway they had taken led to a circle at the end of the path. Several hiking trails sprouted from the circle, leading into the thick of the woods. The circle provided enough of an opening that the sky was visible. The trees blocked any light from neighboring houses or street lights. It really was a perfect place to watch the stars.

Kathy had carefully backed her car in between the trees, hoping that she could hide it from Natalie's view when she showed up. Depending on how powerful she was, she might sense the witches' presence anyway.

"How's he going to come here first? You don't start a date without bringing the girl."

Kathy cast a sidelong glance at Holly. They were waiting in the car. "Natalie probably has a late shift. Josh told her that he'd set up a picnic for them."

"How do you know?"

"He texted me, but that's all he said." She didn't like the way they had thrown this plan together. Despite trying several times to get him on the phone to talk it over, they had only received a few texts from him all day.

"So when is he supposed to show up?"

Kathy peered through her binoculars. "I would assume anytime now. That's what I'm looking for."

A ball of flame in the center of the circle pathway cast light in all directions. Holly and Kathy both shielded their eyes until the flame passed.

"Is that…?" Holly breathed the question, unwilling to raise her voice any higher.

"I don't know."

After a moment, the witches saw that it was Chris standing in the open.

Holly swung open the door and closed the distance between them quickly. "Are you okay?"

He pulled her into a hug. "I'm fine. And I have some news."

"So do we." Kathy took her turn hugging him. "How did you find us?"

"You're family. I just focused on where you were." To be honest, he'd only focused on Holly. It didn't take much effort. She was home. "Your news first."

"Josh found a way to destroy the Chaos."

"How?"

"Combining the magic of both good and evil," Kathy explained. "It's risky, though."

"Where are we going to get someone practicing black magic to help?" he asked.

"That's the risky part. The casters will likely die," Kathy said. "I told him to get a better answer, but I don't think there is one."

"Well, that leads me to my news," he said.

"Good or bad?" Holly asked.

"Both."

"Good news first." She hated feeling this overwhelmed. She needed some ray of hope.

Chris sighed. "It took some time, but I think I've managed to prove that I'm worth something to the Fire Wizards beyond whatever special reason they have for me."

Kathy crossed her arms. "What do you mean?"

"They began training me. Due to my connection with them, my powers have already grown. I can withstand simple flame, breathing smoke no longer bothers me, and I can teleport in the same fashion as them."

"That's a lot of change in twenty-four hours," Holly noted.

"It's all very basic stuff, actually. I guess our connection as a coven advances these new aspects of my specialty."

"If they didn't trust you at first, why would they train you?" Holly's distrust grew again.

"That's what I asked, but if they train me to fight like them, they can disable me easier. They'll anticipate what attacks I'm about to make. That's what they said, at least. Besides, they've been trying to drug me with a potion, which I've been dumping out. A persuasion potion, I believe. I think I do a pretty good job of keeping up appearances, though."

"Still, it sounds like you're walking on thin ice," Kathy said.

He shrugged. "It's what I have to do until I'm able to get what I want."

Holly studied him but didn't say anything. She was so confused about her feelings toward him. She knew a part of her would always love him, but how many warnings did she have to see before she gave up on him completely?

"What's the bad news?" Kathy asked.

"Well," he started, "they're about to recruit the woman who controls the Chaos. A sorcerer."

"So the Fire Wizards will control it?" It seemed too convenient to Holly.

"But that's good," Kathy said. "You're one of them now."

"They still won't tell me any details. I do have a plan, though. But you guys aren't going to like it."

Holly glared at him. "Chris, what did you do?"

A set of headlights flashed down the driveway, and the witches scattered, hiding in the trees around the circle. They all breathed a collective sigh of relief when they recognized Josh's car.

"Where is everybody?"

Slowly, Kathy, Holly, and Chris emerged from their hiding places and joined Josh in the center of the circle.

"Natalie should be on her way anytime now," Josh announced. He passed around vials. "Drink these."

"Wait, what's going on?" Chris asked. He was so wrapped up in catching up with them that he didn't have a chance to ask where they were.

"My girlfriend is apparently the one controlling the Chaos and the one—" He stopped. Chris didn't need to know that Natalie had kidnapped Sophia. Neither did Holly. Not yet at least. Natalie may be evil, but Josh didn't want to see his brother beat her to a pulp out of rage. "She's just not a good person. Not like I thought."

Kathy rubbed his shoulder.

"So what are these for?" Holly raised her vial.

"Protection. She won't be able to sense that you're here. I don't know what kind of magic she possesses, but I thought it'd be better to cover all our bases."

"I have something too." Holly raced to the car.

"You never said you had a girlfriend," Chris said.

Josh shook his head. "Not anymore. Not really ever, I guess."

Chris thought back to his first night back in Erie. He had specifically asked Josh if he had a girlfriend—more out of conversation than anything—but Josh had purposely avoided that question. What else was he hiding?

"And now she's bad?"

"I guess so." Josh wanted to tell him just how bad, but didn't.

Chris's wheels were spinning. Josh's girlfriend not being innocent didn't seem like a coincidence to him. It was deceitful. Deliberate.

"Why don't you tell me the truth?"

Josh narrowed his eyes. "What are you talking about?"

"You're jealous of the amount of power I have." Chris jabbed his finger into his brother's chest. "Always were. I've always had the flashiest power. I could blow things up and now I can control fire. You just couldn't handle that."

"Chris!" Kathy pulled on his arm, but he shrugged her off.

"You don't think I realize just what you've been up to? While you were trying to get sympathy from everyone by allegedly losing interest in magic, you were actually orchestrating everything that has gone wrong in my life."

"*I* did it all? Chris, that doesn't even make sense."

Chris stepped closer and closer, forcing Josh to move backward.

"I thought it was strange that you joined the Pentad—more so that they'd even ask you if you supposedly had lost touch with your magic—but it all makes sense now that I know your girlfriend is a big bad witch."

"I never said she was a witch."

"But you admit that you've been lying?"

"No." Josh didn't want to tell his brother the truth—that would only incriminate him more.

"You were the one who ordered Sophia to be kidnapped. And now you're hiding behind your girlfriend so she can kill us all by releasing the Chaos—all while keeping your hands clean!" Chris pushed Josh's chest.

In a flash of red light, Kathy was between them. "That's enough, Chris."

"Aunt Kathy, don't fall for his lies—"

She pointed over his shoulder. "Go!"

As Chris backed away from them, Holly pulled him aside.

"What's going on?"

Chris's hands shook. "I hate him." He turned to look at Josh and shouted. "I *hate* him!"

She pulled him back to face her. "Chris, stop. These are some big accusations. Where is this even coming from?"

He studied her. "Why aren't you more upset? That man is responsible for our pain and suffering for the last two years. And he's supposed to be family…"

Kathy approached them. "Natalie's on her way. Chris, if you're going to help, you need to put whatever you think about Josh aside. The goal tonight is to stop Natalie."

"This is all because of that asshole." He looked over her shoulder.

"You were going to tell us something before he showed up." Kathy needed to get his attention off Josh. His behavior was very strange, but she didn't have any idea what two years alone would do to someone's psyche. "You said we weren't going to like it."

"I'm going to give that bastard a taste of his own medicine. I'm going to take control of the Chaos."

"You're *what*!?" Both women echoed each other.

"Chris, no. That's crazy," Kathy said.

"How do you plan on doing that?" Josh asked. He took a cautious step closer.

Kathy glared at him but didn't have a chance to say anything.

"I have a spell," Chris said. "Thanks to you, I've had a lot of time on my hands lately."

"I never told you to abandon the family you have left." Now Josh was mad. "Maybe if you weren't such a coward, Sophia would already be home!"

"Enough! Both of you!" Kathy was overwhelmed. They didn't have a concrete plan, and yet Natalie was going to be there soon. They hadn't even studied their enemy that well. They were going in blind and she didn't like it. Not just that, but the four of them had lost their touch. They were out of sync and no longer a team. The odds were against them.

"Okay, Chris," Holly started, "why do you want to take control of the Chaos? Just forget about Josh for a moment."

"You guys said that in order to destroy the Chaos, good and evil need to cast a spell and sacrifice themselves, right?"

"As far as we know, yeah." She didn't remind him that Josh had been the one to discover that.

"What if we can harness the power of the Chaos ourselves? Raven wouldn't stand a chance against us. Everyone would bow to us. We'd have Sophia back in no time."

Kathy put up her hand. "Chris, there are major holes in your plan. We don't even really know what the Chaos is, how are we supposed to control it? Not to mention, it is not our purpose to make people bow to us. That's not why we're doing this."

"*We're* not going to control it." He poked his finger in his chest, careful to avoid the tender spots from the Fire Wizard brand. "*I* am."

Holly shook her head. "Chris, no. That is stupid. You cannot control the Chaos! You're connected to the Fire Wizards. If you get stronger, they get stronger."

"We can't just let this opportunity pass, Holly! It could help us get Sophia back. Don't you want that?"

"I do, but this isn't about getting Sophia back. You've never been able to walk away from power. You just can't let something like the Chaos go. *That* is your weakness and everyone knows it. It's going to get you killed. I just hope it doesn't get the rest of us killed in the process."

Chapter Nineteen

Holly's words had subdued Chris enough that he stopped pushing the idea of summoning the Chaos. It didn't mean he wasn't still thinking it. He figured that sometimes it was better to ask for forgiveness than to ask for permission.

The witches had scattered into hiding spots in the woods around the circle. Josh leaned against his car as he waited and tried to act casual. His nerves were growing. It was a simple plan to formulate, but the execution would be a different story. Would he be able to do just that? Could he actually execute the woman he'd once trusted most? The woman he thought he might love?

That woman didn't exist. Never had. Josh needed to let that dream go. Still, the idea that he had found somebody to share his life with was hard to ignore.

The flash of headlights down the driveway notified him that

Natalie had arrived. He repeated the spell in his mind and tried to establish the mental connection with Zamball. He still couldn't quite get the hang of it, but he knew Zamball was listening.

When Natalie stepped out of the car, she leaned up to kiss Josh, but she pulled away before their lips met. Something in his face had given him away.

"What's the matter?"

He shook his head. Despite his best efforts, all he could ask was, "Why?"

"Josh…" She backed away and saw Chris, who had stepped into view.

Ancient strengths and ancient sorrows,
to my soul, you will follow.
Leave your—

A gunshot stopped Chris from finishing the spell. Holly let out a shriek as she watched him crumple to the ground. She raced to his side. Luckily, the bullet had just gone through his shoulder. Still, his blood was pouring out of the wound. She pulled off her jacket and tied it tight around his shoulder.

"I'm impressed you caught on this quickly." Natalie lowered the gun to her side. "I thought your family was completely broken. Guess it was only fractured. Good for you."

Kathy remained hidden in the shadows behind a tree. She put her hands up to freeze Natalie, but nothing happened. The Chaos must've been protecting her from any magical influence.

From the other side of the circle, Holly charged after Natalie. The two women collided on the ground. The gun fired again, but the bullet never found its target, firing up into the trees instead. Holly wasn't able to find her footing. Natalie knew how to fight.

Kathy watched from her hiding place. Josh had raced to his brother and tried to help him stand. Despite Chris's prior allegations, he let him help. Meanwhile, Holly was taking multiple punches. Even in the dark, Kathy could see Holly's blood splattering everywhere.

In a flash, Kathy was behind Natalie. Lifting her leg, she delivered a good kick into the sorcerer's side, knocking her to the ground. Holly collapsed against the gravel. A soft moan escaped her lips.

"Natalie, don't let your thirst for power corrupt your thoughts." Kathy thought she might be able to reason with her, but she kicked Kathy to the ground instead. Natalie was not interested in talking.

* * *

Josh managed to help his brother around to the other side of his car, away from the fight. Chris's shoulder only had one impact point.

"I have to get the bullet out," Josh said.

Chris nodded and watched as his brother opened the passenger door to his car and dug through his bag. He returned with a long pair of tweezers and a bottle of alcohol.

"This is gonna hurt." Josh poured some of the alcohol on the wound and poked around with the tweezers.

Howling in pain, Chris squeezed his eyes shut tight and clenched his fists. There had only been one time during his exile that Chris had had to stitch himself up. For every bit of alcohol he'd put on the wound, he'd matched it with the same amount of liquor. This time, however, there was nothing to help numb his body.

Finally, Josh got ahold of something hard and pulled. He dropped the bloody bullet on the ground and doused his brother's shoulder with alcohol. He clamped his hand down on the wound and put pressure on it.

"Josh," Chris said through ragged breaths, "you need to perform the spell to consume the Chaos." He handed him a bloody piece of paper. "Someone in our circle needs to have control of it."

"We're not in the same coven anymore. It won't work."

Chris gripped Josh's shirt and pulled him close. "No matter what groups we've joined, nothing beats blood."

Josh hesitated. If he controlled the Chaos, what would that mean for his relationship with the Pentad? It would likely make him a stronger ally and they would need to listen to his demands for his cooperation. Sophia would be their top priority. She was the reason he was here. The reason they all were.

He nodded. "Yeah. I'll do it."

* * *

Kathy shouted in pain as Natalie pinned her against the hood of the car with her arm hanging off the side and brought her elbow down on it. An audible crunch sounded. When she backed away, Kathy crumpled to the ground.

"You witches were most surprising to me." Natalie addressed both Kathy and Holly. She stood over them. "The boys have the fire power, sure, but you two are the most resourceful. The Chaos is what leveled the playing field. I thought you two would be the biggest threats to me."

"Leave them alone!" Josh stepped into view.

Natalie spun around. "Well, baby. It's just you and me."

He shook his head. "How long? How long have you been planning this?"

"Oh, some time now. See, at first it was just a regular hit. A routine job. I had no interest in you or your family."

Josh felt the sting.

"But then the Fire Wizards interfered."

"The night you stole Sophia?"

She nodded. "They attacked and set the house on fire. I need-ed to get out of there quickly before your brother saw me. We were neighbors. He would've recognized me. I grabbed the girl and ran."

"So how did the Fire Wizards get her?"

Natalie shrugged. "They made me an offer. Better than what the Pentad offered me."

"You just handed her over like an *object*?" Josh remembered his little niece. Her innocent giggle. The way she drew all the at-tention in the room. She was special. Not a piece of property for trade.

"I only cared about my bounty. Which I'm still reaping the benefits of. I'm sure you'll remember your neighborly visit the other night."

"The Fire Wizards *gave* you access to the Chaos?"

"Not only that, but Raven showed me the best way to utilize its greatest potential. See, I was just going to use it on as many people as I could. Instill paranoia all over, have people killing themselves so I didn't have to."

Paranoia.

That explained Chris's behavior. He must've been exposed to the Chaos while he was with the Fire Wizards. That could even be where it was hidden. Had the Fire Wizards been hiding it until they found a willing host who was able to control it? How long had they been planning this?

Natalie offered a quick jab to Josh's face before he could put any more thought into it.

"The one thing I wasn't counting on was the Chaos's ability to weaken everyone's magic. I've grown to like real fights." She swung again, but Josh moved in time.

He was not a fighter by any means. Not even when he he'd been a teenager and he and Chris had chased evil more frequently. But he still needed to detain Natalie long enough to cast the spell. Once he had the Chaos himself, he could finally stop her. Maybe even save her. That was, if the Chaos was the thing corrupting her mind. He didn't want to admit that that probably wasn't the case.

She swung again and he dodged. He just needed to evade her long enough for her to get tired. Then he would cast the spell.

* * *

Holly woke with a start. Her body ached and her head throbbed. It took a minute for her vision to stop spinning and to get her bearings. Once she did, she felt like she was being watched.

Zamball hunched over her. She tried to back away, but she was already pressed up against Josh's car. Josh and Natalie's fight led them behind the vehicles, away from where Holly and Kathy lay.

She looked over and saw that Kathy was still out cold.

"I'm not going to hurt you," he said. "But I do need your help. What did Josh tell you about the Chaos?"

When she spoke, her voice was thick. She could taste her blood in her mouth. The side of her tongue was swollen from biting it. "That there is a way to destroy it."

She didn't add that she knew the spellcasters would die as a result. At this point, it didn't matter. Chris was bleeding to death, Kathy was out of commission, and Natalie was going to kill Josh if she wasn't stopped. They had already lost. It was only a matter of time.

He offered his hand. "True, but there's also a way to contain it. Seal it away once again so it can't harm anyone else."

"How?"

"I've devised a spell, but just like the spell to destroy it, I think it'd be more powerful if white and black magic work together."

"Are you sure about this?" She didn't want to trust him, but had no choice.

"The Chaos is interfering with our plans as well. Containing it is the only solution for now. I'm going against direct orders right now. This force is too powerful to be loose."

Holly looked into his eyes. They had had a long history together. She'd known Zamball most of her life. Since before she'd even known him as Zamball. He was not a good person. Even as Elliott. As much as she hated to admit it, though, he was her only hope.

She knew now what Josh and Chris both must have been going through when they'd joined their respective groups. They were out of options and hopeless.

Grasping his hand, she nodded.

He helped her stand. "Here's the spell. Blood needs to spill, but I see you've already spilled some."

Holly's right eye was swollen shut. She couldn't quite see the extent of her injuries, but she knew it wasn't good. She could feel it.

Zamball pulled a knife out from his belt loop and slid it across his arm. His red blood ran down his forearm, contrasting with his blue skin. Gently, he reached up to Holly's cheek and dabbed his thumb in her smeared blood.

"Ready?"

She nodded.

* * *

After a few minutes of parrying, Natalie had visibly slowed. Josh took advantage and swung his foot behind her knees, dropping her to the ground. He fell on top of her, pinning her arms under his knees.

211

She sneered at him. "We've been here before, haven't we?"

"Shut up." He didn't want to think about the times they'd spent together. The times he had enjoyed. The times that had been a lie. He pulled the spell from his pocket.

Ancient strengths and ancient sorrows,
to my soul, you will follow.
Leave your host, let her be.
She is now your enemy.

* * *

Zamball gripped Holly's shaking hand tightly. He pressed his thumb, slick with her blood, against the blood trickle on his arm. Through the windows of the car, Holly could see Josh sitting on top of Natalie. He seemed to be casting a spell himself. She wanted to beat him to the punch. This was hard enough for him. He had lost enough.

Holly followed Zamball's lead and recited the spell.

Magical strength and unity,
we call you now to hear our plea.
Contain the Chaos and its power.
The gifted will no longer cower.

As Holly finished the spell, she looked up and saw the purple Chaos cloud passing between Natalie and Josh. Something was wrong. What spell did Josh cast?

She tried to let go of Zamball's hand and run toward them, but he tightened his grip.

It was too late now. The spell had been cast. The next instant, Holly was thrown backward.

Josh, Natalie, Zamball, and the Chaos no longer occupied her conscious mind. Instead, her thoughts were filled with memories: Josh standing beside Chris as his best man at their wedding. The joy she'd had simply from repainting the living room in their new house. Something she and Chris could finally call theirs. The cruise they'd gone on a year after they got married when she'd discovered she was pregnant.

As she seemed to float above her body, looking down upon herself, Holly was graced with some of the best moments of her life. A part of her she would've loved to get back to.

Bliss.

Chapter Twenty

Chris's ears rang as he rolled to his side. Dust still settled when he opened his eyes. The trees surrounding the circle had all been knocked down. He didn't see where the cars were. What he saw was a small crater where the end of the driveway once had been.

He groaned as he struggled to stand. With the way he'd landed against the trunk of a fallen tree, he was lucky he hadn't broken his back. Once he was on his feet, he leaned against the debris to catch his breath.

Stepping closer to the crater, Chris slowly began to make out what had happened. Closest to him was Natalie. Her body lay twisted in an unnatural position. Her head was crushed under a large branch.

Turning his attention to the other end of the hole, Chris waited until more of the thick dust settled to see. He studied a mound across the crater. The image slowly grew clearer. Then he saw him: Josh lay facedown in the gravel.

Shouting his name, Chris sprinted as fast as he could to the other side. Turning his brother over, he felt for a pulse. Nothing.

"Josh, c'mon." He started chest compressions—as best as he could remember. By the time he came up from giving him a couple of breaths, Kathy and Holly were by his side.

"Let me try." Holly sat on Josh's other side. She waved her hands over him.

Healing spirits, hear my plea,
let this witch return to me.

She repeated the spell over and over again to no effect.

"All three of us have to try. Together." She grasped for their hands, and they recited the spell three more times. Still nothing.

Kathy crumpled to the ground beside him and reached for his limp hand. Holly ran her hand along Josh's lifeless arm. Chris lowered his head down onto Josh's chest and sobbed. The sound of his wails the only thing in the air.

Everything had gone wrong, and yet they'd achieved exactly what they'd come for: the Chaos was gone and Natalie was dead.

But so was Josh.

In the end, the very thing he'd tried to stay away from was what got him killed anyway: magic.

Chris blamed himself. He had been the one with the misplaced rage toward his brother. The Chaos had gotten into his head. Now that he was thinking clearly, he knew Josh wasn't capable of doing any of the things Chris had accused him of, but now it was too late. Josh was gone and Chris would never be able to apologize for everything he'd said. All the time he'd spent away from him. Time that had been wasted.

"He's gone." Zamball's voice snapped them all to attention. He stepped forward with a limp. "I can feel it." He had a gash at the top of his bald head. Dried blood caked with dust covered his face. "Something went wrong."

Holly rose to her feet. "You knew this was going to happen. You *wanted* this to happen! I trusted you!" She threw her fists weakly into his chest. Guilt was tearing her up. She had essentially pulled the trigger that had killed Josh.

Zamball grabbed her wrists. "I did not want this to happen. Josh joined the Pentad, therefore he became my partner. My equal. As a result of his death, myself, and the rest of the Pentad, are all weakened."

"Are you trying to get sympathy from us right now?" Kathy was disgusted. This was their loss to grieve, not his.

"No. What I'm trying to do is get you to see that this was an accident."

"What happened?" Holly demanded. "The Chaos was supposed to be concealed!"

"Josh wanted to consume the Chaos himself," Chris muttered. "I told him too." He looked down at his brother. Chris helped push him off the cliff without even meaning to.

"That must've been the spell they were casting," Zamball said.

"What are you talking about?" Kathy asked.

"The Chaos was transferring from Natalie to Josh when we cast the spell," Holly recalled.

"And with our added spell we must've overloaded the Chaos with too much power and destroyed it completely."

Holly shook her head. "Don't think you're safe just because Josh trusted you. He's dead because of you."

"I never think I'm safe. Not in this world under these circumstances. And neither should you." He lifted his finger to his ear. "At the moment, you three will have some very difficult questions to answer. Very real-world problems that neither the Pentad nor the Fire Wizards have to deal with."

Kathy strained to listen for what Zamball was talking about. A moment later, she could hear the faint sound of sirens.

Panicking, she looked to Chris. "What are we going to do?"

He shook his head. "I'm not leaving him."

"Chris, this isn't going to go away on its own," Holly warned.

"And what are we supposed to say when the three of us walk into the hospital where they both worked and ask to get stitched up without any questions? We need an alibi."

Holly turned to ask Zamball what he was going to do, but the wizard had already left. "Coward," she muttered.

"We can't just play dumb," Kathy said. "The police aren't stupid."

"Then what do you suggest?" Chris asked.

"I don't know." Kathy looked to Holly, who didn't have any answers herself.

The sound of sirens grew louder.

THE BLUE MOON
PART II: ORDER

Chapter Twenty-One

Chris watched helplessly from the back of the ambulance as two policemen lifted Josh's corpse into a black body bag. As they zipped it closed, he caught possibly the last look that he would ever see of his brother. It was witch custom to burn the bodies, but he wasn't sure if they'd be able to get his body back for a backyard funeral pyre.

The bullet hole in his shoulder received the most attention, but Chris barely noticed. He was numb. Broken. No amount of medical knowledge could put him back together. No amount of magical knowledge could, either.

His eyes remained fixated on the bag Josh was now lying in. Soon to be just another number in the Erie morgue. The coroner, the police, they didn't know what Josh was. Nobody knew who he really was. The people who cared about him and truly knew everything about him were now suspects in his mysterious death.

"Mr. Harper."

Chris was sucked back to reality. His shoulder hung in a sling just below his chest. It throbbed with pain beneath the bandage.

Slowly, Chris met the man's eyes. He wore a dark blue blazer and matching slacks. His hand was on his hip, revealing his badge that hung on his belt loop.

"I'm Detective Wendel, I need to ask you a few questions if you're feeling up to it."

Behind him, Chris could see Kathy and Holly still surrounded by the paramedics. He nodded slightly and muttered, "Sure." The sound of his own voice surprised him. Hollow. Lifeless.

The detective studied him a moment. "Well, to start with, what were you doing out here?"

Chris's mouth was thick. What *was* he doing out there? They hadn't quite straightened out their story yet. "Um, Josh—my brother—he said him and his girlfriend were going stargazing tonight, and he asked if we wanted to join."

Wendel nodded. "Could you give me a rundown of what happened tonight and who was here?"

"My, uh—" He hesitated, not sure of which direction to go. He decided to be vague unless details were pushed. "Holly and I were going to go. I guess you could call it a double date."

"And your aunt?"

"She wanted to come too."

Wendel nodded. Chris wasn't sure if he believed him. Still, the story had been started. He needed to continue.

"The three of us met Josh and Natalie here." He had to force out his name. Just the thought of it brought a lump to his throat.

Crossing his arms, Wendel took a deep breath. "And then what happened?"

Chris glared at him. Couldn't this wait? Didn't he have any time to grieve? Why did each tragedy need to be shrouded in accusation?

"I don't know what happened." Chris was angry now. "We were outside watching the stars and… I woke up and saw my brother dead." He readjusted his sling. "If you don't mind, I'd like to stop talking about this." Despite his efforts to show his rough edges, Chris could hear the tremor in his voice.

Wendel nodded again. "Of course. Thank you for your time. I'll be in touch if I have any other questions. I'm sorry for your loss."

Chris watched him leave before he rose to his feet. He just wanted to get away from all the noise. There were too many people. Too many strangers. For someone who had spent his last two years alone—to protect his family, no less—the commotion that surrounded Josh's death was too much for him to take. He needed to escape.

Setting off down the driveway, he tried to walk it off. Josh had died thinking he didn't trust him. He never knew how much Chris—

"Where are you going?" It was Holly.

"I just want to be alone."

"Yeah, well, I don't. I want you." She reached for his hand but he pulled away.

"Leave me alone." He took a step forward.

"Don't push me away again, Chris."

He stopped in his tracks. Things needed to be different. The path they had been on had gotten Sophia kidnapped and Josh killed. He couldn't lose Holly too.

He kept his head down but held out his hand. When she took it, they continued toward the road.

"It hasn't quite hit me that it's real, you know?" Holly was the first to break their silence. "I just keep thinking that I'm going to wake up and everything—"

"Holly, I don't want to talk."

She nodded and they continued without a word. By the time they met up with Kathy again, the scene was quieting down. Forensics was cleaning up, paramedics were rolling out, and only two police cars remained.

Kathy, Holly, and Chris stood in a line. They were captivated by the size of the crater from the Chaos explosion. The same thought filled their minds: Had they done the right thing? The Chaos was gone, sure, but hadn't they caused more damage—at least to themselves—than the Chaos had?

"Do you three have a ride home?" Wendel asked.

They looked at each other before Kathy answered. "No." With their cars overturned, she'd planned on teleporting them back, but the less attention they drew the better.

"I'll give you a ride."

* * *

Returning home without Josh didn't feel right. He had lived in this house his whole life. Chris had moved out just before he and Holly had married and hadn't really called it home since.

Holly helped make the first night without him bearable. It was times like these that Chris realized how much he had really missed her. How much he still needed her and would continue to for the rest of his life.

Especially now that Josh was gone. Growing up, Josh had been his best friend. His partner. The thing that haunted him the most were the insults and accusations he'd thrown at him just before the explosion. They would likely never leave his mind.

Luckily, Kathy had put in a double bed when she'd turned the old magic room into a guest bedroom, which meant nobody had to go into Josh's room just yet.

In truth, he just wanted to lie with Holly. Just like they used to. Even before Sophia had been born. When they wouldn't get out of bed on the weekends until the afternoon and spent the rest of the day lounging around the house watching Netflix and ordering a pizza.

He just couldn't be alone anymore. His world had been shattered twice before. He didn't want to go through it a third time. Couldn't.

Chris and Holly lay in bed with the lights off. The streetlight making shadows dance on the ceiling. His head rested on her shoulder. She stroked his long hair, brushing it back along the top of his head. "I've missed this."

"Yeah."

"We have to get Sophia back."

"Yeah." It was all he could manage.

"We've both lost so much from magic," she said. "It's time it starts giving back, too."

While Chris was so concerned with his own loss, he didn't think about Holly's. She had lost her entire family. Her uncle was the only one still alive. Still, it was because of magic that she never saw him. Chris at least had an aunt and, until tonight, a brother. He had had a family.

Thinking back, though, Chris had been to blame for the destruction of his family. He had been the one to give Josh the spell to summon the Chaos. He had been the one watching Sophia when she had been taken. He had been the one who hadn't developed his powers early enough to save his mother. It was all him. Whatever sadness he felt was a result of his own actions or inactions.

He felt the tears sliding down his cheek and soaking into Holly's T-shirt.

"I've messed up everything, Holly."

She looked down at him. "What are you talking about?"

"Josh is gone because of me. You even said it yourself: I'm addicted to power. I can't just let things go."

Tugging at his arm, she said, "Come here." Slowly, he shifted and lay side-by-side with her. She took his face in her hands. "In the last week you have shown me something I never thought I'd admit. Definitely not to you."

"What's that?"

"That I was wrong. I jumped to conclusions the night Sophia

was taken, and even after I apologized, I still judged you based on the man I thought you had become. Someone who would betray me and let his own quest for power lead him to do stupid things. Not the man I knew. This past week has shown me that you are a much different person than I thought you were. You're who I saw when we were fifteen and fighting Toxanna: a strong man. A powerful witch. Someone who cares a lot about his family."

He smiled. "Do you think Josh saw that too?"

"Are you kidding? He was the one trying to remind me who you were—even after you disappeared off the face of the earth. Every time I would talk to him, he would ask if I'd talked to you or if I'd forgiven you. And after each time I told him no and that I wanted nothing to do with you, he tried to remind me of all the reasons you're worth keeping around. He never stopped being your big brother. He loved you, Chris. No matter what you said to him, he never stopped seeing who you really are."

* * *

Kathy couldn't sleep. For one, she couldn't get comfortable with her makeshift cast. For another, she couldn't stop replaying the events of the night in her head. And she wasn't sure when the ringing in her ears would finally go away.

The cup of tea she made didn't do any good, even after she spiced it up with a few herbal aids to help induce sleep. Nothing seemed to be working. What she needed to do was talk about everything. Even if that was the last thing she *wanted* to do. She knew herself well enough by now.

She considered writing it all down, just to get it out, but decided that a cold notebook wouldn't be as comforting as someone to cry with. Chris and Holly were both sound asleep. Kathy peeked her head in and saw them lying together. Despite everything, it brought a smile to her face. At least something was going right. They still had a long road to go, though.

Sitting in the dark quiet kitchen with her tea, she sent a text to Jeremy asking him to come over. It was three in the morning and she didn't expect him to answer, but surprisingly, he did. Half an hour later, she heard the soft knocking at the front door.

"What's going on? Is everything okay? What happened to your arm?" He wore a pair of jeans and a white T-shirt. Glasses, too. Those were new.

Kathy pulled her bathrobe over her sling a little further. "Do you have time to talk?"

He rubbed her arm—the one without the cast. "You're scaring me, what's going on? Who hurt you?"

She turned toward the couch and motioned for him to follow. "You know how I said I had two nephews?"

Jeremy nodded. "Sure. Uh…Josh and Chris, right?"

She squinted her eyes. "How did you—"

"My dad saw Dr. Harper last year when he had a heart attack."

Kathy felt her shoulders begin to shake. She had to call the hospital, the insurance company, make arrangements for his memorial—she had so much to do. Meanwhile, Josh's patients would be without their doctor with no solid reason. Who would explain to them what had happened?

"Tell me what's going on." He reached for her free hand.

"Josh is dead."

"Oh, Kathy." He pulled her into a hug. "How? When did this happen?"

She wiped at her nose. "Tonight. It's a long story. I'm sorry I missed your party."

"Doesn't matter. What happened tonight? Is that how you broke your arm?"

Even in the darkness, she could see the worry in his eyes.

"Kathy, who hurt you?"

"The woman who did this, she's dead too."

"You should've called me! I would've been there if I had known!"

She shook her head. "It's not like that. The last few days have been…bad."

"Why?"

"I spent the other night in the hospital. I was…sort of attacked."

"By who? Are you all right?" His eyes scanned over her.

"I'm fine. It doesn't matter who did it." She knew Greg was still in the hospital. Judging by Jeremy's growing rage, mentioning him would put him in danger too, and she wasn't about to do that.

"Kathy, tell me." His voice grew louder.

"It wasn't his fault."

"The guy who attacked you and put you in the hospital wasn't responsible?"

"You don't understand!" She regretted texting him. He was angry now, and he had a right to be. Right now he was showing how much he cared for her and she wasn't being honest with him. She couldn't. Magic was the direct cause of so much loss; she couldn't bring someone else into the mix. Not if she could help it.

"Kathy, this is insane! Someone hurt you. On more than one occasion. I can't help you if you won't even tell me the truth. Who was it?"

She looked out the window onto the street. Her lips sealed shut.

"You know what? Never mind." He released her hand and stood. "I'm sorry about your nephew. I just…need to get some sleep."

Kathy reached for his hand again before he was out of reach. "Please don't go."

She looked at him with moisture in her eyes. She looked like a mess, but it didn't matter. She was desperate. Scared.

He studied her for a long time. Outside, the sound of a dog barking was the only noise. Finally, she felt his hand squeeze hers and he retook his seat.

"We'll talk tomorrow?"

She nodded and moved so she was leaning back against him. His arms around her. As they drifted to sleep, she wondered if she could ever tell him the truth.

Chapter Twenty-Two

Things were going to have to change. The events from the night before proved to Chris that the fight still wasn't over. They had work to do.

He had work to do.

The stitches in his shoulder limited his mobility, but he knew he couldn't very well walk into the Fire Wizards' camp with a sling. After one look at him they wouldn't take him seriously.

When he removed the sling, however, he could feel the stitches pulling. As soon as he returned home, he was going to have to put it back on. Just another setback.

After Holly awoke, she kissed him gently before heading off to the shower without a word. His depression was likely very evident on his face. He tried to hide it with determination, but it was obviously not working.

Her sudden absence gave him the perfect window to leave. There was no way Holly would approve of his idea. Better to tell her about it later once he got back. He considered leaving before she even woke up, but he needed to see her before he could go. If things didn't go his way…he just needed to see her.

In a swirl of flames, he was gone.

He appeared just outside of the camp. Several of the other familiar blue-robed wizards meandered throughout. Chris hadn't gotten his blue robes yet. He still had training to finish.

Raven entered a tent on the opposite side of camp. Chris circled back through the trees and entered in the rear of the tent. Luckily, she was alone.

"Where's my daughter?"

She didn't jump at all, as if she was expecting him. "How was your trip home, Mr. Harper?"

He stammered. He thought he had taken all the appropriate precautions when he'd gone back to Erie. Apparently they had been watching him closer than he thought. Then again, he had been gone longer than he'd anticipated. Spending the night hadn't been on the agenda.

"Not good," Chris finally said. "I'm done working with you. Tell me where Sophia is."

Raven finally turned and looked at him with a sneer. "You're done working with us? Please, Mr. Harper, tell me when *did* you ever work for us? You have been a prisoner and an escapee—and only briefly a trainee—since you were admitted to the coven. Need I remind you of the oath you took when you joined? The vow you took to remain loyal to us? You're one of us forever. That brand on your chest is there for a reason."

"To show your oppression."

"However I choose to get things done is irrelevant. You don't have a say. Your job is to serve the coven. I held up my end of the bargain and saved you from rotting in that desert. Don't make your betrayal my thank you."

"*My* betrayal? What about the manipulation you used to get me here in the first place?" He wanted to tell her that he knew the Fire Wizards were involved with Sophia's kidnapping, but he held his tongue.

"My manipulation put me closer to the very thing I'm after: your family." Raven kept her hands locked together, and her body was composed, while her mouth spewed venom. "Based on your lack of foresight, your brother cost the Fire Wizards two assets: Natalie Quinn and the Chaos. Don't think I'm naïve enough to believe that you, Holly Bowen, and Kathy Walker didn't have a hand in her demise. I won't be quick to give you the only leverage I hold over you."

Before Chris could offer his retort, two men entered the tent from behind him and took him by the arms. He could feel the stitches in his shoulder pulling, so he gave in.

"I guess I'll have to take more severe steps to ensure your cooperation. You're really making this worse on yourself, Mr. Harper." Raven watched smugly as the guards dragged Chris away.

The rest of the camp watched as they carried him to the cage he had twice been imprisoned in. When he was within two feet of the cage, he lifted his legs and used the iron bars to vault himself over and out of the men's grasps. The tear in his shoulder sent blood pouring down his arm. It didn't stop him from turning and running out of the camp before disappearing in a swirl of flames.

* * *

Kathy's sewing kit sat bloody on the kitchen counter. Chris had administered his own stitches before, but he never liked doing it. Still, it had to be done. There was no way he would properly heal if he kept abusing his body like this. He slipped the sling back on and cleaned up what he could. It's not like his aunt really sewed anyway.

He found Holly in Josh's room. She had an empty box and a garbage bag beside her, and was sorting through the various papers and knickknacks Josh had deposited on the top of his dresser.

"What are you doing in here?" Chris didn't dare pass the doorway. Just the entryway threatened to cripple him with sadness.

"Cleaning." She didn't look at him. He knew she must be mad. "What did Raven have to say?"

"I wasn't—" He stopped himself. Lying to her was something the old Chris would've done. Things were different now.

"Did it solve anything? Did all of our problems suddenly go away because you went there?"

"Holly…"

She pounded the top of the dresser with her fist. "Damn it, Chris! You keep going on these suicide trips and they're only making things worse. Meanwhile, we're stuck here worrying whether you're going to get yourself killed and instead…"

She brought her hand to cover her mouth as her shoulders began to shake. She moved to walk passed him, but he grabbed her with his good arm. Finding comfort in his embrace, she leaned against his chest.

"This is real, Chris. I don't think you get that. Sophia is gone. Josh is dead. Getting yourself killed will only add to our problems. Mine and Kathy's. We're the ones who will be left to pick up the pieces if you're dead. Don't do that to us."

They held each other for a long time. Both of them thinking the same thing, neither of them having to voice it. It was as if they had never spent any time apart. Both of them found comfort with familiarity, and despite everything not being as it should, there was no place either of them wanted to be more.

Chris motioned to the box. "You already started going through his stuff?"

The idea was a little morbid. Josh's body wasn't even out of the morgue yet and they were already erasing him from their lives. But he was glad somebody was doing it. Without Holly, Chris might've never stepped foot in Josh's bedroom again. Having a shrine to him wasn't healthy, either.

Holly pulled away from him and wiped her eyes. "Yeah. When I saw that you were gone, I needed something to do, and I figured I was better off going through his stuff than you or Kathy. I know how hard it must be." She remembered what she'd gone through when her dad died.

He nodded. "Yeah. All of this," he motioned to the room, "I just can't think about it right now."

They walked to the guest bedroom and sat on the bed. "So what happened this morning?"

"Nothing good. I even tore my stitches out."

Her eyes flashed to his shoulder. Once he'd come home, he had thrown his blood-soaked shirt in the trash. He hadn't had a chance to put another one on yet. Her eyes scanned his wound then snapped back to his eyes.

She gave him a look that said, *I told you so.*

"I'm done working with them, though. Even if Raven thinks that she has me."

"How are you going to do that? You're a part of the coven. Sooner or later she's going to force you to do what she wants. Besides, she hasn't taken *everything* from you. Not yet."

"Might as well have," he muttered.

She sighed. "The Fire Wizards. The Pentad. These supergroups are on the wrong side. They're going to win. They have too much united power. Too bad there wasn't a group like that fighting for white magic."

Chris's head perked up. "What if there was?"

"What do you mean?"

"I mean we should start one. We've got allies. You could talk to your uncle, see if he can get some witches from wherever he is to join."

"How are people from Australia supposed to get here?" Holly shook her head. "And why would they care?"

"Because if we don't stop these groups, who else is going to? They're only going to keep growing until they've destroyed every-thing. Somebody needs to stop them. Better yet, somebody needs to keep an eye out for any other supergroups. Put a stop to them before they get a chance to do anything."

"How do we know there will be other supergroups?"

"The Fire Wizards and the Pentad are not new groups. They've been around for years. Not to mention, just in our lifetime we've seen other alliances." He squeezed Holly's hand. "You said Toxan-na was married before she married Axon. It's the same way Will recruited Aunt Kathy to his side. They were forming groups. Power in numbers. Remember back when Aunt Kathy was released from the hospital after the Queen put her there? We couldn't get in the house because all of our enemies worked together to keep us out. We could do the same thing."

"Chris, this is dangerous, though. We can't ask people to put their lives at risk if they're not targets. That's selfish." She knew that if she had been asked to join before Sophia was kidnapped, she would've said no.

"But how do they know they won't be targets in the future? *That's* what I'm saying."

"I mean, it's a good idea—definitely something we should con-sider—but how are we going to recruit trustworthy people who are willing to put forth an honest effort to help us take down these supergroups? Especially when they're not in direct danger? I don't see what would make it worthwhile for them."

Chris rubbed his hairy chin. "I don't know yet. But we have to try. The way we're living now is not the future I want for our daughter. She should be able to take a day off instead of living in fear that the people she loves are going to die unexpectedly." He could feel the lump forming in his throat. Josh's memory surrounded him. He wanted to get out. Away from it all.

But then Holly locked her fingers between his. Despite how he felt, he wasn't alone.

She nodded. "Okay. Let's talk to your aunt and see what she thinks."

The idea seemed too far of a stretch to offer any real outcome. But they were out of options. They were down to three witches while the other groups had an endless amount of power. Forming their own supergroup might put a target on their backs, but then, the target was already there.

* * *

Greg had his own room now. That was all the information Kathy was allowed. At least he wasn't in ICU anymore. She was glad, not only for his survival but also for the relief of her guilt. Adding more stress to her life was something she couldn't take.

She debated whether or not she wanted to visit, but she needed to get out of the house. She couldn't stand to be reminded of their loss. Getting out made things feel normal. As if Josh would be home just as soon as he got out of work.

Greg was still heavily sedated when she visited. It was refreshing to hear the regular beeps from the monitor indicating his heartbeat. The easy rise and fall of his chest as he breathed.

She didn't stay long. She just needed to see with her own eyes that he was okay. That the evil that had only temporarily possessed him didn't completely ruin his life.

In the parking garage, the headlights flashed on her car after she hit the unlock button. It was a rental. The trip to the insurance company was only one of the many errands she was running to keep her mind busy.

"Ms. Walker."

The voice startled her, and she swung with her good arm. Detective Wendel caught it before she could do any damage.

"Oh. Sorry. You scared me." She readjusted her sling.

"That's actually what I tracked you down for," he said.

"To scare me?"

He smiled. "Not quite. You were attacked twice in the same week. We only know the one perpetrator. There's a possibility the two cases could be linked."

"You think he was hired by someone?"

"We don't know for sure." He indicated her sling. "Judging by the pain both attackers have caused, cooperating with the district attorney's office will help put this maniac—or two—behind bars and might even help you get some closure."

Kathy wanted to say that the two incidents were unrelated, but that would show that she knew more about the cases than she'd let on. Instead, she shook her head. "No. Greg is a friend. He needs therapy, not a criminal charge."

She could tell by Wendel's face that it wasn't the answer he was looking for. "I'd strongly advise against that. The DA is already drafting up the paperwork."

Blood drained from her face. "What?"

"He attacked you, Ms. Walker. There are witnesses and security footage to prove that. In fact, it's because of the witness testimonies that charges aren't being brought against you for putting Mr. Martin in the hospital."

"That was self-defense!" she blurted.

"I know that," he said with a nod. "Right now what's stumping everyone on the case is the motive. Now, you said he showed interest in you romantically, correct?"

She nodded. "But that's not what we were talking about at the time. It wasn't even on his mind."

"Well, that's for the court to decide. It's my understanding that once Mr. Martin is conscious enough, the DA plans on putting him under a seventy-two hour psych evaluation."

"Why?"

"If he's as harmless as you say he is, something else must be going on. It's usually just to cover some bases."

"What's going to happen to him?"

He hesitated. "Off the record? I'm thinking he'll get at least a misdemeanor. Spend some time in jail. Your cooperation plays a big part in that." He looked down at his watch. "I've gotta go. Don't do anything rash, Ms. Walker. We can offer protection if that's what you're worried about. Mr. Martin or anyone else he's associated with won't be able to hurt you."

If only that were true. If only she could be protected from

harm and still serve justice. From the outside, everything seemed so simple. Kathy was the one standing in her own way. But there was no explaining reality to Detective Wendel. She couldn't.

"No, Detective. I'll be fine."

Chapter Twenty-Three

There was so much to do to get ready for Josh's memorial. Kathy wished she had made a list of things she'd done when she'd prepared Samantha's. But that had been eleven years ago. She'd never thought she'd need to plan another one. Certainly not for her nephew.

After sending an email to the newspaper about his obituary and stopping by the hospital's main office to fill out some paperwork, she hurried home to grab something to eat. Hunger panged her stomach, and with the amount of money she'd be spending on everything for the memorial, she couldn't afford to go out. Her books had made her life comfortable, but it wasn't a bottomless pit.

"Hey guys," Kathy said when she walked into the kitchen. Chris and Holly were seated at the table.

"You were up early this morning," Chris said.

Kathy fumbled through the cupboards. She wasn't sure what she wanted. It was a little after 11:00. She poured herself a glass of water. "Yeah. I had some errands to run."

"Why don't you rest for a bit? Take a day off," Holly suggested. "I think we could all use a break." She shot a look at Chris.

"Can't. Too much to do." Kathy guzzled her water down.

"Do it tomorrow then. Both of you," she pointed to Chris and then to Kathy, "need to come to grips with Josh."

"Holly, don't…" Chris protested.

"No. Kathy, you're walking around like everything is okay when I know for a fact it isn't. And Chris, you nearly got yourself killed this morning. I can't imagine you were like this when your mom died."

The sound of glass shattering cut into her speech. Kathy's hand was bloody, but she paid it no mind. She glared Holly and said, "Don't talk about things you don't understand."

"*I* don't understand?" Holly rose from her seat. She was angry now. Leaning onto the table, she said, "My whole life has been surrounded by death. I had more misery before I was even able to drive than most people have in a lifetime. If anyone here understands what you guys are going through—or *should* be going through—it's me!"

Kathy turned and ran her hand under cold water at the sink. She was ignoring Holly, afraid of what she might say.

"So neither of you is going to say anything?"

Chris shrugged. "What do you want us to say? Sorry we're not grieving the way you think we should be?"

"You're not grieving at all!"

"It's barely been twelve hours!" he countered.

"And what have you done in the meantime? Almost jumped in the grave with him!"

Chris looked away from her. Kathy knelt down and began picking up pieces of the broken glass.

Holly knew she wasn't going to get anywhere with them—especially not by yelling at them—but she didn't want to keep it to herself, either. They needed to hear this. They needed to deal with it. She remembered when her dad had died and she'd felt so numb to everything. It wasn't until the pyre that everything had hit her. Kathy and Chris probably just needed more time. Still, their self-destructive behavior worried her.

After taking a deep breath, she said in an even tone, "Chris and I have an idea."

"What's that?" Kathy muttered from the floor behind the counter.

"Well these groups like the Fire Wizards and the Pentad got to be as powerful as they are by growing gradually. And they're likely not the only ones uniting for a common cause. We were thinking that there needs to be a supergroup of white magic. Someone to regulate these demonic supergroups and put an end to them before they get out of hand."

Kathy rose and deposited the broken pieces of glass in the trash. She struggled with only one arm, but she managed. Her appointment to get a real cast was in two days. That had been another part of her productive morning.

"We wanted to start one ourselves," Chris added quietly.

Still, Kathy's attention was on the mess.

"What do you think?" Holly prodded.

"Well…I don't think you two have done your research." Kathy picked small pieces from the palm of her hand and dropped them in the trash.

"What do you mean?" Chris asked.

"I mean, there's a balance between good and evil that needs to be maintained. Right now evil has the upper hand, which means eventually someone on our side is going to get strong enough to stop them and shift the balance back to neutral."

"Like yin and yang?" Holly remembered her Uncle Ken mentioning something about balance when he'd been studying Asian witch cultures. Based on her experiences with Toxanna, it didn't seem to hold true.

"Similar, yeah." Kathy struggled with the broom but wouldn't let Holly take it from her. "I got it."

Holly huffed and leaned against the counter. "So you're saying we shouldn't even try?"

Kathy shrugged. "Well look where trying has gotten us. A missing baby and a dead brother."

"So you mean give up?" Chris asked.

The broom slipped out of her hold and slammed into her makeshift cast. The pain made her cuss loudly. Tossing the broom to the floor, she finally met their eyes. "Well what happens when this new supergroup you want to form gets too big? What if the balance shifts out of our favor? How many people are going to die then? How many *innocent* people?" She wiped at her face. Her arm was throbbing now. She needed to take it easy.

"That's still better than not even trying!" Holly argued. "Now that we know there's a balance, we can form the group to account for that. Make it a defensive group rather than an offensive one."

"And how can you be sure you're not going to get someone who's corrupt? Someone who's going to make you trust them and then smile while they stab you in the back? Look at the Fire Wizards."

"How can you be sure of anything?" Holly asked. "I thought I knew for sure that I would be married to Chris forever. I thought for sure that I would be able to tuck my daughter in every night. I thought for sure Chris would always have a brother, Sophia an uncle." She shook her head. "Nothing is certain. That doesn't mean we stop trying."

Kathy leaned on the counter with her good arm. She didn't say anything for a long time. "And what happens if we're targeted because we're leading this group? We can't keep doing this. We were out. I thought we were safe. All of this nonsense just keeps creeping back into our lives."

"So let's create the group so we can be alerted to threats before they attack," Chris said. "If we have a group of people monitoring, we'll spread the responsibility out over a number of people. We'll all be looking out for one another, helping each other carry the weight."

Kathy sighed. "I need to think about it. I still think it's too risky.

But I do want to talk to you guys about something else." If she was going to avoid more arguments like the one she'd had in the middle of the night with Jeremy, he needed to know everything. She needed to tell him she was a witch.

"What is it?"

"I don't know if you guys even know this, but—" She didn't know where to begin. Chris and Holly hadn't even met Jeremy. Why would they trust him with their secret? Especially since the last man who had known their secret had ordered Samantha's murder.

"But...?" Chris asked.

Kathy shook her head. Asking them to trust someone they had never met was too much. Especially since she wasn't positive Jeremy would be sticking around. How would he react when he learned the woman he thought he knew had not only grown up but also been lying to him since she'd known him? Would he be okay with her being a witch? Would she be okay if he wasn't? There were bigger problems to ponder at the moment. Any potential romantic relationship she might have could wait until things with Josh had settled down.

"Never mind. I have to go attempt to take a shower with one arm."

"Wait," Holly called.

Kathy spun around.

"What about the arrangements with Josh? What's going on?"

"The funeral home is bringing his body here for the memorial. Afterward, we can do our ceremony."

* * *

With everything they needed to plan for Josh's memorial, Chris and Kathy busied themselves with preparations. Holly had taken it upon herself to clean up Josh's bedroom and sort through the old photo albums to find the best pictures to document his life.

The sadness she felt as she sorted through everything surprised her at first. Josh wasn't her nephew or her brother, but he was certainly a friend. For a time, she'd called him family. He had been someone to talk to when Chris was driving her up a wall. He and Kathy had been there for her when she'd felt the most alone. For all intents and purposes, he *was* her brother.

Josh's passing just meant another member of her family had been taken from her. Magically. She couldn't believe she had lost someone else she cared for.

Holly forced herself to keep her composure. She didn't want Chris or Kathy to see her fall apart. She knew it sounded stupid, but she felt guilty. She wasn't Josh's blood. Chris and Kathy had more of a reason to mourn him than she did. If they weren't visibly upset, why should she be?

During the memorial, not only were people offering their condolences, but just as many people were looking for gossip. How did Josh *really* die? What was going on with the investigation?

Holly tried to be the mediator for these invasive questions. Kathy and Chris didn't need to deal with it. Not today.

What surprised her, though, were how many questions she

got about the state of her relationship with Chris. She had been so consumed with trying to get her family back that she didn't think about what the rest of the world would think. From the outside, it looked like nothing had changed. Chris, Holly, and Kathy were all under the same roof again. Holly and Chris were kind of back together. They hadn't discussed it, but the neighbors expected concrete answers.

Throughout the day, Chris and Kathy were dry-eyed and, occasionally, even happy. When would they get hit with the overwhelming sadness Holly knew was coming? Chris had broken down a few times, but outside of that, he appeared to be fine. She wondered if the Chaos had had an effect on them from the explosion, but she didn't feel any differently. Not just that, but the spell *had* destroyed the Chaos. Any traces of it would be gone, too.

Everyone left after the sun had set. Silently, the three of them put away the leftover food, cleaned up plates and napkins, broke down tables. All without a word to one another.

Once everything was cleaned up, the elephant in the room was the only thing left: Josh's open casket.

"Is the pyre made?" Holly asked.

Chris nodded. "I did it this morning."

She wondered how he'd managed with only one arm but didn't say anything. She was glad it was done. Now all they needed to do was send Josh off in the traditional witch way.

"I think I'm going to call the funeral home and see if they can take him back." Kathy had her phone in her hand already.

"What? Why?" Holly asked.

Kathy shrugged. "I mean, does the pyre really make that big of a difference?"

"Yes! With the number of enemies we still have, don't think that they won't take advantage of his corpse to torment us."

Kathy rolled her eyes. "You're being overdramatic."

"At least I'm *feeling* something! You lost a loved one. Get angry, get sad, do something! Don't just sweep it under the rug as if his death didn't mean anything. Don't disrespect him like that."

Anger flared up in Kathy. "Disrespect? Forgive me for not following your set of rules, Holly."

"Carting away his body so you don't have to deal with these emotions seems like the cowardly way out," Holly said.

"Do you think it's easy for me to deal with this? He deserved to live! To fall in love, start a family, continue saving lives!" She took a deep breath. "He didn't need magic to do that. He didn't deserve this."

Holly could see Kathy begin to lose it, but she escaped upstairs instead of accepting comfort.

Chris stared at the floor, still silent.

"Josh does deserve better," Holly said. She hooked her arm around his waist and kissed his cheek. "The memorial today was beautiful. Everybody loved him. It shows what kind of life he had and the legacy he's leaving behind. But his legacy is more than what can be put in the paper. We know just how great he was."

Chris had a somber look on his face, which Holly was glad to see. Still, she knew how much of a loose cannon he could be. Especially when he was upset. She just wanted him to talk about it. Talk to her. There was a crack in the wall he put up, but still, he was shutting her out.

Later that night, Kathy leaned on Chris's shoulder as Josh's body was consumed in flame. They had cast the incantation to let his spirit rest in peace and sat silently for a long time until the flames had subsided.

"Let me check your stitches," Holly said later that night. She and Chris were getting ready for bed. The way he'd pulled them the day before, she was worried they would get infected. Kathy's sewing kit was not exactly sanitary.

After helping him pull off his shirt, she knelt behind him on the bed and ran her hands gently over the wound. From what she could tell, Chris had done a nice job. They were tight and the knots held up. His skin was still a little red, but there didn't seem to be any sign of infection.

"I think you're good." She wrapped her arms around his chest from behind him and kissed his neck.

He held her hands but didn't say anything.

"You okay?"

He shrugged. "According to you I'm not."

She pulled away from him. "That's not what I said. You're not out on the road anymore. You're home. You have a family again. Let us help you."

He rolled onto his back. "Come here."

She lay beside him and rested her head on his good shoulder.

"It's not easy, you know," he started. "My whole life I've always had a brother. A built-in best friend. We were complete opposites, but we were always there for each other."

Holly smiled. She wished she had a sibling. Growing up, there were times when she had been so lonely. She couldn't imagine what Chris was going through.

"I guess I've always been trying to make him proud. Not just him. Everyone who was responsible for me, you know? My mom, Aunt Kathy, Josh…even you sometimes."

She kissed his chest.

"After I lost my mom, that shifted more to my aunt and my brother. Now that he's gone…"

Holly felt his chest shudder. She moved to kiss his cheek and then his lips. "Just because you can't see your mom or your brother anymore doesn't mean you can't still make them proud. Show them the man you can be. I've seen it. He comes and goes now and then, but I know he's in there."

He stared at the ceiling. "How am I supposed to do that? Today people were shocked to see me. I have no life here anymore—"

"Don't say that. You have me. You have your aunt. Soon we'll have our daughter. People are going to talk. Ignore them. We need to do what makes us happy. Right now, *you* make me happy. We've lost a lot, but the war isn't over. We can still have everything we want. Sophia is waiting."

CHAPTER TWENTY-FOUR

I want to thank you for coming in again, Ms. Walker." Detective Wendel sipped his coffee from his white mug. The words "World's Best Dad" were scrawled across it in thick black letters.

Kathy felt uncomfortable sitting in the plastic chair beside his desk. The police station was crowded, but nobody seemed to be paying attention to her. Still, her back was in knots from the stress.

"Yeah, no problem."

"I read about your nephew's memorial in the paper. I heard it was very nice."

She nodded. "Thank you."

Wendel seemed to just notice his pad of questions in front of him and changed the subject. "That's actually part of the reason I called you down here. There were a couple of points that were left unclear the other day. I just wanted to get your take on them before we continue our investigation."

"Did you catch whoever did it?"

"No." He took a deep breath with the word. "Your nephew wasn't a hated man."

She shook her head. "No, he wasn't."

"Which makes us think that you were the target."

Her eyes snapped to his. "Me?"

"This was the second incident you were involved with in a matter of a few days."

"What happened with Greg Martin was completely unrelated." She had called down to the hospital. He was in the midst of the psych evaluation. It wouldn't show Greg was mentally ill, which, according to Kathy's research, meant they'd be back to square one.

Wendel flicked his pen against his pad of paper. "Okay. If you don't believe you're the target, what about your nephews? Do you know of anyone who would want to harm them?"

Kathy shook her head. "No. Everyone loved Josh, he never said anything about anyone giving him a hard time. And Chris…" How would she explain Chris's innocence? He was the one without an alibi or any character witnesses. "No, Chris doesn't really talk to a lot of people."

Detective Wendel gave her a curious look. Still, he pressed on. "Holly Bowen? What about her? Her neighbors in Lily Dale said she left rather abruptly. Is there any chance it was out of fear?"

"When Holly moved away, we fell out of touch for a while. We finally reconnected and I offered to have her move back here." Kathy shrugged. "We all keep to ourselves for the most part. Holly probably never even told her neighbors about us. To them, it seemed like she left in a hurry."

He nodded slowly and jotted down a few notes. Kathy didn't think he was buying her story. He closed his eyes and rubbed his face. He was growing tired with her and her excuses. "What about Natalie Quinn? She might've been the target that night."

"Why would you say that?"

"Well, she and your nephew both worked at the same place. It could be possible that the perp overheard them making plans for the night," he explained. "Do you happen to know if Natalie Quinn had any enemies?"

Kathy paused. She didn't really know much about Natalie, neither her cover story nor her real story. Josh would have known more about her cover story. Chris would know more about her real story. She racked her brain trying to think of some detail that would not only help Detective Wendel out but also lead him off their trail. And she needed an answer fast.

"Uh…I only met her a few times—maybe twice. Josh didn't really talk about her much. He was always busy."

Wendel nodded. "Right. Well, I can't seem to get ahold of her family, so could you tell me what you know about her? Anything at all."

She smeared her sweaty palms on her jeans. The room suddenly felt ten degrees warmer. "Well, she was a nurse at UPMC. She's pretty new. Just moved from New York, I guess. I think the Bronx maybe."

"Oh, New York City?" He scribbled on his pad.

Kathy tried to glance at what he was writing without being obvious, but she couldn't see. "Yeah, why?"

"Her records show she was from out west."

Sweat dribbled down her back. "She was?" Had she been wrong? Did this incriminate them more?

He nodded. "Yeah. It's all right. Sometimes the information just hasn't been updated. Go on."

Trying to clear her throat, Kathy asked for a cup of water. Her mouth was dry and her heart was racing, but mostly she just wanted to cool down. Her hands were clammy, her back was sweaty, and she didn't want it showing. The skin under her new cast itched badly.

Detective Wendel fetching her a cup of water gave her time to think of a better way to steer the conversation away from them. Make Josh out to be the victim. Maybe even lead the police away from her and Chris and Holly so they wouldn't have to come down here anymore. Kathy had volunteered to come down solo so that Chris and Holly wouldn't have to deal with it.

After the drink, she said, "There is one thing I feel like I should mention."

He nodded. "Sure, what is it?"

"About a week before…it happened, Josh said that on his way to his car he was stopped." She could be hurting her story further by saying this, but she had a hunch she needed to follow.

"What do you mean 'stopped'?"

"By a person. A man and—" She stopped from saying a woman. For all she knew, Zamball was the only one with a human identity.

"…And?"

She shrugged. "It was weird. It was late. He texted me after midnight to tell me he was on his way home, and the next morning he told me about the man."

"What did the man say to him? Did your nephew know who it was?"

Kathy shook her head. "I don't think he knew him. But he mentioned a first name: Elliott."

Wendel scribbled on his pad. "What did he say?"

"I don't know exactly." She tucked her hands under her legs to keep them from shaking. "Josh made it sound like this Elliott guy wanted something from him."

He raised his eyebrows. "Something like what?"

"Josh didn't say. Maybe drugs? Maybe information on a patient? I don't know."

The detective nodded. "Okay."

Okay? What exactly did that mean?

They were quiet for a moment. The sound of a phone ringing, papers shuffling, and low murmurs filled the space between them.

"We'll find who did this, Ms. Walker."

She tucked a strand of hair behind her ear and looked up. "I hope so."

"What about you?"

Her throat went dry again, but the water in her cup was gone. "What do you mean?"

"Are you sure you feel safe enough?"

"Is this because of Greg Martin?"

Wendel leaned back in his chair. "Ms. Walker, I want you to think clearly here. You know who your attacker is. Hospital or not, he still deserves to be held accountable for his crime."

Kathy closed her eyes and licked her lips, trying to think of a plausible explanation. She had done her best to keep everyone safe, but everything seemed to be slipping through her fingers.

She sighed and stared at the floor. "I just want Greg to get better and go back home. Everything will be fine after that."

He crossed his arms. "I disagree. But that's for the district attorney's office to figure out. I just want to remind you that we can protect you if he's threatening you in any way."

Kathy met his eyes. "Is that all you need, Detective?" She refused to respond to his nagging about Greg. She just needed to stall long enough until she figured out how to make it all go away. If only Samantha were still alive, she would know what to do.

Detective Wendel leaned back and studied her a moment. "Yes. I'll give you a call if I need anything else."

* * *

Chris was nervous. Some of the people he was meeting with weren't suited for civilization—too long on the run. Others he hadn't seen in well over a year. He used to be one of them. Identify with them. Share in their suffering. Now that he was back home, calling them for a favor seemed rude.

At a greasy dive bar on Twenty-Sixth Street, Chris was surrounded by three people who had never been in the same room with each other before. Each of them had connections to their own powerful covens, and each of those covens had connections to others. Whether they would work together remained to be seen, but it was a start.

This meeting was strategic. Holly was right, he needed to be smart if they were ever going to get Sophia back. The supergroups needed to be dismantled. Allying with other covens who all fought for the same thing was the first step in doing so.

To Chris's left sat Delano Shephard. His specialty was the mind, though he mostly focused on persuasion. Whether his specialty would be able to work on the combined power of the Pentad or the Fire Wizards was yet to be determined. That was, if he even agreed to help Chris form the white magic supergroup.

The other flamecaster at the table was Cyrus Graves. While he was able to ignite particles in order to create flame in the same way Chris could, his specialty focused more on increasing the temperature of a person's blood. It was deadly, no doubt, but Chris couldn't be the only one on their side with a strong fire power.

Chris wasn't completely sure what Orchid Stone's specialty was, but he was most certain about her cooperation with his proposed group. Like Chris, she had lost her family to Q. She was a single mother of three and had awoken in the middle of the night to find her children slaughtered. Just another hit for Josh's former girlfriend. The event turned Orchid into a killer. Her hand-to-hand combat was powerful and skillful and graceful all at the same time. When that wasn't an option, she had a perfect record with her pistol. That was something she never went anywhere without.

None of them were hungry, but they each ordered a drink of some sort to appear more casual. Orchid was especially uneasy. After she'd skipped town, she'd heard that the police suspected her of murdering her children. She tended to stay away from cities of any kind now.

Chris wasn't sure how to start the conversation. The bar had filled enough so the low murmur of their conversation couldn't be overheard, but he still wondered if they would've been better off meeting some place more private. He wanted the added protection of a crowd. They had helped each other out in the past, sure, but people change.

"It's been a while since I've seen each of you, so thank you all for coming," he started.

"What is this about, Harper?" Cyrus's arms were covered in tattoos, and his straggly, greasy hair hung around his face. Chris had hitched a ride with him from Milwaukee to Minneapolis almost two years ago.

"The Fire Wizards and the Pentad."

"Aren't you one of them now?" Delano asked. Chris could feel the push from his magic trying to sway his words, but he had taken the appropriate potion before coming to prepare for that.

"Yes and no."

"Tell us the truth," Orchid said. She maintained the look of a mother in the way she dressed, only with a scowl on her face instead of a smile. The sight of her in a bar with a beer in her hand was strange. But Chris knew her better than that.

"Raven, the leader of the Fire Wizards, tricked me into joining them. She hurt me, knew I'd be desperate for help, and then made promises she had no intention of keeping." Chris's hands hugged the glass bottle between them. He took a sip. "Anyway, I found out she has my daughter too—"

"I thought she died?" Orchid asked.

Chris nodded. "So did I. But Raven admitted that she's still alive."

Delano held up his hand. "How can you be sure?"

"I can't. But if there's any chance that my daughter is alive, I need to double- and triple-check to make sure before I make any rash decisions." Chris met Orchid's eyes briefly. "Anyway, after I escaped from their imprisonment, the Fire Wizards focused their attention here. Specifically on me."

"Why would you even come back here?" Cyrus asked. "Last time I saw you, you said you'd never come back to Erie. Said you'd do anything to keep the rest of your family safe." He shrugged. "How are we supposed to believe anything you say if it's obvious your words have no meaning?"

Chris looked down at his hands. Cyrus had a point. He had made that declaration before. But things had changed. How could he promise them he wouldn't change his mind about the supergroup too? Especially once he had Sophia back.

"Well, I guess you can't really believe me. But believe this: because of these supergroups, a powerful force called the Chaos was released. My family and I went to stop the person who was controlling it." His eyes flickered to Orchid, knowing Natalie had been her children's murderer. That would be a conversation for later.

"And my brother died as a result."

The three looked solemn. Despite their hard exteriors, they were all in similar situations. They all empathized with Chris, not only because they had been where he was, but because they each knew how much he cared for his family.

Chris cleared his throat. He couldn't think about Josh right now. The meeting needed to continue. They weren't leaving without making a decision.

"Turns out he was a part of the Pentad—not because he was bad, but because the members of it made him think I was dead. Once he found out I was alive, he was stuck." He looked up and scanned the table. "These groups are manipulative, powerful, and deadly. If we hadn't stopped the Chaos, there's no telling what damage could've been done without them ever getting blood on their hands."

"I don't get it," Delano said. "What do they want?"

"Power," Cyrus answered. "Why else would they release the Chaos?"

"But what were they doing with it?" Orchid asked. "Just killing random people?"

Chris shook his head. "More like infecting. Causing innocent people to act violently. My aunt was attacked by our neighbor and one of her friends."

"That still doesn't answer why they have your daughter," Delano said. "What do they want with her?"

"Leverage. For me and Holly. And even my aunt. It worked for the Pentad on Josh. Now that he's gone, they're going to use Sophia as our weak spot so they can kill us. Once we're out of the way, they can slink back into obscurity—especially the Pentad. Not many people know about them. Most people think the Fire Wizards are dormant. They're not."

"So now that the Chaos is gone, the Fire Wizards will go away," Orchid said. "Which means they'll stop hurting people."

Chris shook his head. "They'll just be out of the limelight. They'll still be working."

"So what do you have in mind?" Delano asked. Even though Chris had protected himself from having his mind invaded, his old friend had a knack for reading people.

"I think it's about time there's a supergroup for white magic. Not a vindictive, power-hungry, evil-killing supergroup, but one that regulates the power of demonic activity so that any future groups don't get as big and unstoppable as the Fire Wizards or the Pentad. Obviously, they'd be our first concern, but I think by sticking together, we have a real chance at beating them."

Silence filled the table. Chris was nervous and tightened his grip on the half-empty bottle to keep his hands from shaking.

Cyrus was the first to say something. "So what you're saying is that you want us to fight your battles for you?"

"Not *for* me. *With* me."

Delano sat back and scrunched his face. "I don't know. It sounds like it's shifting the target to us."

"Okay, you guys might be targeted. I'm not going to deny that. But these groups aren't expecting you. If we continue to meet in secret like this and come up with a plan that recruits all of our covens, then we can keep you guys in our back pocket until we're ready to strike. They'd be surprised. Once we take down the Fire Wizards, we can shift our attention to the Pentad. By then, we will hopefully have gained more followers."

Orchid shook her head. "It's suicide. They're too strong."

"They're too strong for a three-witch coven like the one I'm in. If you add my three, plus your five, Cyrus's six, and Delano's five, then we can match their power. Not to mention, everyone in our covens has different specialties. The Fire Wizards are mostly contained to fire magic."

Orchid began to shake her head. "No, Chris. We all have baggage. Sooner or later, these groups will find that and exploit them. One by one they'll pick us off."

"But we're dead in the water if we don't even try!" Chris leaned over the table. He was getting desperate. Watching his plan slip through his fingers.

"She's right," Cyrus said. "We can't defeat them. We've each had our own missions through the years. We've each worked hard to stay undercover. I know I don't want to expose that."

Delano shook his head. "No. I'm out." He stood and the other two followed suit. "I really hope you make it through. I really do."

Chris watched as they each left. Orchid lingered a moment and offered her apologies, but in the end Chris was left sitting at the table.

Alone.

CHAPTER TWENTY-FIVE

One week.

It had been one week since Josh had died. Chris had gone weeks, months, even years without seeing his brother before, but he hadn't missed him even half as much as he had in the seven days since his passing.

The permanence of it all was what struck him the most. Before, Chris had always had the option to go home. Now he knew that no matter where he went, he'd never get to see his brother again. This wave of sadness hadn't struck him since he'd mourned the loss of his mother. It wasn't ever something you got over. Just something you got used to.

Each day when the sun went down, he dreaded attempting to sleep. Even though Holly was right beside him, he was alone in his head. Nothing to distract him from the tragedy he was struck by.

Luckily, Holly picked up on this. She had stopped pestering him about his grieving process. He let her see him fall apart. After all, what other secrets did they have between one another?

It was good for him, too. He needed to lose himself. In his sadness. In Holly. Each morning he woke with more clarity and determination than he'd had in years. Holly's words rang in his head: *Show them the man you can be.*

It was what drove him now. He had been knocked down countless times, but he was still breathing. Still fighting. Still had things to work toward.

The week had not only allowed him to mourn his brother and readjust to life with a family again, but it had also given his shoulder time to heal. His full mobility still hadn't returned, although the sling was no longer necessary.

With the meeting for a white magic supergroup having failed, Chris and Holly were putting their heads together to try to come up with a new way to defeat the Fire Wizards and the Pentad. It was only a matter of time before they struck.

Kathy had a plateful of her own problems, so they tried not to worry her more than they had to. She had been in and out all week for meetings about her book, final arrangements for Josh, and wherever else she disappeared to. They decided it was best to give her space.

"Camphor!" Holly exclaimed. She was huddled over the magic book at the kitchen counter.

Chris fussed with a pot of boiling water. "What about it?" Some of the roaring water shot out of the pot, splattering his hand

and sizzling on the burner. He shook his hand at the sting. He was out of his element in the kitchen. Potions weren't his thing.

"It causes persuasion." Tapping her finger on the page, she said, "I know the potion has camphor in it." Holly was searching through *The Art of Magic* for the potion recipe she had been thinking of. Something that would help give more weight to their power.

"Yeah, because that shouldn't be hard," Chris said sarcastically.

Holly opened her mouth to retort, but the doorbell stopped her.

Turning off the burner, Chris wiped his hands on a towel. "I'll get it. You keep looking."

It was likely a neighbor stopping by to bring some sort of food dish. Mrs. Kors had been bringing over enough sweets that Chris was beginning to think she ran a bakery out of her home. It was nice to see how much the neighborhood came together to support them while they mourned Josh, but Chris had noticed a shift in the number of visitors. The first few days the doorbell seemed to be ringing every five minutes. Now, they only got one a day. It was usually Mrs. Kors, too.

Chris's jaw dropped when Orchid stared back at him. After her dismissal at the meeting, he wasn't expecting to hear back from her. Not anytime soon, at least.

"Hey." She wasn't alone. Another woman stood with her. A petite blonde with a sleeveless denim blouse and the tattoo of a snake curling up her right arm.

When Chris didn't offer an intelligent response, she added, "I thought about what you said. About standing together. You're right. It's about time we make a change." She stepped aside and the blonde stepped up. "This is Paula. She's a shapeshifter."

Chris shook her hand. "Why don't you guys come in? Holly and I were just working in the kitchen." He led them through the house and introduced them to Holly. "Orchid was one of the people I met with last week about forming our own supergroup."

"I thought that didn't go well?" Holly asked.

Orchid nodded. "I had my reservations—still do—but you can't expect change to happen if you're not willing to do anything about it. With Chris's brother being gone, I wanted to give you guys some time before I came back. But time is not on our side. As you said last week, Raven is holding your daughter over your head. Now that she knows for sure that you won't cooperate, there's no telling what she'll do." She shook her head. "I can't let anything like that happen to another child."

Holly could feel the lump forming in her throat. After the emotional week she'd had, she couldn't help it. In the short time since she'd learned Sophia was alive, this was the first person outside of her family who could help and was willing to.

She recognized the look in Orchid's eyes. The pain of a mother who had lost a child. For two years, Holly had seen it every time she'd looked in the mirror. Soon, that would change.

With Orchid's urgency, Chris didn't want to wallow in emotions longer than he had to. They made him uncomfortable. Besides, they still had work to do.

"So, Paula, you're a shapeshifter? That will be very helpful."

She nodded. "My whole family are shapeshifters. We live down in Meadville. The Chaos infected my neighbor. Long story short, my husband killed him."

"Oh, I'm so sorry." Holly remembered Ray attacking Kathy because of the Chaos. Not to mention Greg.

Three men in blue robes suddenly appeared in a swirl of flames in the kitchen. A moment later, another man appeared in a similar fashion, only he wore a khaki jacket with holes at the elbows.

Fire erupted as the four of them summoned attacks against one another. The kitchen was large, but still didn't contain enough space for eight people, half of whom were throwing flames from the palms of their hands.

Orchid and Paula dropped behind the island counter. Holly closed the magic book and joined them. Chris stood and watched, holding a fireball in his hand.

"Chris, don't provoke them!" Holly tugged at his pant leg. "Get us out of here!"

One of the men in blue robes crashed out the window, propelled by a large stream of fire. The other two moved in on the man in the jacket.

Dropping behind the safety of the counter, Chris took the book from Holly. "I need one of the banishment spells in here somewhere." He flipped through the old pages. Drew had left them with a list of the short charms and spells he'd used. Powerful magic contained in just one ancient word.

Holly pulled the book from him. "Give me it." She had been through the book so many times since she'd been back in Erie that she remembered where the spell was.

A burst of flame shot overhead, scorching the backsplash above the stove.

Paula placed her hand on Chris's arm for a second. "I'll distract them." They watched as her body morphed into Chris's. She swept her new long red hair out of her face. Racing through the kitchen, she led them out the back door, and the commotion ceased.

"That was cool." Holly smiled.

Orchid shook her head with wide eyes. "That was her only power. All she can do is dodge their attacks. Hurry, find the spell."

A minute later, the three of them were out in the backyard where the battle had moved. Paula was trapped behind a tree in the yard. The trunk had burn marks up the sides from the relentless attacks.

Wherever you have come from,
we never called to you.
Return to where you came from,
it's time to bid adieu.

The four intruders turned as Holly and the others cast the spell. Moments later, the ground opened beneath them and swallowed them up.

* * *

Kathy sat by the window at the Starbucks downtown. She cradled her coffee in her hand and let her mind wander. The static noise of the people in the background offered a reminder that she wasn't alone. Crowds were the only place she found solace now. Grief consumed her in the quiet moments of her life. Numbness slipped in. A dangerous road that she'd been down before.

Jeremy was supposed to be on his way. He had texted her and asked if she was okay. They hadn't spoken in the last week and she wanted to apologize. The morning after Josh was killed when she'd called Jeremy for comfort, Kathy had snuck out before he'd woken up. She'd purposely stayed out until later that evening to make sure he would be gone. She hadn't given him a straight answer about what had happened. He deserved one.

Looking for another excuse to leave the house, Kathy invited him to lunch. Truth be told, though, she just wanted his comfort. Jeremy was her connection to a world outside of her heartbreak. It was ironic, really. The first time they were together, she had needed an escape from him. Now, he was the escape.

By the time he arrived, her coffee had gone cold. She wasn't sure how long she had been sitting there, but her legs were stiff when she stood to hug him.

"How are you doing?" He took a seat on the bench beside her.

She shrugged. "Okay, I guess."

He grasped the fingers sticking out from under her black cast. "I'm glad you got this taken care of."

"I didn't really have a choice."

They were quiet for a moment. Neither knowing what to say. Kathy didn't even really want to talk. She just wanted to be with him. But that wasn't fair to him, because she hadn't been completely honest. Besides that, they still hadn't defined exactly what their relationship was. Did she even have a right to find comfort in his arms? He had confessed his love, but Kathy never made her feelings clear.

Finally, she cleared her throat. She kept her eyes on the street outside as she spoke. "There've been things I've wanted to tell you. About us. About me. Every time I've tried, I just couldn't bring myself to say them because of our history. Because of who I am now. Because of the way I feel about you."

He let go of her hand and leaned on the counter. Their arms just barely touched. He tried to find what she was looking at. Cars whizzed by.

"Kathy, I told you that I love you," he said. "I don't think I ever stopped. Just forgot, I guess. Seeing you on the pier brought back all the emotions and memories I had of us, and I can't help but feel ashamed of the way I treated you before."

"You've already apologized for that."

He shook his head and met her eyes. "I'm not just talking about when we were younger. I'm talking about last week. You had just lost your nephew and I got mad at you for not giving me details. As much as I'd like to think I've changed, I haven't."

She studied him. "So what are you saying?"

"I'm saying I think you should keep what you're about to say to yourself." He motioned between them. "This isn't ever going to work."

Kathy rested her mouth against her fist. Her eyes were welling up again. She thought she had found someone she could have a future with. Someone she knew she could love. But she hadn't. She was still lonely. What had she thought was going to happen with her ex-boyfriend?

She wiped away the tears from her eyes. "I want to show you something."

"Kathy…"

Turning to look at him, she tugged at his hand. "Come on. Can we go to your place?"

He shook his head. "What is this?"

"You'll see."

* * *

Jeremy gave her the short tour of his house. It was small, but he didn't need much. A spare room for his daughter when she wasn't at school or her mom's, a small backyard, and a home office. With the amount of money Kathy guessed he brought home, he certainly didn't show it. The house was nice, but it wasn't otherwise noteworthy.

When they returned to his small kitchen, he leaned on the counter and asked again what she wanted to show him.

"Can I trust you?"

"You tell me."

The corners of her mouth turned up slightly. She closed her eyes and disappeared in a flash of red light, reappearing behind him.

He jumped, staring blankly at the space where she had just been standing.

She tapped him on the shoulder from behind, and he backed against the counter. His eyes were wide with confusion.

"How did you—"

"I'm a witch," she said with a deep breath. He looked terrified, and she immediately regretted leading with magic.

"What? Kathy, I'm being serious—"

Grabbing a porcelain bowl off the counter, she tossed it in the air, put up her hands, and froze it in place.

"This is what I've been keeping from you. Not just this past week, but my whole life." She pointed to the frozen bowl. "This has been my life for as long as I can remember. Why do you think I never went to college? I had my sights set on a lifelong career as a witch."

Jeremy raised his hand to the bowl but didn't touch it. "I don't even know where to begin…"

She snatched the bowl out of the air and placed it back on the table. "Then listen: Magic is the reason my sister died so young. Magic was involved with my marriage. Magic is what got my nephew killed. I don't want magic to get you killed too."

"Kathy…"

"No, you don't understand. The people who have made us their enemies are foreign to us. We don't know much about them or how to defeat them. They're strong, too. They'll find a way to tear us down—including you. They took my nephew's daughter and have been enslaving her for two years. They have no limits."

He tapped his fingers on the counter and stared at the floor. Kathy waited while everything sank in.

"So what made you tell me?" he asked.

She shrugged and wiped more tears from her eyes. She hated being this sensitive. "Because I could love you too. Most men want something from me: power, sex, money. You just want me. That's all you've ever wanted."

"What about our history?"

"I don't care about our history. That was thirty years ago. We're two different people now. Besides, we had fun. Even through the bad years."

"That's true." He smiled. "So you're a witch, huh?"

"Yes, sir," she said with a deep breath. Her chest felt lighter. She was more relaxed, yet nervous and a little scared at the same time.

"It's definitely weird, I'll give you that. But you've always been eccentric. It's part of the reason why I was drawn to you."

She smiled and rolled her eyes.

"My one concern with all of this is that you're going to get hurt." He pointed to her arm. "You're already sporting an injury. And with everything you said that's happened to your family—"

"Jeremy, the day that we reconnected and you saw me on the pier? I had a black eye. Covered it in makeup. My being in danger is not new. I've always been in danger from one thing or another. The one good thing about magic is that I can protect myself with it."

"You're not protected from the law."

She dropped her eyes to the floor.

"I saw you coming out of the police station last week," he said. "Does that have anything to do with the two attacks?"

Closing her eyes, she nodded. When she opened them, Jeremy had his arms around her.

"It's happened before. With my ex-husband," she said. "My sister was able to help me get out of it. But this time…"

"You're still getting out of it this time."

"How can you be sure?"

"Because you're a good person. You've had your share of sadness. I think good karma will come your way sooner than later."

Kathy wanted to tell him that he should keep his distance until her good karma kicked in. Being associated with her wouldn't be safe for him.

Instead, she found herself kissing him. Giving in to the temptation she had been fighting since they'd first reunited. When she'd made up her mind to tell him, she'd told herself that she wouldn't hold back anymore. Not with Jeremy. Being with him was familiar and comfortable but also new and exciting. They were grown-up versions of the same people. Maybe timing had been the only thing wrong with their pairing before.

As they moved to the couch, all of Kathy's pent-up stress was slowly peeled away. Giving in was not a sign of her weakness. She realized that now. Giving in meant a missing piece of the puzzle had been found. She was no longer alone. Now she had a partner.

Chapter Twenty-Six

Kathy rushed in the front door. "What happened? Are you guys okay?" They had sent her a text saying that she needed to come home because they'd been attacked. It was probably not the best way to tell her with everything that had happened, but it was certainly effective.

Chris nodded. "We're fine. But the Fire Wizards *and* the Pentad attacked at the same time." They were in the kitchen cleaning up the mess from the attack.

"What did they want?"

Chris shrugged. "I don't know. We got rid of them before they could explain."

"It was weird, though," Holly added. "They seemed more interested in each other than they did us."

"Well, they're each other's enemies too. They both want power," Kathy said.

Holly chewed on her thumb. "Yeah, I guess so. But the shift of power has changed."

"What do you mean?" Chris asked.

"Well, the Fire Wizards no longer have control of the Chaos. It's gone."

"Yeah, but the Pentad has also lost a member," Kathy added. "Josh said that unless it has five members, it isn't up to full strength. So they're both weakened."

"But the Pentad has strength in magic whereas the Fire Wizards have strength in numbers," Holly explained. "So even without a fifth member, the Pentad is still powerful. And the Fire Wizards are just as strong, even though they don't have the Chaos. They're evenly matched."

"So what should we do then?" Chris asked.

Kathy crossed her arms. "We go after the Pentad. Even if what Holly said is true—about them both being down—the Pentad has a chink in its armor. It has a weakness we know about and can exploit. Besides, we have an inside man with the Fire Wizards."

"Actually…that is likely a done deal," Chris said with a cringe. "Raven pretty much cast me out of the group."

"Because of your flip-flopping?"

He nodded.

"Still, we have some inside intel that we wouldn't have had without your involvement."

Chris was surprised. Kathy had had a change of heart with his involvement with the Fire Wizards. But then, the circumstances had changed, too.

"Did Josh leave any information on the Pentad in the magic book?" Kathy asked.

Holly shook her head. "I wasn't looking for that, but I can."

Kathy nodded. "Do that. We're going to need as much information as we can get. Chris, did you have any luck putting together a group of allies?"

He stammered, shooting a look to Holly. "Uh…you said that you needed to—"

She rolled her eyes. "Come on, you and I both know you didn't let it go."

With a smirk, he nodded. "Not at first, but earlier, just before we were attacked, two people agreed to help us. They each have nice-sized covens, so we already have more people in our camp."

She nodded again. "Good. Can you trust them?"

"Absolutely. I knew them when I was out west. They're good people." He didn't mention that he had just met Paula today, but after two years with only himself to trust, he had developed a knack for reading people. Paula didn't seem to be the type to do them harm. She had a family to protect. Chris sympathized.

"We should ask them to try to get more allies to join," Holly suggested. "The more witches, the stronger we'll be."

"I agree," Kathy said. "For now, we just need numbers. After that, we can consider putting together a group to moderate like you suggested."

Chris smiled. "So you agree with me?"

"I'm just tired of always looking over my shoulder and still getting knocked down," she said.

"We'll get there."

Kathy hesitated. She needed to tell them about Jeremy. Should've asked them before she'd told him her secret. Their secret. The one that could get all of them in trouble if he decided to tell anyone about it.

Although things were different now between her and Jeremy, Chris and Holly still didn't know him. How were they supposed to trust him with their secret?

Still, she had to tell them. She had made a decision for them without even running it by them first. The least she could do was tell them now before they found out later.

"Do you guys remember that thing I was going to tell you last week?"

"Sure," Chris said.

Kathy tucked some of her hair behind her ear. "I sort of reconnected with an old boyfriend. Someone I used to date when I was younger. Younger than you guys are now."

Chris shrugged. "Okay, so is he your new boyfriend?"

Holly smacked his arm and gave him a look. She turned back to Kathy. "That's great. It definitely helps to have someone—especially now."

Nodding, Kathy said, "Yeah, it is. Um, but that's not it. Well, not completely."

"What is it then?" he asked.

"Today I told Jeremy I was a witch." She looked up and met their eyes before quickly dropping them again. "Which means he knows that you guys are witches too."

"Oh," Holly said.

"Yeah." She felt like a little kid who had just gotten in trouble. "I'm sorry. I should've talked to you guys about it before I told him. I wanted to, but it was right after Josh and it never seemed like the right moment. I just—Jeremy thought I was lying to him about why I couldn't see him. He didn't accept the fact that I couldn't tell him what was going on. How I broke my arm, why I'm not pressing charges against Greg. I just needed to simplify my life a bit."

Chris and Holly were quiet. For a long time, no one said anything. The silence was eating Kathy up. She just wanted things to be normal. Well, comfortable. She already had enough on her plate with everything with her books, and her whole writing schedule had been thrown out the window within the last few weeks. She had lost control of everything in her life and she hated it.

"Do you trust him?" Chris broke the silence.

Kathy nodded. "Yeah, I do."

"Good." Chris reached for Holly's hand. "Then we trust him too."

She smiled and pulled them both into a hug. "That's good. I'm glad. As soon as things have calmed down, I'm going to invite him over so you guys can meet him." She pulled away. "I'm going to go call him." Turning on her heel, she raced up the stairs.

"I think we're all tired of living this life," Holly said to Chris.

"Yeah. But we're not done yet." He wrapped his arm around her and kissed her head.

"No. We have a daughter to bring home."

"We'll get her back. Soon. Orchid and Paula and the rest of the allies we recruit will help us."

Holly gave him a sad smile. "I'm worried—scared, really. We've made a move and pissed them off. Now we're trying to back off while we regroup and I'm afraid something is going to happen to Sophia."

He brought her hand to his lips and kissed the back of it. "Don't think like that. She'll be fine." He had to believe that for his own sanity.

"How can I not? Raven told you that you're out. Just like that, we just lost our only connection to her! They could do whatever they want with her."

Chris never told Holly how Raven had threatened to take more severe steps to get him to cooperate. She didn't need to hear that. She was already beating herself up enough. They would get Sophia back before Raven could do anything to her. He just didn't know how they were going to do that in such a tight time frame. They needed more people and a plan, which would take time. Time they didn't have.

"No. I'm going to go back to the Fire Wizards—"

"Chris, you can't do that. You just got home. Don't give in to their demands."

"What other choice do I have? She has our daughter! I've always said that I would die for her. Now it's time I follow through with that." He stepped toward the door.

She tugged on his arm. "Don't! Think of another way. You know the camp. Isn't there a way to find her without giving your-self up?"

He shook his head. "I'm not a shapeshifter, Holly. If they see me, I'm dead. I've already told them to go to hell. Raven's not going to give up Sophia." He didn't want to risk using Paula's shapeshifting abilities, either. Even if she could get to the camp, the rest of the coven would sense she wasn't one of them.

"Then what good is going to come from you going back there? I want nothing more than to have our family back, but don't make me choose between you and Sophia—"

"I'm not."

"So give me both."

"I don't know how, Holly! I can't guarantee that everything is going to work out how we want it. Look at Josh. I thought he'd be able to see his niece again."

Holly shook her head. "We need a different approach. The Fire Wizards have to have a weakness."

"Maybe it's Raven. I don't know."

"So let's take her out."

"Even if she is the key to taking down the coven, how am I supposed to get around her bodyguards? And even if I could, I can't defeat her. Her magic is more advanced than mine is."

"Didn't she train you?"

"For what? Two days? I learned how to teleport. That was about it."

Holly ran her hands through her hair and collected it to one side. "Maybe the best way to approach this isn't getting stronger, maybe it's just relying on our instincts."

"What do you mean?"

"When was the last time you blew something up?"

Chris shrugged. "I don't know."

"Exactly! Your powers have grown so much that you forget you're even able to do it."

"Holly, you're not making any sense."

She grabbed his hands to get his attention. "We need to go back to basics. Maybe magic isn't the solution. Instead of taking down the Fire Wizards to draw out Sophia's whereabouts, why don't you find her without using your magic at all? I mean, you'll have to use it to go to the camp, but once you're there, rely on your instincts. Listen in on conversations. Look for signs of a four-year-old. Find Sophia and bring her back home. Once we have her, then we can worry about taking down the Fire Wizards and the Pentad. By then, we'll have more people on our side."

Chris sighed. He liked her plan, but it was risky. He could get caught, tortured, killed. But the risk was worth it. Sophia had been gone long enough. There was no telling what she had gone through. She must look so different now. Would she even recognize him? It didn't matter. She belonged with them. Not Raven.

"Okay. I'll go. But there's something I need to do before I leave."

"Chris, I can tell Orchid and Paula to try to recruit more people. You need to go."

He lifted her hands and kissed the back of each of them. His fingers traced over the finger that had once held her wedding ring. "This will only take a second." He went down on his knee. "I know I don't have a ring—"

She pulled her hand away. "Stop," she said with a giggle.

He looked up at her, confused. "What?"

"Stand up."

When he was back on his feet, she took his face between her hands and said, "I love you, but this is way too fast."

He interlocked his fingers with hers. "I don't know if you realize this, but we've kind of been married before."

"I'm not saying I don't want to ever remarry you. I'm just saying that we need to get things back to normal before we make that kind of decision."

He scrunched his face. "Um…normal?"

"Well, our version. Let's get Sophia back. Get *jobs* again. Be a little more self-sufficient and pick up where we left off two years ago. Once we've had a taste of reality, then we can talk marriage."

Smiling, he said, "Okay. That makes sense."

"But I do want you to promise me something."

"What's that?"

"Bring our daughter home."

He squeezed her hands. "I'll do my best."

She held up her pinkie.

Wrapping his finger around hers, he said, "Promise."

Holly smiled once again. "You better."

He returned her smile and let out a laugh when she squeezed his face and smothered him with kisses. It was another glimpse of the life they had shared. The happiness they had once had. Soon, hopefully, they would have that life again.

Chris just needed to be willing to die for it.

Chapter Twenty-Seven

Whatever relief Kathy had felt from telling Jeremy the truth was gone the next morning. Not only was it another morning without Josh, but it was also a morning without Chris.

The night before, he'd told her about his aggressive plan to get Sophia back—yet another in their long list of attempts. Reluctantly, she'd let him go. He didn't really need her approval anyway. He was an adult. He was the parent now. Kathy wasn't anymore.

Just as she poured her first cup of coffee, her phone began to buzz beside the newspaper on the counter. The number wasn't programmed in, but she still recognized it.

"Hi, Detective Wendel."

"Good morning, Ms. Walker. I hope I didn't call too soon."

She decided to leave out the part that she had just gotten out of bed. It was almost 9 a.m. on a weekday. "No, you're okay. What's up? Do you have more questions?"

"No, we actually have some security footage from the hospital parking garage that we think may be of the perpetrator."

Kathy's hand began to shake, and she set the mug on the counter. "You do?"

"Well, we think so. We were hoping you could come down with your nephew and Ms. Bowen to help determine whether we have the right guy."

She tried to recount what evidence the police could go on. Josh's and Natalie's bodies didn't have any bullet holes. They likely had broken bones, but that could've been from the impact after the explosion. Forensics would've likely been able to determine that.

Kathy was far from a CSI detective, but based on the size of the crater, they were probably looking at the possibility of a bomb. The gunshot Natalie fired at Chris wouldn't be linked to them. If anything, it would be linked to whoever the gun was registered to. If it looked like the gunman had instigated the attack, maybe the whole case would go away for them. That seemed too good to be true, but Kathy still wondered if they had pinned the wrong person.

"Do you think the three of you will be able to come in?"

"Uh…today? Can it wait a few days?"

"Today would be best. The sooner we can identify the perpetrator, the sooner we can book him."

Kathy nodded. "Right. Okay, well I don't think it's going to be today. I have a ton of things to do, and I don't even know what Chris and Holly have planned. But I'll try to round them up by this weekend at the latest."

She knew it was a lousy excuse, but she needed to buy herself time to figure out a Plan B if things didn't go their way.

"Ms. Walker, the longer we wait on this case, the longer he's out there to hurt more people. I've got men trying to track him down, but in the meantime I'd like to know if we're even chasing the right guy."

"We can't come in today," she said a little more forcefully.

He sighed heavily into the phone. "Okay. Give me a call when it'll be more convenient. Thank you, Ms. Walker."

Kathy felt horrible for lying to him. He was only trying to help, and it looked like she didn't care.

She picked up her coffee again and stared out the window—which had magically reformed after the attack from the two supergroups. Perks of the house absorbing their magic through the years.

There was no telling how long Chris would be gone or whether he'd even come back. If he never came back, Wendel would begin to suspect foul play. Two brothers die within a few weeks of each other? Even Kathy had to admit that that would sound strange. And she was used to strange.

"What was that about?" Holly bounded down the stairs.

"Oh, the detective working on our case wants us to come down to the station to identify a potential perpetrator."

Holly raised her eyebrows. "They got Zamball?" She knew they couldn't. He wouldn't change back to his alias without a proper reason, and he definitely wouldn't sit in a jail cell for long.

"No, just a camera still. Whomever it's of, though, whether he's a criminal or not, it's not fair for him to be punished for a crime he didn't commit."

Holly shook her head.

"We have to think of another way out of this," Kathy added.

"Maybe we can bargain with Zamball. Get him to play along long enough to be sent to prison, and then once he's there he'll break out and the case will be focused on his alias and not us. Or him."

"There are a *lot* of 'ifs' in that theory. Even if we could get Zamball to help us, there's nothing that would ensure his cooperation. Besides, we have nothing to offer him. And I don't want to work with him again."

"You're right. But that's the best I've got. How's the case going otherwise?" Holly asked. "Do you think they suspect us?"

"Not that I can tell. But that might change if Chris doesn't come home soon enough. I told the detective all three of us would be down at the station this weekend."

Holly's eyes grew wide. "What happens if Chris isn't back by then?" She didn't know the details of the Fire Wizards, but she feared that if Chris wasn't back by the weekend, he wouldn't be coming back at all. Not with the way he had left things with them.

Kathy shrugged. "I don't know. But while we wait for him and fend off Detective Wendel, we need to make sure this war going on between the Fire Wizards and the Pentad doesn't kill anyone. Have there been any other disturbances?"

Holly shook her head. "I don't think so, but I'll double-check."

"Good. Keep on that. I'll try to keep Wendel pacified until we hear from Chris."

"Okay." The distraction would be good for her, but surveillance didn't seem like she was doing enough. She had already contacted Orchid and Paula earlier that morning to try to get their help recruiting new people. But at this point all she could do was sit and wait.

And worry.

She wanted to talk about the conversation she'd had with Chris the night before. Wanted to acknowledge it and share their renewed union. But not only did they have bigger things to worry about, she couldn't give Kathy a sense of hope. Not if Chris never came back. It was best if she kept that to herself. Maybe if nobody knew about it, and if he never came home, it would help Holly forget that they had ever talked about remarrying.

* * *

Chris knew that if he spent the night with Holly, he wouldn't leave in the morning. And he had to leave. Not only to get Sophia back but also to show Raven and the rest of the Fire Wizards—even the Pentad and whatever other group that thought they could threaten him or his family—that he would not back down. If the white magic supergroup was going to be successful, it needed to be feared. It needed to showcase the extent of its power.

This was just the first test.

Knowing there would be scouts out, he spent the night a half a mile away from the Fire Wizards' camp. That way he wouldn't be seen, but he was still close enough to hear if anything big happened.

THE BLUE MOON

Earlier that morning, he caught one of the scouts sleeping and was able to sneak up on him. Luckily, he didn't get any blood on his robe. That was an essential part to Chris's plan. He couldn't mosey around and listen in on conversations without some sort of a disguise.

Prior to leaving his house, he raided the kitchen for any potions that might help him. He stuffed them in a satchel he wore at his waist. The glass from the vials clinked together when he walked. That was stifled once he donned the traditional coven robe.

The potion he needed most was fortunately one that they had on hand. It subdued the presence of his magic to anyone advanced enough to sense it. If he stuck to a moderate-sized crowd, he could go undetected.

However, the fear that the Fire Wizards' camp was too small still crept into his mind. For the most part, everyone knew everyone else. They would recognize an outsider.

As he approached, he heard Raven's distinctive voice. She stood in the center of camp in front of the fire that always burned blue. The whole camp seemed to congregate around her.

Still, there was no sight of Sophia.

"...threat is the Pentad. While the ancient coven has had its share of members through the years—even dabbling into white magic as of late—it has also made its weaknesses known. The destruction of the Chaos has set us back. However, it may have crippled the Pentad forever. *Now* is the time to strike! If we can kill all the members before the next harvest moon, there will be no more Pentad. And *that* is the legacy we want to leave!"

Chris dropped his head down. Raven's speech drew his attention and made him let down his guard. If someone recognized him as the prisoner they'd recently had—or the person whose house they'd just broken into—he would be dead before he could do anything.

"I'm sure you've all heard the screams of the little girl," Raven continued.

There were groans and complaints throughout the crowd. Chris had to fight the urge to look up at Raven.

"As I've said before, she's a part of our mission. It's time we use her to our advantage."

"The brat won't shut up!" someone called from behind him.

Raven sneered. "While it is true that the Harper girl has been less than cooperative, she does have value. The power she wields is more than any of us could imagine. If we are to fulfill our rightful destiny, we must withdraw our hesitations and annoyances. We all knew the challenges of kidnapping a girl so young. It was a sacrifice worth making for the end goal. She will lead to the destruction of her family, which, if done correctly, will grant our coven the powers of *all* the Harper witches. We will be a force that the Pentad cannot compete with."

Chris balled up his fists until his fingernails nearly made his palms bleed. Raven was directly responsible for the destruction of his family. She was going to pay.

The sound of a child's screams drew Chris's attention. He meandered through the crowd and walked along the outside of the tents, just outside of camp until he drew closer to the sound.

THE BLUE MOON

This was his chance. The entire Fire Wizard coven was distracted by Raven's speech. He could grab Sophia and run someplace safe. The Fire Wizards would no doubt be on his tail, but he could outrun them. He'd done it before.

Still, he'd have to get a message to Holly and Kathy to figure out a way to defeat them while he kept Sophia safe. He couldn't resume the life he'd had on the road. He couldn't skip meals and spend hours traveling. A four-year-old couldn't handle that.

Chris stood outside of a nondescript white tent. Sophia's wails came from inside. He was sure it was her. Even though her age had doubled since he'd last heard her, he could recognize his own daughter's cry.

Chancing a look around the tent, he saw the crowd still fixated on Raven. Her speech was long and emphatic, and the crowd seemed to be fired up from it.

It was now or never. Just as he reached for the canvas flap, he heard a man's voice shout from behind him.

"Where do you think you're going, witch?"

Chris froze, which crucified him. His return home had killed the instincts he'd learned on the road. He should've turned and said that he wanted to shut the kid up so he could hear Raven. Should've acted like any other member of the Fire Wizards would.

The guard pulled back Chris's hood and pushed him to the ground. Chris's face was pushed into the dirt. His arms were bent at an odd angle behind his back.

He felt the restraints clamp on to his wrists, and he awaited the public execution that was sure to follow. The crowd was already there. Already riled up.

Strangely, Chris's hood was lifted once again and he was brought to his feet. The guard began leading him away from the camp at a pace that suggested he didn't want to be followed—or seen.

Chapter Twenty-Eight

Chris had a hard time keeping up with the swift pace of the guard, who must've been much taller than him. He hadn't gotten a good look before he was dragged away like a rag doll.

They walked farther than he expected. Past the spot where he had spent the night before and into the thick of the woods. By the time they stopped, Chris was tired and ready for a break from the quick march.

The guard pushed him to the ground and pulled back his hood.

"If you just wanted to kill me, why didn't you do it back at camp?" Chris asked, breathless.

"I'm not going to kill you." The guard was a tall, burly man with white-blond hair and a round face. His neck had burn marks on it. Apparently it was a common injury among the Fire Wizards.

"Then what do you want?"

"You've been busy since we last saw you."

Chris narrowed his eyes. This guy had something to say. It would come out eventually.

"What's your name?"

"Warren." He crossed his arms and stood intimidatingly over Chris. "I'm sorry to hear about your brother. Despite Raven's brash demeanor, Josh's death was not our intention. As you heard, she plans to use that to our advantage. The nimble ones are the successful ones."

"And you're one of the people she holds counsel with?"

Warren chuckled. "Raven doesn't hold counsel with anyone. No, I'm in charge of one of her infantries. I'm among the first to hear what she has in store."

"And what is that?"

"You've heard everything I know."

"Then what are we doing here?"

Warren studied him. "I heard you wanted to start a supergroup yourself. Something that could regulate groups like the Fire Wizards."

Chris froze. If Raven or any of the Pentad caught word of his plan, it'd be dead before it started.

Clearly, he'd put too much trust in someone with loose lips. Maybe Cyrus? He didn't think Orchid would say anything to anyone who might be connected with the Fire Wizards. And he didn't really know Paula, but Orchid trusted her and he trusted Orchid. Delano didn't have any connections to the Fire Wizards or the Pentad, so he was out too. It must've been Cyrus then.

"Don't look so nervous. I didn't say anything. At the moment, I'm the only one among the wizards who knows about it. Well, technically you too. But you're an outcast."

Chris glared at him. "So what do you want?"

"I want in. I want to help."

"Really?" Chris was skeptical. "Why would you want to help us?"

"The Fire Wizards are not the same coven we once were. Not since Raven. You're not the only one who has joined under false pretenses. Usually after some time in a jail cell—"

"*Cage.*"

"Whatever. Eventually, they come around to follow her like an obedient dog. It's part of her process. That was, until you."

Chris stifled a smile. "Why would you risk your high rank among the wizards to join some grassroots effort? What's in it for you?"

Warren squatted in front of him. "About ten years ago, the Fire Wizards changed. Raven took over. Turned the coven into a dictatorship. Whoever didn't follow was killed. My apprentice at the time was a young wizard I believe you knew very well. Or, your ex-wife did."

"Drew?"

Warren studied the ground. "He didn't agree with the way Raven wanted to do things. And like a fool, he spoke up." He closed his eyes tight. "The things I did to him to keep *me* alive…I've never forgiven myself."

Chris was speechless. He had a newfound respect for Drew as

well as a deeper hatred for Raven. Ten years ago was when Chris had known Drew. They had been teenagers. How could she condone doing something to a kid? Worse, what did that mean for Sophia?

"Anyway, I've played her game since then for my own survival. For a long time, I thought I was the only one who didn't agree with Raven's reign. Then I began hearing murmurs among my infantry as well as others. People want change. They want out of an oppressive coven."

"And why would they want to join a group of white magic practitioners?"

"Think what you will, but the Fire Wizards are not demonic. Raven is. Even she doesn't prefer to kill people—especially innocent people who don't have magic. It's always a last resort."

"Tell that to my brother."

"It was never the intention of the Fire Wizards for either of them to die. Natalie Quinn went rogue."

"Then how do you explain infecting innocent people with the Chaos and turning them into murderers?"

"That was also Q."

"Sounds like you're placing a lot of blame on everyone but yourself."

Warren gripped Chris's chin in his hand and squeezed. "I'm not the one calling the shots! I know what I've done and I'm trying to correct it!" He let go of him and cleared his throat. "Whatever arrangement we work out in the end doesn't matter. Your goal is to take down the Fire Wizards, no?"

"First I want my daughter back."

"I may be able to help you with that. But you still intend to eliminate the wizards, correct?"

Chris glared at Warren. He was suspicious of his claims. It seemed too good to be true. Not to mention, he assumed Warren had a hidden agenda. He didn't want to set himself up to be stabbed in the back.

"I'll take that as a yes. Between me and my soldiers, we can devise a plan to crack the Fire Wizards from the inside."

"And if I don't agree to work with you?"

"You'll have no chance of getting your daughter back. I'll deliver you straight to Raven myself."

Chris's chest puffed and he could feel his face flush with anger. Warren could be leading him right into a trap. Just like Raven had. Yet again, there was no other option.

"Sophia's safety needs to be guaranteed."

Warren smirked. "As long as we agree that I get to work with you, I can promise you that you'll have your daughter back by tonight."

Chris sank back onto the ground. No matter how much he distrusted Warren, he couldn't pass up the opportunity. It had been so long since Sophia had been taken from him. For a long time, she had been dead to him. The thought of seeing her again, holding her, raising her to be the woman she could be—none of that had seemed possible. But now it was. Holly would be ecstatic.

"So, do we have a deal?" The wizard offered his hand, but

drew it back when he realized Chris was still bound.

Instead, Chris nodded. "Sure, it's a deal."

* * *

Between herself, Chris, and Kathy, Holly felt like she didn't have enough to do. Chris had taken a huge risk returning to the Fire Wizards' camp to rescue Sophia—which she had asked him to do—and Kathy was handling the brunt of the police investigation the three of them were faced with. It made the two phone calls Holly had made earlier seem insignificant.

She had resorted to placing protection spells and charms throughout the house. The magic book was filled with them. Even if they didn't all work against covens as strong as the two they were facing, it was something. Definitely would keep her busy for the day as well as help with peace of mind.

The inside was thoroughly cloaked. There was so much incense throughout the house that Holly was glad to get outside to work on the house's exterior. She needed the fresh air.

"You're wasting your time, you know."

Holly spun around at the sound of Zamball's voice.

"These protection spells only cloak the house to folks like me if the house hadn't already been discovered." He stood several feet away from Holly with his arms stiffly behind his back. "It may protect you from future threats, but for the people I'm assuming you're trying to keep out at the present moment, it's not going to work."

Holly dropped the talismans on the ground. "What are you doing here?"

"Can't I just pay a visit to an old friend?"

"Answer the question. What do you want?"

He smirked, which made her skin crawl. "Leverage." In a series of swift moves, he lunged at her. As soon as their skin touched, each of them erupted into puddles of water that trickled down the driveway and into the storm drain on the street.

* * *

Kathy wasn't sure if she should see Greg on his release day. The doctors were wary of him traveling, but he insisted on getting back to work. She wanted to see him, but since she had one investigation to deal with, she didn't want to raise any suspicions with Detective Wendel. He had already shared his concerns on the matter. It was better for Kathy to keep her distance.

Still, she needed to talk to Greg. She decided to settle for a phone call instead. The Starbucks on State Street had become her makeshift office. The dining room used to be her home office, but since Holly had moved back in and they'd become wrapped up in several magical affairs again, being home was a distraction.

Wherever she set up her work space, she always slipped into her business state of mind easily. It made her feel like herself again. She needed to get back to that. Writing the next book, talking with her publisher, and working with Greg. She needed to smooth out their relationship.

"Oh good, I didn't think I'd be able to reach you," Kathy said into the phone when he answered. "I wasn't sure if they moved you to another room."

"No, I'm still here," Greg said on the other end. His voice was raspy. Tired.

"Well, I heard you're being released. That's great news!"

"I'm still going to need physical therapy, but I should be okay."

Kathy tried to lighten the mood with a chuckle. "I'm sure you've used up all your vacation time."

"Yeah."

There was a distinct change in their dynamic. Things were different now, and she wondered if they'd ever be able to find that comfortable working relationship again.

"Well, I'm going to get back to my book. Give me a call when you get back to New York and have worked your way out from under the pile on your desk. Maybe I'll have my new book ready for you by then."

"Kathy?"

"Yeah?"

"Thank you for not pressing charges." He chuckled. "That was a sentence I never thought I'd say."

"Well, it's not really up to me. Has anyone been in to talk to you?"

"You mean after the loony bin determined I wasn't crazy? Yeah, a detective. He said I should expect files charged."

"Oh Greg, I'm so sorry. You don't deserve this."

"I just don't know what got into me. I hope you know I'd never want to hurt you."

She smiled. "I do."

"Anyway, the detective told me that because you refused to testify against me that I'm probably just going to get a plea deal."

"Well, hopefully it's nothing too harsh. I just feel so awful."

"Don't. I'm the one who did this." He paused. "Do you know what happened? I swear I must be blocking something out. I can't remember it at all."

"Uh…it all kind of happened so fast. I was nearly unconscious before another guest came by and knocked you off."

"Right. Yeah. Sorry, you probably don't want to be talking about this."

She could hear the hesitation in his voice.

"No, it's okay." An awkward silence filled the space. "Well," she finally said, "have a safe trip home and a speedy recovery."

"Thanks."

Chapter Twenty-Nine

Kathy didn't want to lie to Jeremy anymore. That's the reason she'd told him her secret. If she was going to have a future with him, she needed to tell him everything. She just wondered if it was too soon to reveal *all* of her dirty laundry. But this wasn't their first shot at dating. He already knew some things.

Even though she wanted to try to avoid Jeremy's house for his safety, she was sure that's where he'd be. She had been working all day and her back was aching from hunching over her computer. If she went home before she talked to Jeremy, she'd sit down and never get up. This needed to be done sooner than later. Especially with Wendel's call that morning and Chris and Holly turning to Kathy for guidance. She still felt like she should have all the answers.

"Come on in. I made dinner," Jeremy said when he answered the door. "Jo should be by later."

"Jo?"

"My daughter."

She had never met his daughter before. All she really knew about her was that she was a senior in high school. And now her name.

Kathy fussed with her hair, gathering it up and moving it from one shoulder to the other. She tried to come up with excuses so she didn't have to tell him about the investigation, but it needed to be said.

"You look nervous." He set two places at the small table in the kitchen.

"Uh…yeah, I am. I need to tell you something."

"More secrets?"

Kathy could see disappointment flicker across his face. That decided it.

"Sit?" He took the seat opposite her and waited. "Kathy, what's going on? Does this have to do with you being a witch?"

"Uh, not really. Well, sort of."

Jeremy raised his eyebrows in confusion.

"I told you how the police are investigating Josh's and Natalie's murders, right? Now they think they've got a suspect, and they want the three of us to go down and ID him."

"Do you think it's the guy?"

"Unless they somehow captured a blue-skinned water-bending wizard, I don't think so. Besides, it wasn't *technically* only his fault. I'm afraid that eventually they're going to look to us. I don't know what I'm going to do."

Jeremy scrunched his forehead. "Why don't you just go down there and explain what happened?"

"They want all three of us. Chris is gone." She considered telling Jeremy the whole story, but decided against it. Not until everything was cleared up and he no longer had to worry.

"Where?" he asked.

"To get his daughter back."

"What?"

Kathy gave him a sad smile. There was so much more that he needed to know. Not enough time to tell him properly.

"It's a long story. Basically, we thought his daughter was dead; turns out she was only kidnapped. He went to try to figure out a way to get her back. But we don't know how long he's going to be—or if he'll even be successful."

He shook his head. "First of all, don't think like that. Chris *will* be back and he *will* have his daughter. Second, I have to be honest with you: everything I've learned about you in the last couple of days scares me."

She dropped her eyes. She'd been afraid of that. Too much had been thrown at him at once. It wasn't fair for her to expect to lean on him.

"You're being threatened," he continued. "That's obviously not good. The fact that you have magic puts me a little more at ease. But all of this with the police—that won't just go away because you're a witch."

She shrugged. "I know."

"Okay," he exhaled. "Well, let's figure out a plan." He stood and grabbed their plates. At the stove, he dished out their food. "What about the guy who did it? Is there any way you could point the police in his direction?"

"It wouldn't be fair to put him in a situation where he could very well hurt the police officers."

"He's the blue-skinned wizard?" He set Kathy's plate in front of her and took his seat.

She nodded. "He has a human form too. Sometimes. It's more like an alias that he goes to when he needs to use it."

"Is he…" He chewed his food while searching for the right word. "I mean, is he a person? Like, to the government?"

"I think so. Problem is, he'll still have his powers in prison. And what if he doesn't even get convicted? The fingerprints for his alias might be different than his true form."

Jeremy waved it off. "Fingerprints aren't always conclusive. There are other ways he can be set up."

Kathy raised an eyebrow.

"I watch a lot of cop shows. Anyway, if we can get him in there, is there something you can do to cut off his magic?"

"We could take away his wand—"

"You guys use wands?"

"*Wizards* use wands."

Jeremy smirked and took another bite.

"He'd still be able to use simple charms. That would probably be enough to unlock the gates. And piss him off."

"There's gotta be another way then."

Kathy twirled her fork in her food. Some sort of pasta dish. It was delicious, but she wasn't that hungry.

"I suppose I could probably come up with a potion that could permanently bind his powers. But we'd still need to watch him."

"Why?"

"He's got connections. If he can't find a way out, there's no doubt he can get in touch with someone who could." She tapped her fork against her plate. "But watching him might not be as bad as it sounds."

"Why's that?"

She smiled. "We've got connections too."

* * *

Warren had instructed Chris to wait outside of camp until he made the signal. Chris hated not having control of the situation. For all he knew, Warren was setting him up.

He considered just running in and grabbing Sophia. He knew which tent she was in. But that would be impossible. The sheer number of wizards in the coven would prevent him from making a clean getaway. Even if he made it out of the camp, he would be followed. He'd never truly be free. Never get the life back he wanted.

The most frustrating part was that he needed to trust Warren to keep an eye on Sophia until he could get in there himself. Chris was used to doing things alone. Even relying on Holly or Kathy for support was hard on him. He was only beginning to learn to let people help him. But this was his daughter. He had waited long enough. Not to mention, Warren had admitted to personally attacking Drew before. Betraying the trust they had. Still, after they came to an agreement, the wizard had freed Chris. At least there was some level of trust between them.

Warren hadn't specified what the signal would be, which made Chris even more uneasy. He'd simply said, "You'll know when you see it."

Cryptic.

Shouts echoed from the camp. Chris peered through the trees, trying to decipher what was going on. Half of the congregated Fire Wizards took off through the trees in the opposite direction without a second look at Chris, who was perched in a tree. The other half of the coven swarmed around the central fire pit.

This was it. This was the signal.

Chris hesitated. Raven wasn't stupid. Hadn't their camp ever been attacked before? Doubtful.

Then he spotted her. Raven stood by the fire pit with her arms outstretched and her eyes closed. The flame rose, licking the branches of the trees momentarily until it subsided. When she opened her eyes they were different. Illuminated somehow. In a swirl of flames she was gone.

He made his move.

Hopping to the ground, he ran at full speed, avoiding any sticks or fallen branches that would give away his location.

He failed.

Miserably.

His feet seemed to collide with everything along his path that made noise. But it didn't matter. He had his target set and nothing was going to get in his way. Not this time. He was so close. Warren had promised him Sophia. Chris had promised her to Holly. He wasn't leaving without her.

The Fire Wizards in the distance paid him no mind. They were too consumed with whatever attack they were preparing for. Whether it was real or not, Chris couldn't tell. He wasn't sure how far Warren would go to create a distraction.

The anticipation made the tent seem farther away than he imagined. When he finally reached it, he pulled back the curtain and saw Warren holding Sophia.

His baby.

Only she wasn't a baby. Not anymore. She was tall, with long red hair just like him. She screamed and kicked at Warren in pure terror.

Chris shushed her and said, "Soph, it's okay. It's me. It's Daddy."

She ignored him and continued to holler.

Warren passed her to him. "You have to go."

Chris struggled to get a good grip of her as she wiggled.

"Go!" Warren bellowed. "Don't let them see you!"

Darting out of the tent, Chris held his daughter close and ran. She squirmed and pushed at his chest to get away from him. Both of them crying. Each for different reasons.

He ran and ran until he thought his legs were going to betray him. He didn't want any of the wizards to see where he went.

In a swirl of flames, Chris was back at the house. With his heart pounding and a lump in his throat, he sank to the floor.

Sophia immediately pushed away from him. "Let me go!"

THE BLUE MOON

"Sophia, it's Daddy."

She ran to the next room and hid behind the wall. Peering around the corner, she hid once again when she saw him looking at her.

Chris wasn't expecting this. He hadn't really thought about it. Why would she hug him and accept him back into her life? Even he hadn't done that when he'd come back to Erie. He couldn't expect his four-year-old—who was probably so confused—to be so comfortable going home with a strange man.

They hadn't seen each other in two years. Half her lifetime. The thought made him sick, especially knowing that for most of that time, they had thought she was dead. Really, she had been in the same camp he had been held prisoner in.

Chris knew she just needed time. Hopefully seeing Holly and Kathy and spending some time in a familiar place would bring back the memories she had of her life before the Fire Wizards. Until then, he just needed to give her space.

But that didn't mean he was any less heartbroken. The life he was trying so hard to get back was even further out of reach than he expected. Raven had already caused irreparable damage to his family. For that, he was going to make sure she couldn't cause any more.

Leaning against the back of the couch, he closed his eyes and wept. Everything he felt came rushing out. The mistakes he had made, the damage he had done, the stress he was under, the loved ones he had lost.

Whenever he took one step forward, he seemed to take two

steps back, and he couldn't ever get ahead. Not with the Fire Wizards. Not with the Pentad. Now, not even with his own daughter. Wasn't he allowed just one victory?

Chris looked over and saw that Sophia had come out of her hiding spot. She was still on the other side of the room, but she sat cross-legged and watched him.

He only hoped that pieces of her memory were coming back to her. Maybe it was an instinctive level of trust she had for him. Maybe it was pure sympathy. Either way, it was a step forward. A sign that he could still achieve small victories.

Sophia was home.

CHAPTER THIRTY

Chris's show of vulnerability had obviously warmed Sophia up to him a little bit. She had inched closer to him until she was within arm's reach. But curiosity drew her to him more than anything else. She studied him but still remained silent. A sense of recognition somewhere in her mind.

The fire had destroyed all of her toys. Kathy had had a small collection of them, but they were likely up in the attic. Or had been sold at a garage sale.

Instead, Chris pulled a throw pillow off the couch and slid it across the floor to her. It originally started as a test. He didn't want her to think he was throwing things at her.

Within five minutes, Sophia picked up the pillow and tossed it back to him. She stood but took several steps back. Clearly, she still didn't trust him.

The two began a silent game of catch. Chris tried to liven the mood with smiles and laughter, but Sophia maintained her blank stare. She watched him with nervous anticipation.

Kathy's entry brought the moment to a screeching halt. When she walked in with Jeremy not far behind, Sophia took off toward the kitchen.

Chris stood and watched to make sure Sophia didn't run out the door. She had hidden in the small pantry. When he returned, Kathy was wiping away tears.

"When?" she snorted out.

"About an hour ago." Chris smiled and wiped the moisture from his own eyes. Kathy pulled him into a hug and squeezed him tight. "But she's scared. Really scared."

"Well, it's been so long." Kathy seemed to just remember Jeremy was with her and said, "This is Jeremy. He's—"

"Your boyfriend who now knows we're witches?" Chris shook his hand. "Sorry. We're not usually this sappy. It's just—"

"A special moment," Kathy finished.

Chris nodded. "Yeah."

Jeremy held up his hands. "No, it's okay. I'd probably be the same way. I'm really happy to see that she's back. I can't imagine what it must've been like."

Kathy's heart swelled. He really was different.

"Thanks," Chris said.

"I'm so glad both of you are okay." She rubbed Chris's back. "Can I see her?"

He hesitated. "Um…why don't we wait for her to come to us?"

She nodded, a hint of disappointment on her face. "Okay, yeah. That's probably a good idea. Has she said anything?"

"No. I'm hoping that seeing you and Holly will help her remember. Familiar faces, you know?"

Kathy nodded. "It's too bad you couldn't take her back to your old house. I'm sure she would remember more than anyone would expect. Have you told Holly yet?"

Chris shook his head. "I haven't seen her. Where is she?"

Trading looks with both Chris and Jeremy, Kathy said, "She was home when I left this morning. I've been gone all day."

The two sprang into action.

"I'll start a searching ritual," Chris said.

"I'll look to see if she left a note."

"What do you want me to do?" Jeremy's words stopped both witches in their tracks.

"Um…" Kathy knew there'd be a few hiccups to dating a non-magical man.

"Turn on *Mickey Mouse Clubhouse* or something. Sophia used to like that. Maybe it'll draw her out."

Kathy nodded. "Good idea."

No note had been left and Chris couldn't find any trace of Holly with the searching ritual. Sophia had come out of the pantry and clung to the doorway in the kitchen to watch the commotion the adults were making.

"Guys!" Jeremy called. "Get in here!"

Kathy and Chris raced to the living room. Jeremy had the TV set to the news. The words, "Breaking News: Riots Attack

Downtown Erie" flashed across the bottom.

Chris's eyes widened as he looked closer. The group attacking the city were all wearing blue robes with the familiar triangle on their chests. The same one that was branded into Chris's skin.

"That's the Fire Wizards!"

Kathy covered her open mouth as she watched fires ignite from the palms of the robed figures. People ran for cover as policemen tried to usher everyone to safety.

After several policemen were struck by the wizards, Kathy said, "They can't beat them."

Chris shook his head. "They don't know what they're up against. They're not going to shoot them. Not unless they have to. Even then, it might not do anything."

"Do you know these people?" Jeremy asked.

"They're the same people who took Sophia," Chris said. "And they tricked me into joining them."

Jeremy pointed the remote at the TV. "You're one of them?"

"Sort of. Exiled."

"What do you think they want?" Kathy asked.

Chris shrugged. "Attention? Maybe they're pissed because I have Sophia now."

He wondered what had happened to Warren. He wouldn't be out in the mess fighting if he was truly interested in helping Chris. The fact that the Fire Wizards were attacking downtown and not the house might be a sign that he hadn't betrayed him.

"Do you think they're trying to draw out the Pentad?" Kathy asked.

"In public?"

"Why not? If Raven is truly after complete power, the world will know about the Fire Wizards sooner or later."

Chris thought about the rally he'd overheard. "Maybe. I over-heard them talking while I was there. I think they were going to use Sophia as leverage to get us to work with them. Now that we have their leverage, they're using something else we hold closely over us."

"The city."

Chris nodded.

"So what are you going to do?" Jeremy asked. "The two of you can't fight all those people. And what about your wife?"

Chris took in a deep breath. This might not have been Raven's original plan, but it was definitely playing out exactly how she wanted it. They would be forced to save the city, potentially even exposing themselves in the process. Even if the Harpers somehow beat the Fire Wizards, the witches would still lose.

Chapter Thirty-One

The sound of dripping water met Holly's ears as she woke. She felt groggy, and her head throbbed. Zamball must've given her something to make her pass out. Her hands were suspended above her head and bound in chains. The tips of her toes barely reached the floor.

The room was dark. It took her a minute before she could make out where she was. A glimmer of light shone from a crevice at the top of the wall opposite her. Otherwise, the walls were wet. Slimy even. She felt a trickle of water run down her arm and send goosebumps across her body.

A creaking metal door swung open, and Holly was momentarily blinded by the sun.

"Well," Zamball's voice met her ears, "you're finally awake."

The door swung shut, but Holly still only saw spots. She

wanted to say something to the wizard, but she was still too tired. Whatever potion or drug he had used on her hadn't yet left her system completely.

"I hope you were comfortable." He laughed.

"What do you want me for?" Her chest was heavy, like someone was sitting on it. Just getting out those six words left her gasping for more air. The rancid smell of the room wasn't welcoming either.

"I told you back at the house, I need leverage." He pulled a short stepladder to the middle of the room and took a seat. "It's an even playing field. The Chaos is gone and the Pentad needs more powerful players on our side if we're going to properly execute our plan."

"Which is?" Holly gasped. Her eyelids were heavy, and she fought to keep them open.

"None of your concern." He pointed a finger at her. "You're the pawn. I'm sorry to say, but you're probably not going to make it out of here alive." He smirked. "Guess my mother's vendetta will be complete after all."

She tried her best to glare at him. If she was the pawn, then that meant the person they were trying to draw out would be Chris. Maybe even Kathy, too. But if she was dead, why would Chris and Kathy continue to work with him?

Unless it was a trap.

"You're not at all like your mother," Holly said, regaining some of her strength.

Zamball shrugged. "I mean, she was a witch, whereas I'm a

wizard. Not to mention that I look at the bigger picture. My mother was too consumed with you to worry about any other threats—namely, the Harpers. But I think you and I knocked them down a peg together, didn't we?"

Holly gritted her teeth. As if she didn't have enough guilt already that she'd played a part in Josh's death. She hadn't even really talked about that with Chris yet. It was still too soon. Their relationship was still fragile.

He stood and stepped toward her. "Don't be too hard on yourself. You got what you wanted too. The Chaos is no more."

The back of his hand stroked her face but she pulled away.

"It's a shame we never got married. I tried a couple of times. I thought you and I could be a powerful couple. We certainly made a great team with the Chaos."

"Go to hell."

Zamball laughed. "There's that fire! If only we could've—"

The metal door swung open again, and Holly turned her head to protect her eyes.

"Z, leave the girl. We need you." It was a woman's voice. Young. Probably no older than Holly was.

"What is it?" Zamball barked.

"It's urgent. Eleanor is calling a meeting."

He grumbled. Grabbing ahold of Holly's face, he leaned in close and said, "Don't get comfortable."

* * *

This was bad. The city had never been openly attacked before. The Fire Wizards were not only dangerous, but they were reckless too. They didn't care about the silent standard among all things magic: secrecy. It was an unwritten rule that those with special abilities needed to prevent nonmagical attention. The way the Fire Wizards were marching downtown showed that they didn't play by the rules.

Chris worried about Holly. The timeline didn't add up to indicate that the Fire Wizards had taken her. It must've been the Pentad—unless another enemy was approaching.

No.

Any other enemy would stay far away from the Harpers because they likely knew they had a double target on them. Kidnapping Holly would be interfering with the Fire Wizards and the Pentad. Other enemies would stay away. Which meant she was with the Pentad.

But where? Unlike the Fire Wizards, the Pentad didn't have a standard base of operations. Not to Chris's knowledge, at least. The searching ritual he had performed earlier had come up with nothing. They needed a different plan.

The luxury of time was not something they had, though. The longer they waited, the longer the Pentad had to kill Holly. Not only that, but the Fire Wizards would slaughter more innocent people.

They needed help.

"What's the status of your supergroup?" Kathy asked, as if reading his thoughts.

Chris shook his head. "Not enough people yet. Besides, even the folks who have agreed to work with us would be skeptical of jumping into battle right away."

"But it's an option."

"We don't have time!" Chris shouted, exasperated. "How are the two of us supposed to save the city *and* Holly while making sure that neither group swoops in and takes Sophia from me again?" He shook his head. "We can't do it! They're too strong."

Kathy sighed. She let Chris's snap slide. They were under a lot of stress. Him especially. This whole mess had snuck up on them.

But something still needed to be done. And someone needed to have a level head in order to properly delegate assignments. For the time being, Kathy put the investigation from her mind. None of that would matter if the city burned to the ground.

"Okay, this is what we're going to do." Kathy clapped her hands together to get Jeremy's and Chris's attention. "Chris, you're going to go up and search the magic book until you find the best way to get Holly back."

"Do you think we have time for that?"

"It's Holly. There's always time."

He nodded.

"I'm going to head downtown and try to fend off any attacks. Hopefully, by stopping time, I can work my magic without even being seen."

"Don't you think my fire power would be better against them?" Chris asked.

Kathy shrugged. "Maybe. But we need you elsewhere. Once you get Holly back, then you two can join me."

"What about Sophia?" Chris asked.

"Jeremy can watch her." She turned to her boyfriend. "If you don't mind."

He nodded. "Sure. Should be easy, with her hiding from us and all."

In the doorway to the kitchen, Sophia still hid behind the wall. Although, she was curious enough to continue her watch from a distance.

While Chris went up to grab the book, Kathy took a seat beside Jeremy. Her night was about to get a lot more dangerous. She wanted to steal as many peaceful moments as she could. Her hands were already shaking from fear.

Jeremy put his hand on her knee. "Be careful."

She placed her hand on his. "Always."

"I mean it. You worry me. I don't want to see you with another broken arm—or worse."

She leaned in and kissed him. "I'll be back."

"You better. Now go save the city."

Chris came bounding down the stairs. "I think I have an idea to find Holly. I just need to find the right spell."

Kathy stood. "Good. Be careful. You have a daughter to come home to."

He stole a glance to the kitchen. Sophia tucked out of sight when he met her eyes. "Yeah, hopefully she'll talk to me again."

"She will. Just give her time."

He kept his eyes on the book. "Currently that's something we don't have."

"We will soon."

"Oh look, there's more now." Jeremy pointed at the TV.

Chris and Kathy gathered around.

"Oh no. The Pentad is there now," Chris said. "This is an all-out war."

"How can you tell?"

He pointed out the blue man. "Well, there's Zamball. Aunt Kathy, are you sure you don't want me to come down there?"

She didn't answer him right away. She was taken by the sight playing out on the TV. "They seem to be fighting each other."

Chris nodded. "Good. That will buy us some time. Maybe you can get down there and just start moving people to safety. We'll really start attacking if I get Holly back."

"*When* you get Holly back," Kathy corrected.

"Right." He looked at his aunt. "You ready?"

She shook her head. "No. But it doesn't matter what I'm feeling. I can help, so that's what I have to do."

Chapter Thirty-Two

Most of the civilians were gone by the time Kathy got downtown. That was good news. However, she wondered just how many people had died before they could get to safety. The bodies lining the streets were hard to fathom. It was heartbreaking. This was her home. She had never seen such destruction, let alone in the places she'd once thought were the safest.

Among the carnage, the street was eerily still. Blood was splattered across a news van parked on the street. Flame and smoke billowed from several of the office buildings. Clearly, the fighting had just been here. They must be moving throughout the city.

Kathy forced herself to look away. She needed to find the source of the attack. Survey the action until Chris could join her.

She crept to the corner, peered around a building, and saw them. At least fifty men and women in blue robes. The flames they wielded illuminated the sky, and Kathy could smell the acrid smoke from the burning.

Lifting her hands, she worked her magic. Fireballs were frozen in place until they were in line with another wizard, and then she would unfreeze the attack to eliminate one enemy at a time.

The building gave her enough protection to keep from being seen and from being hit with a stray fireball. This would have to do until Chris and Holly joined her.

Windows above her smashed, and one men fell screaming from the top floor, only to be silenced once he hit the pavement. Kathy closed her eyes and pressed her fist to her mouth. There was no point to this riot. Only a showcase of power against people who weren't properly equipped to defend themselves.

Across the street she saw two teenaged girls cornered in the crook of another building. A man in a blue robe loomed over them, striking up a fireball from the end of his wand. He raised it, and Kathy froze all three of them from where she stood.

In a flash, she was beside the wizard. She hesitated before unfreezing the girls. That would expose them to magic. But hadn't they already seen enough? Besides, their safety was most important.

"Do you have someplace safe nearby to go?" Kathy noticed that the one girl had burns up her left arm. "Never mind. Cut through the alley and get to the hospital. You need to see a doctor. Run. Don't stop until you're inside."

The girls huddled together and studied her.

"I'll cover you, but hurry!"

Still apprehensive, the injured girl nodded and reached for the other one. Together, they ran through the alley. Kathy watched them until they rounded the corner.

Turning back to the wizard, the words to a defensive spell rolled off her tongue:

Fires that burn from a magical source,
will reverse their original course.

Kathy was thrown onto the sidewalk as the supernatural flames redirected back to the casters, creating a blast right beside her. The wizard lay smoldering on the ground, dead. Kathy's ears rang from the blow.

Scrambling to her feet, she ran just inside the alley for cover.

The fighting resumed. Not all the wizards took a direct hit from the spell she'd cast, but a lot of them were now burning on the ground.

The only one she knew among the Pentad was Zamball, and he had yet to show his face. However, the fighting stretched along State Street, which went all the way to the lake. He could be any-where.

Police sirens sounded in the distance. She wondered where the policemen she saw on the news were.

Then she saw them: several policemen lay burning in the street. She hadn't noticed them before, trying to ignore the mass of corpses.

"Pretty foolish to ride solo."

Kathy spun around. A black woman in blue robes with the familiar triangle approached her. She had short-cropped hair and a scowl.

"How do you know I'm solo?"

The woman flashed her brilliant white teeth. "My name is Raven. I'm the leader of the Fire Wizards."

"Yeah, I've heard about you."

"Then you know that I'm patient, Ms. Walker. I've kept my tabs on your entire coven—even the castaway."

"Why are you doing this? Why are you killing innocent people? This isn't going to get you any power in the magical world."

"That's *exactly* what it's going to do!"

"How?"

Raven grinned again. "Take over a city, then another, and another. Eventually the whole country. Meanwhile, we're building our forces—as we have been for years—and the magical world is taking note of our domination of the nonmagical world. At that point, we'll have conquered both worlds."

"So why were you so hell-bent on keeping Sophia?"

"We need to recruit forces. Mr. Harper is a part of our coven, whether he cooperates or not. Now that he's joined us, we can force him to follow us."

"How?"

"We have our ways. The child was one of them."

"So you kept her for two years!?" Kathy thought about the scared little girl back at the house. Her capture had permanently scarred her. She'd never be the same.

"I told you I was patient. But the young Harper girl was actually to lure Ms. Bowen, not Mr. Harper. Once he joined, we thought that if the sight of his imprisonment wasn't enough to get her to join, the imprisonment of her daughter would be." She tilted her head to the side. "That didn't go as planned. We didn't even have a chance to show her the girl."

Kathy waved her hand around her. "So you're just going to kill everything in sight until you get what you want?"

"No, Ms. Walker, we're going to kill the protectors of this city—the police force, city council, the mayor, witches. We're going to hang you all in the center of town to show the true extent of our power." She waved her hands to someone behind Kathy. "Now, we've had enough—"

Two men grabbed Kathy's arms, and she felt a thick cord of rope against her wrists and another around her throat.

The sound of gunshots rang in Kathy's ears. The men's grasps loosened and she was free.

With nowhere else to hide, she dropped to the ground and covered her head until the ringing in her ears dissipated. When she looked up, she saw a policeman standing a few feet away, his gun still raised with both hands. Raven lay on the ground beside her, a pool of blood surrounding her head.

Dead.

* * *

The metal door swung open once again. With no other way to brace herself for Zamball's return, Holly tensed up and prepared for the worst.

"Holly, are you okay?"

Slowly, her eyes adjusted and she could make out Chris's face among the near-blinding light.

"Chris? How did you find me?"

He cracked a smile and set to work on the chains around her wrists. "The spell I cast led me to the woman I loved."

She couldn't help but return the smile.

"Yeah, yeah." He focused his attention on her restraints, not wanting to look her in the eyes. "It's stupid."

"It worked."

Pausing, he leaned in and planted a kiss on her lips.

Chris motioned to Holly's restraints. "They're welded around your wrists. I'm going to have to blast them."

"Be careful."

"Of course." He took a step back and took a deep breath. He hadn't used the explosion part of his specialty in a while. Before the flamecasting side of his powers had manifested, he'd had excellent precision. Since then, fire had taken precedence.

"If you're nervous, we could try a spell." Holly wanted to get out of the restraints as soon as possible, but she wanted to keep her hands in the process. The metal was digging into her wrists. The tips of her fingers had gone numb.

"No, I can do this. Just hold still."

Raising his hands, Chris jerked two fingers in the direction of the chains. He focused all of his energy on the part that he wanted to break—the only part. Time seemed to stop as he waited for the split-second to pass to see the outcome of his magic.

A silent *snap* signaled that he had been successful. He breathed a refreshing breath of air—despite the gruesome stench—and focused on the other clasp.

Another success.

Chris rushed to Holly and wrapped one arm around her waist as he worked her arm out of the clasps with his other hand. Once she was free, she collapsed in his arms. He held her close.

She was so tired. The sedative had worn off, but her body ached.

"You okay?" he asked.

She nodded. "I will be."

"I've got some news."

"Good or bad?"

"Both."

Resting her head against his chest, she didn't press him for details. Not yet. She wanted to savor the moment she had with him. But the fact that he'd come alone meant that Kathy was busy somewhere else. Busy with something magical. Holly couldn't be selfish.

"All right then. Good news first."

He beamed. "I got Sophia back."

"You did!?" Holly pulled away and studied him. Tried to determine if this was real or a dream. The pain throughout her body told her it wasn't a dream. She didn't know whether to jump with excitement or cry with happiness. Her baby girl was home. Finally safe and sound.

She wanted to see her. She needed to. They had been apart too long already. Sophia shouldn't have to get reacquainted with her family, but that's not the way the cards had been dealt.

But if Chris had left Sophia to come rescue her, something must still be wrong.

"It's the Fire Wizards, isn't it? That's the bad news?"

Chris dropped his head. "Yeah."

"They tricked you into going back, didn't they?" Moments after her elation, she felt her heart breaking. When would this roller-coaster of emotions be over?

He shook his head. "No. Holly, they're attacking the city. Aunt Kathy is fighting them off right now—the Pentad showed up too. I saw Zamball."

So that's where he'd gone.

"What do they want? We don't even know how to defeat them!"

Chris took her hands and kissed the backs of them. "I know. We have to figure it out soon, though. We have a daughter to get home to." He wasn't sure when he'd stop smiling at the mention of Sophia. Probably not for a while. And that was okay with him. He only hoped Sophia would be able to adjust to them. But that wasn't the chief concern at the moment.

"If Kathy's fighting the Fire Wizards, where's Sophia?"

"At the house with Aunt Kathy's boyfriend. We figured it'd be safer that way." He left out the fact that Sophia had barely said two words to him. If they were going to fight, Holly needed hope.

Still, fear crippled her. "Chris, this is so dangerous. We're completely unprepared." She thought back to when she'd been a new witch and had to face Toxanna for the first time. She'd felt the same uncertainty then as she did now.

"And Aunt Kathy is? We can't just leave her in the midst of a battle!"

"But we can't get ourselves killed in the process! What good would that do? Besides Sophia, we've already given everything we have: your mom, your brother, my *entire* family."

He squeezed her hands. "Holly, that's *exactly* why we need to fight. I killed my mother's killer. You got justice for your family's death. It's time to do the same for everyone else we've lost. Fight to make Josh's death mean something. Fight to give our daughter a safe future to live in."

She took a deep breath. "You're right. One last fight."

He held out his hand. "Let's go get 'em."

Chapter Thirty-Three

The destruction of the city was far worse than Chris had anticipated. On his way to Holly, he'd bypassed the carnage. Now he was in the midst of it and couldn't believe what he saw.

The worst were the corpses, but that wasn't all. Smashed cars, burning buildings, shattered glass. The city was trashed. Police sirens roared nearby, though Chris couldn't make out where exactly they were yet. Smoke filled the air, casting the downtown area in a foreboding haze.

There were fewer members of the Fire Wizards than Chris expected. He saw many of them on the ground, slain from one attack or another. Kathy's body was still nowhere to be found, which was a very good sign. Chris couldn't stand to lose her too.

The few members of the Pentad were scattered around State Street. The three Chris spotted were all surrounded by clusters of

Fire Wizards, each moving in attack.

"We need to find Kathy." Holly's words pierced his thoughts.

He nodded. "Can you create a diversion to buy us some time?"

"Look!" A shrill voice came from one of the Fire Wizards' clusters. Someone from the Pentad drawing attention away from them.

The Fire Wizards all turned and began marching toward Chris and Holly. The witches backed away, increasing their speed until they each turned and took off in a sprint.

Balls of fire whizzed by their faces as they ran. The stopped cars and other debris scattered across the street and sidewalk slowed their pace. Eventually, Holly hunkered down behind a tipped car and pulled Chris with her.

"What are we going to do?"

He shook his head. "I don't know."

"Well, didn't we come here to fight?"

"Yeah."

"Then we fight."

Chris still worried about his aunt, but there wasn't anything they could do for her right now. For the moment, they needed to put an end to this madness and face their enemies head-on.

He kissed the back of Holly's hand. "Be careful."

In a swirl of flames, he was down the street, behind the group of Fire Wizards marching toward Holly. Raising his hands in the air, he shot a stream of flames out of each of his palms, igniting two of the wizards.

The four who remained turned their attention to him. The odds were still not in his favor.

"Traitor." The word from one of the oncoming wizards was loud. Chris didn't even realize the wizard had fired an attack until he was on the ground. He patted out his leg and struggled to stand, but the wizards were standing over him now.

"Raven should've never tried to recruit a witch," one of them said. He delivered a kick to Chris's side that left him slumped over and coughing.

"Not so tough without your girlies, huh?" Another one kicked him. Hard. This time Chris collapsed on the ground.

One of the wizards grabbed a fistful of Chris's long hair and pulled him to his feet. "I want your girl to watch as your blood trickles out of your neck, *witch*." The wizard's breath grazed Chris's ear. The cold metal of the blade brushed against his throat.

Suddenly, Chris was thrown to the ground again. He rolled to his side and watched as Orchid drove a knife into the bellies of two of the wizards in quick succession. The final one, she sparred with shortly until she raised her hands beside his face, casting tiny streaks of lighting from her palms. The wizard's eyes rolled to the back of his head and he fell to the ground beside Chris.

Orchid offered her hand. "We have some new recruits."

Once he was back on his feet, Chris gripped Orchid's shoulder and squeezed. His other hand was still cradling his side. "Thank you," he said softly.

She pointed down the street. "Your wife needs help. Can you fight?"

Chris moved to take a step forward but stumbled.

"Stay here, then. My coven will protect you. There are enough others to help fight now. The enemy's numbers are dropping."

Before Orchid had a chance to move, Chris reached for her. "No, I'll go." Wasn't that what this was all about? Fighting for his family? He couldn't stop just because he was hurt. He wasn't dead. Not yet.

* * *

After some time, the illusions Holly cast lost their effect. No matter how real they looked, Zamball knew they weren't. His reactions to the scenarios she created gave away her secret, and the others walked right through them.

Her skills at combat had dwindled through the years. The confidence she'd once had to inflict physical damage was gone. So she tried to run, but the littered street got in her way.

Two cars pinched together created a dead end. She could try to leap over them, but the Pentad was too advanced in magic to let her get away so easily. She needed cover. Right now they were testing her. Ratcheting up her anxiety and fear until they could strike. It was working.

Holly needed to stop reacting and start acting. Running away meant she was doing exactly what they anticipated. That's what she had been doing since she'd come back to Erie. The tables needed to turn.

Whirling around, she faced the trio. She still didn't like that she was in a corner, but she couldn't let that show.

"This isn't your style, Zamball. What would your mother

think? She would never be this sloppy." If he could play with her mind, she could play with his. "She tormented my family in secret for eighty years without this level of exposure. You've been after me for what? Two weeks? And now look at you."

"You should've cut out the bitch's tongue," the woman beside Zamball said. She planted her foot on the street and the ground shook. A crack formed in the road until Zamball put his hand in front of her.

"Enough." Turning back to Holly, he said, "You are my prisoner. I've been a little tied up with things, but it's time I took you back."

"Now that we've fought your battles for you?" She tried to mock him, but her fear was taking prominence. She still had no idea how to get away. "Afraid the Fire Wizards were going to get too powerful?"

Zamball moved within arm's reach of Holly. An ear-splitting screech drew everyone's attention. Holly covered her ears. She felt hands lift her up and over the hood of the car blockade.

When the scream stopped, Holly's ears still rang. Paula sat beside her, clutching her arm.

"Cassidy has them. We need to find your coven."

Holly didn't ask questions. She followed Paula through the labyrinth that had become the street until they nearly collided with Chris and Orchid.

Chris wrapped his free arm around Holly.

"You're hurt!"

"I'll be fine." He tilted his head in Orchid's direction. "Looks like my friend came through."

"We've got ten covens interested in joining the supergroup," she added.

Chris and Holly exchanged smiles.

"I like it," she said.

"Only my coven and Orchid's coven are here now, though," Paula continued. "If we're not smart, the Pentad and the Fire Wizards can still get the upper hand."

Scanning the street, Chris couldn't see any sign of Warren. Maybe the wizard hadn't been truthful in wanting to join the group. But then why did he help rescue Sophia? Unless he was at the house…

"We need to get home."

"What? No, Chris, we need to find Kathy," Holly said.

"I need to make sure Sophia is okay."

"Why?"

"I'm afraid this is all a distraction. I'm going home." He grabbed her hand, but Orchid gripped his arm.

"Wait. Find your aunt first. Running around with our heads cut off is only going to get us killed. That's the whole reason for this group, to have a united front. Do the same with your coven—your true coven. Find your aunt. Then while you're checking on your daughter, we can stay behind and make sure no one else gets hurt."

He didn't want to wait any longer—he had waited long enough—but she made a good point. Going in without a concrete plan wouldn't do Sophia any good.

Orchid slid her knife into the holster on her side. "I'm gonna go hunting. Be safe. We'll find you when it's over."

Before she could run away, he called to her, "Thank you."

Chris and Holly raced as fast as they could with his injuries along the side streets. It was important to stay as hidden as possible. Eventually, this would all be over. In the meantime, if either of them were seen displaying their powers, there would be major consequences. Consequences that the Fire Wizards likely wanted to happen.

Rounding the corner onto French Street, the couple nearly collided with a group of four men in blue robes. In an instant, Holly created a hundred knives in the air, threatening to stab the men.

"Warren…" Chris said wearily.

"Tell your little girlfriend to keep her daggers away from us."

Holly eyed him suspiciously.

"He helped me get Sophia back," Chris told her. He hesitated before he added, "He knew Drew, too."

"We were planning our own rebellion until Ginger came into the picture," Warren said.

She looked to Chris. "You trust him?"

He shrugged. "Have to. He gave us Sophia back. Besides, if he helps take out the Fire Wizards, he's on our side as far as I'm concerned."

"Okay," she said slowly. The knives faded, the illusion gone. "How did you know Drew?"

Warren looked at Chris for a moment and then bowed his head. "I was his trainer when he first joined the Fire Wizards. He talked a lot about you. I believe you were the girl he went out of his way to learn tarot cards for." He smiled and met her eyes. "I'd never seen him more infatuated."

She chanced a look at Chris and then dropped her head. "Well, it's nice to know he had a friend in such a corrupt coven."

"The rest of the wizards are just around the corner," Chris said, changing the conversation. Now was not the time to tell Holly the truth about the end of Warren and Drew's friendship. "I haven't seen Raven, so look out for her."

Warren looked confused. "Raven's dead. Can't you sense it?"

Chris was stunned. "She's dead? How?"

"I don't know. But I definitely felt a shift in the coven. She had more power than any of us realized. That's why the numbers of Fire Wizards has dropped so quickly. We're not as strong as we used to be."

"Oh." He stood speechless for a moment. Then he remembered the rush they were in. "Well, the Pentad is still over there, so are a couple of witches in our new group—" He stopped abruptly, his brow furrowed.

"What is it?" she asked.

"There were only three members of the Pentad there. Josh was their fifth. One of them is still missing."

"Which one?" Holly asked. "I don't even know who is all in the Pentad. Just Zamball."

"They represent the five major magical elements," Warren said. "Fire, air, water, earth, and spirit."

Chris's eyes grew. "The spirit branch is missing."

Chapter Thirty-Four

Chris and Holly found Kathy in an alley on the outskirts of downtown. She was pressed against the wall, peering around the corner.

"Aunt Kathy!" Chris exclaimed.

"Chris! Holly! You guys are okay!" Kathy wrapped her arms around both of them. "I was worried. I hadn't heard from you or seen you."

"What are you doing?" Holly asked. "Everyone is on the next street over."

"We've got some new allies too," Chris added.

"Good. The police showed up. I'm making sure none of them get hurt and making sure they don't see me."

"They don't seem to be fighting, though," Chris said. "At least, I didn't see any officers."

"They must just be doing crowd control until the big guns come in." They all wondered what would happen if any part of the military got involved.

"Well, hopefully Orchid and the others can get rid of them before anyone else shows up," Holly said.

"We need to—" Chris started.

Kathy's phone interrupted him. She pulled it out and looked at the display. "It's Jeremy. Hello?" She pressed a finger to her opposite ear. The sound of the police sirens muffled his voice.

"There's someone in the house." His voice was a whisper.

"What? Jeremy, honey, who is it?"

"There's a—" The line went dead.

"We have to get home."

* * *

The house was a mess. The front door had been kicked in, and the glass from the window lay shattered on the hardwood floor in the foyer. Chairs were knocked down, the middle cushion on the couch had been slashed, the various knickknacks Kathy had collected were now smashed on the floor. In the living room, the TV still played Mickey Mouse.

The screams coming from the basement drew the witches' attention. Most clearly of all were Sophia's wails.

At the door to the basement the witches watched as Eleanor tore through the wooden staircase to get to whatever was behind it. Likely Jeremy and Sophia.

Kathy tried to freeze her but it didn't work. Chris threw his arms in the direction of Eleanor and cast blazing flames into the dark basement.

"Careful," Holly nearly whispered.

Chris's magic threw Eleanor back away from the staircase. The witches bounded down them, leaping over the hole.

"You don't deserve her!" Eleanor shouted. Her hands shook and a crazed smile stretched across her face. Her bandana had slipped off her bald head, revealing a bad scar across the top of it. One of her ears bled from having one of her heavy earrings ripped out. "You don't know what kind of power she wields."

The witches looked at her skeptically.

"And who says that *you* deserve her?" Holly asked.

"She needs to be properly trained," Eleanor continued. "Something that had been neglected when she was in the care of the Fire Wizards."

"And you're the one who's going to do that?" Kathy asked.

"You witches have already proved that you can't handle something with this kind of power," Eleanor spat. "Look at what happened with the Chaos. That was only half the power of what I sense in this child. Clearly, you've shown you don't care to contain that power or you wouldn't have sacrificed one of your own."

Chris lost control. Before anyone could stop him, he pounced on Eleanor, slamming his fists repeatedly into her face. Strangely, with each hit, whatever injury she sustained quickly healed before he could throw the next punch. That only enraged him more.

Holly and Kathy both struggled to pull him off, but it wasn't until Orchid, Paula, Warren, and the others came down the stairs that he stopped, his knuckles covered with his own blood.

Eleanor struggled to her feet. "You witches really don't understand what kind of power I wield, either."

"It's over, Eleanor," Warren said. "You lost. Myself and a few others are all that's left of the Fire Wizards. Your coven's as good as dead too."

She shook her head. "You truly don't understand. The Pentad has been around for ages. I've been a member since its inception. Long before Zamball, Collie, Ignatius, or Joshua joined. I'll rebuild my coven. I have many times before."

Paula shook her head. "Not this time. There's a new super-group. The Pentad is officially over."

Eleanor raised her hand and twisted. With a crunch, Paula's body crumpled to the ground, her spine snapped in half.

Holly let out an involuntary yelp.

"I can't freeze her." Kathy's hands attempted to work her magic.

"Of course you can't. Do you see how easy it was for me to kill her? I can do the same to any one of you. Quick deaths, slow deaths, it doesn't matter. I've unleashed plagues to the world, epidemics. Your little group here—"

Chris was on top of Eleanor again, throwing his bloody fists into her face.

Orchid pulled everyone in close while Chris distracted Eleanor. She pulled out a piece of paper.

"Been working on this for a while," she said. "Ready?"

Spirit, water, earth, air, and fire,
your demonic rule is now over.
Magic united, we speak as one,
it's time to end your destruction.
With our strength and with our will,
your defeat is inevitable.

Chris repeated each line after the rest of the group. Once the spell was cast, there was a brief moment where nothing happened. The room was still and silent, except for Sophia's cries. Chris sat back and looked down at Eleanor. She cracked a smile at him.

A moment later, she erupted. The burst sent the group flying into the cinder-block walls in all directions. Holly and Kathy bumped into each other as they hit the brick wall. Orchid, Warren, and the others crashed farther throughout the room. Chris landed on his back against the stairwell, splinters piercing into him.

There was another moment of silence as debris fell into place and everyone surveyed the damage. Ears rang and dust filled the air as the group struggled to see if the spell had worked the way they'd intended it to.

Creaking floorboards from overhead sounded. Kathy shouted, but nobody heard her. The support beams gave, and the dining room table from the room above came crashing through the ceiling. Everyone hunkered for protection.

A single cry sounded.

Sophia.

Chapter Thirty-Five

You're sure about this?" Detective Wendel asked. Kathy, Chris, and Holly were down at the police station identifying the image of the man the police considered a suspect in Josh's death.

Chris nodded. "Yeah. That's definitely not the guy."

Holly echoed his thoughts.

"Okay, that settles that then." He rummaged through a few folders on his desk and pulled out a photograph. "What about this guy?"

The witches peered down at the image on his desk. Another security camera still. The name of the hospital parking garage could be read in the corner. The same garage Josh used to park in.

"Yeah, that's him," Holly confirmed.

Wendel looked up to Chris and Kathy. They each nodded.

"We found his body downtown after last weekend's terrorist

attacks. Based on eyewitness accounts that put him in contact with Mr. Harper and the type of ammunition found on his body, we have reason to believe he was involved with the terrorist group that initiated the attack. The reason for attacking Mr. Harper and Miss Quinn is still unknown." He eyed them skeptically, but continued, "The FBI is leading that case."

Kathy nodded. "That's good. At least we could all get some sort of closure for Josh's death."

It was true. With everything going on, none of them had properly processed everything that had transpired. Now that things had settled down again, they could move on. Start moving forward.

"Thank you for all your work, Detective," Chris added.

"Just doing my job. There is one thing I do want to ask you three—off the record."

They eyed each other suspiciously. Wendel continued before they could respond.

"What were you doing downtown last weekend when everything was going on?"

Nobody said anything or made eye contact. They didn't want to confirm what he probably already thought.

They'd only magically-altered one thing: Zamball. His body, along with the others of the Pentad, had been completely destroyed after the spell to destroy them had been cast. Magic's way of protecting its secrecy.

The witches had cast a spell that created a dummy body. Holly used her power of illusion to give the dummy the appearance of Elliott Dale. The dummy would only last for about a week. By then, it would be in the ground somewhere. Nobody would be any wiser.

Still, the possibility of them forgetting something loomed over them. Being spotted downtown hadn't occurred to them with the victory they had celebrated.

"Never mind." Wendel gave them a knowing smile. "I'm just grateful to everyone who helped save so many lives in all the chaos."

* * *

Luckily, only part of the house had caved in after defeating Eleanor. However, that didn't make climbing out of the rubble and wondering who had survived any less fearful. Two died from the cave-in: the witch with the banshee scream from Orchid's coven and one of the remaining Fire Wizards from Warren's. Both were properly laid to rest the following day in true witch fashion: a burning pyre.

The loss of another member of the Fire Wizards brought the total count from the original coven down to three. Four, if you counted Chris. His remaining connection to the coven allowed him to notice if there was a shift in power among them. He wanted to trust Warren and the two remaining wizards, but he wasn't going to be fooled into being outplayed.

By the next morning, the house had begun to fix itself. The floor reassembled itself, yet the dining room table still lay smashed in the basement. By day two, the shattered windows had been fixed. Piece by piece, the house returned to its normal pristine condition.

After the house was mostly back to its original state, the various covens that had agreed to form a white magic group were all gathered in the Harper house. In celebration as well as remembrance.

They had work to do, too. The group had not been officially established yet. Things needed to be settled. Their mission, the system they would employ to achieve that mission, and who would be leaders of the group, among other matters.

"I want to thank you all for helping with the attack here in our city," Chris said to the room. "Your willingness to put your own lives at risk means more than any promise of action ever could. The fact that we were able to take out two demonic supergroups in the same day shows that we can accomplish more as a team than separately. So thank you. This is the beginning of a change. Something positive. Something that can restore a sense of order to the chaos the world has seen lately."

"What are we going to call this thing?" someone from Paula's coven asked.

"I like the sound of the Witches Order," Kathy said.

"Uh, some of us aren't witches," Warren noted.

"I was a witch and I joined the Fire Wizards," Chris said. "It's just a name."

"Our group shouldn't exclude any other magical being," Orchid said. "Witches are the most likely to fight evil due to our varying powers, but that doesn't mean we're the only ones."

Chris nodded. "Orchid's right. This group will regulate all magic and be an end to any growing shift in power—even ourselves. We can't let our collective power become the very thing we just defeated."

"So what's the name?" someone from the Fire Wizards asked.

"What about simply: The Order of Magic?" Kathy suggested.

"All in favor?" Chris asked.

Hands shot into the air throughout the room.

"All right then. Our first order of business is settled. From now on, we'll be called The Order of Magic."

The rest of the night was spent creating the structure for The Order. It was going to take time, compromise, and many revisions, but they were going to get it. Chris was sure of it.

What he was most sure of, however, was that he was creating a future that he could be proud of. A future where he and Holly could potentially bring in more children. One where Sophia wouldn't have to suffer the same losses her parents had. More importantly, Chris knew they were each becoming the people—and witches—Josh, Samantha, Danielle, and everyone who had died as a result of magic would want them to be.

MORE BY THE AUTHOR

To find the rest of the books in the Under the Moon Series as well as
more books by the author, visit
davidnethbooks.com/books

* * *

Subscribe to his newsletter to be the first to know of new releases and
special deals!
davidnethbooks.com/newsletter

* * *

If you enjoyed the book, please consider leaving a review on Goodreads
or the retailer you bought it from. Reviews help potential readers
determine whether they'll enjoy a book, so any comments on what you
thought of the story would be very helpful!

About the Author

David Neth is the author of the Under the Moon Series. He lives in Batavia, NY, where he dreams of a lofty writing career and opening his own bookstore.

Follow the Author

www.davidnethbooks.com
www.facebook.com/davidnethbooks
www.twitter.com/davidnethbooks
www.instagram.com/dneth13

www.ingramcontent.com/pod-product-compliance
Lightning Source LLC
Chambersburg PA
CBHW030552170726
48283CB00002B/286